Also by Philip Reeve

MORTAL ENGINES

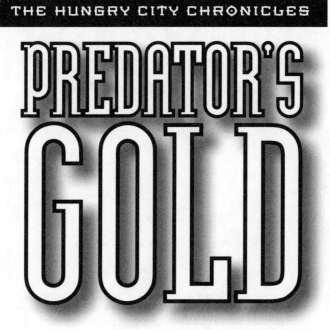

THE HUNGRY CITY CHRONICLES

PREDATOR'S GOLD

A Novel by

PHILIP REEVE

An Imprint of HarperCollins *Publishers*

Acknowledgments

I would like to thank everyone at Scholastic, and particularly Kirsten Skidmore and Holly Skeet for their help and advice during the writing of this book.

—Philip Reeve
Dartmoor, 2003

Eos is an imprint of HarperCollins Publishers.

Predator's Gold
Copyright © 2003 by Philip Reeve
All rights reserved. No part of this book may be used or reproduced in any manner whatsoever without written permission except in the case of brief quotations embodied in critical articles and reviews. Printed in the United States of America. For information address HarperCollins Children's Books, a division of HarperCollins Publishers, 1350 Avenue of the Americas, New York, NY 10019.
www.harpereos.com

Library of Congress Cataloging-in-Publication Data
Reeve, Philip.
  Predator's gold / Philip Reeve.— 1st ed.
    p.   cm.— (The hungry city chronicles)
  Sequel to: Mortal engines.
  Summary: In the distant future, when cities move about and consume smaller towns, Tom and Hester hope that the ice city of Anchorage will reach the rumored haven of the Dead Continent—America—before the savage Huntsmen of Arkangel find them.
    ISBN 0-06-072193-6 — ISBN 0-06-072194-4 (lib. bdg.)
    [1. Science fiction.] I. Title.
PZ7.R25576Pr 2004
[Fic]—dc22   2003025435
                                                                CIP
                                                                AC

Typography by Henrietta Stern
1 2 3 4 5 6 7 8 9 10
❖
First American Edition
First published in the UK by
Scholastic Children's Books, 2003

For Sarah and Sam

CONTENTS

PART ONE

PART TWO

PART THREE

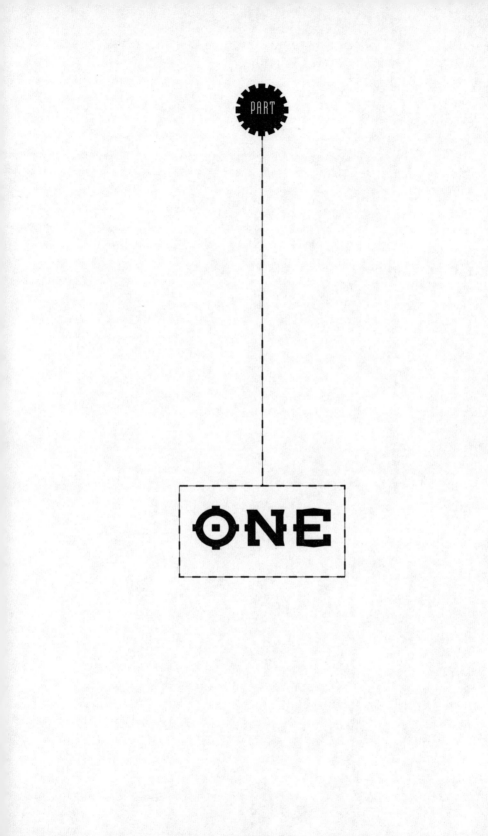

PART

ONE

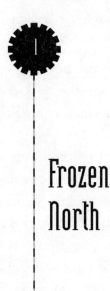

Frozen North

FREYA AWOKE EARLY AND lay for a while in the dark, feeling her city shiver and sway beneath her as its powerful engines sent it skimming across the ice. Sleepily, she waited for her servants to come and help her out of bed. It took her a few moments to remember that they were all dead.

She threw off the covers, lit the argon lamps, and waded through dusty mounds of cast-off clothes to her bathroom. For several weeks now she had been working up the courage to have a shower, but once again this morning the complicated controls in the shower stall defeated her: She couldn't make the water come hot. In the end she just filled the hand-basin as usual and splashed her face and neck. There was a sliver of soap left, and she rubbed some into her hair and plunged her head under the water. Her bath-servants would have used shampoo, lotions, salves, conditioners, all sorts of pleasant-smelling balms; but they were all dead, and the rack upon rack of bottles in the walk-in bathroom cabinet intimidated Freya. Faced with so much choice, she chose to use nothing.

At least she had worked out how to dress herself. She picked one of her crumpled gowns from the floor, laid it on the bed, and burrowed into it from the bottom, struggling about inside until she got her arms and head out through the right holes. The long, fur-trimmed waistcoat that went over the gown was much easier to put on, but she had a lot of trouble with the buttons. Her handmaidens had always done up her buttons very quickly and easily, talking and laughing about the day ahead and never, ever getting a button through the wrong hole; but they were all dead.

Freya cursed and tugged and fumbled for fifteen minutes, then studied the results in her cobwebby mirror. *Not bad*, she thought, *all things considered*. Perhaps some jewelry would make it look better. But when she went to her jewelry room, she found most of the good pieces gone. Things were always vanishing these days. Freya could not imagine where they went to. Anyway, she didn't really need a tiara on her sticky, soap-washed hair, or a necklet of amber and gold around her grubby throat. Mama would not approve of her being seen without jewelry, of course, but Mama was dead too.

In the empty, silent corridors of her palace, the dust lay thick as powder snow. She rang for a footman and stood staring out of a window while she waited for him to arrive. Outside, dim Arctic twilight shone gray on the frosted rooftops of her city. The floor trembled to the beat of cogs and pistons down in the engine district, but there was very little sense of movement, for this was the High Ice, north of north, and there were no passing landmarks, only a white plain, shining slightly with the reflection of the sky.

Her footman arrived, patting his powdered wig straight.

"Good morning, Smew," she said.

"Good morning, Your Radiance."

For a moment she was seized by an urge to ask Smew into her quarters and tell him to do something about all the dust, the fallen clothes, the lost jewelry; to make him show her how the shower worked. But he was a man, and it would be an unthinkable break with tradition for a man to enter the margravine's private quarters. Instead she said what she said every morning: "You may escort me to the breakfast room, Smew."

Riding with him in the elevator to the lower floor, she imagined her city scuttling across the ice cap like a tiny black beetle creeping over a huge white plate. The question was, Where was it going? That was what Smew wanted to know; you could see it in his face, in the way his gaze kept flicking inquisitively at her. The Steering Committee would want to know too. Running this way and that from hungry predators was one thing, but the time had come for Freya to decide what her city's future was to be. For thousands of years the people of Anchorage had looked to the House of Rasmussen to make such decisions. The Rasmussen women were special, after all. Had they not ruled Anchorage ever since the Sixty Minute War? Did not the Ice Gods speak to them in their dreams, telling them where the city should go if it was to find good trading partners and avoid trap-ice and predators?

But Freya was the last of her line, and the Ice Gods did

not speak to her. Hardly anybody spoke to her now, and when they did, it was only to inquire, in the politest possible way, when she would decide upon a course. *Why ask me?* she wanted to shout at them. *I'm just a girl! I didn't want to be margravine!* But there was no one else left for them to ask.

At least this morning Freya would have an answer for them. She just wasn't sure that they would like it.

She ate breakfast alone, in a high-backed black chair at a long black table. The clatter of her knife against her plate, her spoon in her teacup, seemed unbearably loud in the silence. From the shadowy walls, portraits of her divine ancestors gazed down at her, looking slightly impatient, as though they too were waiting for her to decide upon a destination.

"Don't worry," she told them. "I've made my mind up."

When breakfast was finished, her chamberlain came in.

"Good morning, Smew."

"Good morning, Light of the Ice Fields. The Steering Committee awaits Your Radiance's pleasure."

Freya nodded, and the chamberlain swung open the breakfast-room doors to let the committee enter. There used to be twenty-three of them; now there were only Mr. Scabious and Miss Pye.

Windolene Pye was a tall, plain, middle-aged lady with fair hair done up in a flat bun that made her look as if she were balancing a Danish pastry on her head. She had been the late chief navigator's secretary, and seemed to understand his charts and tables well enough, but she was very nervous in the presence of her margravine and bobbed little curtsies every time Freya so much as sniffed.

Her colleague, Søren Scabious, was quite different. His

family had been enginemasters for nearly as long as the city
had been mobile, and he was the nearest thing Freya had left
to an equal. If things had been normal, she would have been
getting married to his son, Axel, next summer; the margravine often took a man from the engine districts as her consort, to keep the city's engineering classes happy. But things
were not normal, and Axel was dead. Freya secretly felt quite
glad she would not be getting Scabious as a father-in-law; he
was such a stern, sad, silent old man. His black mourning
robes blended into the darkness of the breakfast room like
camouflage, leaving the white death mask of his face hanging
disembodied in the shadows.

"Good day, Your Radiance," he said, bowing stiffly, while
Miss Pye curtsied and blushed and fluttered beside him.

"What is our position?" asked Freya.

"Oh, Your Radiance, we are almost two hundred miles
north of the Tannhäuser Mountains," twittered Miss Pye.
"We're on sound sea ice, and there has been no sighting of
any other city."

"The engine district awaits your instructions, Light of the
Ice Fields," said Scabious. "Do you wish to turn back east?"

"No!" Freya shivered, remembering how close they had
come to being eaten in the past. If they went back east, or
turned south to trade along the edges of the ice, the
Huntsmen of Arkangel were sure to hear about it, and with
only skeleton crews to staff the engines, Freya did not think
her city could outrun the great predator again.

"Maybe we should bear west, Your Radiance?" Miss Pye
suggested nervously. "A few small towns overwinter along the
eastern edge of Greenland. We might manage a little trading."

"No," said Freya firmly.

"Then perhaps you have another destination in mind, Your Radiance?" wondered Scabious. "Have the Gods of the Ice spoken to you?"

Freya nodded solemnly. In fact, the idea was one she had been turning around in her mind for a month or more, and she did not think it had come from any god; it was just the only way she could see of keeping her city safe from predators and plagues and spy ships forever.

"Set course for the Dead Continent," she said. "We are going home."

Hester
and Tom

HESTER SHAW WAS STARTING to get used to being happy.
After all her muddy, starveling years in the ditches and scav-
engervilles of the Great Hunting Ground, she had finally
found herself a place in the world. She had her own airship,
the *Jenny Haniver* (if she craned her neck she could just see
the upper curve of her red envelope, behind that Zanzibar
spice freighter at Strut Seventeen), and she had Tom: gentle,
handsome, clever Tom, whom she loved with her whole
heart and who, in spite of everything, seemed to love her too.

For a long time she had felt sure it wouldn't last. They
were so different, and Hester was hardly anyone's idea of
beautiful: a tall, graceless scarecrow of a girl, her coppery hair
done up in too-tight plaits, her face split in half by an old
sword blow that had robbed her of one eye and most of her
nose and twisted her mouth into a snaggle-toothed sneer. *It*

won't last, she had kept telling herself all the time they were waiting on the Black Island for the shipwrights to repair the poor battered *Jenny Haniver. He stays with me only out of pity*, she had decided as they flew down to Africa, then crossed to South America. *What can he see in me?* she had wondered while they grew rich ferrying supplies to the great oil-drilling cities of Antarctica and then, suddenly poor again, jettisoning a cargo to outrun air pirates over Tierra del Fuego. Flying back across the blue Atlantic with a merchant convoy, she whispered to herself, *It cannot possibly last.*

And yet it had lasted; it had lasted for more than two years now. Sitting in September sunshine on this balcony outside the Crumple Zone, one of the many coffeehouses on Airhaven's High Street, Hester found herself beginning to believe that it might last forever. She squeezed Tom's hand beneath the table and smiled her crooked smile, and he looked at her with just as much love as when she had first kissed him, in the fluttering light of MEDUSA on the night his city died.

Airhaven had flown north this autumn and now hung a few thousand feet above the Frost Barrens, while small scavenger towns that had been up on the ice during the months of the midnight sun clustered below it to trade. Balloon after balloon rose to moor at the docking struts of the flying free port, disgorging colorful Old Tech traders who started shouting their wares the instant their boots touched its lightweight deck plates. The frozen north was a good hunting ground for diggers-up of lost technology, and these gentlemen were selling Stalker parts, Tesla gun accumulators, nameless odds and ends of machinery left over from half a dozen different civilizations, even some pieces of an Ancient flying machine that had lain undisturbed in the High Ice since the Sixty Minute War.

Below them, to the south, east, and west, the Frost Barrens stretched away into the haze: cold, stony country where the Ice Gods ruled for eight months of the year, and where patches of snow already lay in the shady bottoms of the crisscross town tracks. Northward rose the black basalt wall of the Tannhäuser Mountains, the chain of volcanoes that marked the northernmost limit of the Great Hunting Ground. Several were erupting, their plumes of gray smoke like pillars holding up the sky. Between them, faint behind a veil of ash, Hester and Tom could just make out the world-wide white of the Ice Wastes, and something moving there, vast, dirty, and implacable, like a mountain gone rogue.

Hester pulled a telescope from one of the pockets of her coat and put it to her eye, twizzling the focusing ring until the blurry view came suddenly sharp. She was looking at a city: eight tiers of factories and slave barracks and smut-spewing chimneys, a sky train riding the slipstream, parasite airships sifting the exhaust plume for waste minerals, and down below, ghostly through veils of snow and powdered rock, the big wheels rolling.

"Arkangel!"

Tom took the telescope from her. "You're right. It keeps to the northern foothills of the Tannhäusers in summer, eating up scavenger towns as they come through the passes. The polar ice cap is much thicker now than it was in olden days, but there are still parts that are too thin to take Arkangel's weight till summer's end."

Hester laughed. "Know-it-all."

"I can't help it," Tom said. "I was an Apprentice Historian, remember? We had to memorize a list of the World's Great Traction Cities, and Arkangel was right near the top, so I'm not likely to forget it."

"Show-off!" grumbled Hester. "I wish it had been Zimbra, or Xanne-Sandansky. You wouldn't look so clever then."

Tom was peering through the telescope again. "Any day now it'll lift up its tracks and lower its iron runners and go skating off in search of ice cities and Snowmad scavenger towns to gobble up. . . ."

For the present, however, Arkangel seemed content to trade. It was too vast to haul itself through the narrow passes of the Tannhäusers, but airships were lifting from its harbors and flying south through the haze toward Airhaven. The first of them cut an arrogant swathe through the swirl of balloons around the floating town and swooped in to dock at Strut Six, just below Tom and Hester's perch; they felt the faint vibration as its docking clamps gripped the quay. It was a lean short-range attack ship with a red wolf painted on its sable envelope and its name underneath in Gothic script: the *Clear Air Turbulence.*

Men swaggered out of the armored gondola, stomping along the quay and up the stairways that led to High Street. Big, burly men with fur cloaks and fur hats and a chilly glitter of chain mail under their tunics. One wore a steel helmet from which sprouted two huge, flaring gramophone horns. An electric cord led from the helmet to a brass microphone, clamped in the fist of another man, whose amplified voice boomed out across Airhaven as he climbed the stairs.

"Greetings, airlings! From Great Arkangel, Hammer of

the High Ice, Scourge of the North, Devourer of the Spitzbergen Static, greetings! We have gold to exchange for anything you can tell us about the locations of ice cities! Thirty
sovereigns for information leading to a capture!"

He started to push his way between the Crumple Zone's
tables, still booming out his offer, while all about him aviators shook their heads and made sour faces and turned away.
Now that prey was in such short supply everywhere, several
of the big predators had begun to offer finders' fees, but few
did it this openly. Honest air traders were starting to fear that
they might soon be barred altogether from the smaller ice
cities, for what mayor would risk giving docking permits to a
ship that might fly off the next day and sell its course to a
greedy great urbivore like Arkangel? Yet there were always
others, smugglers and demipirates and merchants whose
ships were not bringing in the profits they had hoped for,
who were ready to accept predator's gold.

"Come and find me at the Gasbag and Gondola if you
have traded this summer aboard Kivitoo or Breidhavik or
Anchorage and know where they plan to overwinter!" urged
the newcomer. He was a young man, and he looked stupid
and rich and well fed. "Thirty in gold, my friends; enough to
keep your ships in fuel and *luftgaz* for a year. . . ."

"That is Piotr Masgard," Hester heard a Dinka aviatrix at
a neighboring table tell her friends. "He's the youngest son of
the Direktor of Arkangel. Calls that gang of his the
Huntsmen. They don't just advertise for snoops; I've heard
they land that ship of theirs on peaceful little cities too fast
for Arkangel to catch and force them to stop, or turn
around—force them at swordpoint to steer straight into
Arkangel's jaws!"

"But that's not fair!" cried Tom, who had also been listening, and unluckily his words fell loudly into a momentary gap in Masgard's speech. The Huntsman swung around, and his big, lazy, handsome face grinned down at Tom.

"Not fair, airling? What's not fair? This is a town-eat-town world, you know."

Hester tensed. One thing she could never understand about Tom was why he always expected everything to be fair. She supposed it was his upbringing. A few years' living by his wits in a scavengerville would have knocked it out of him, but he'd grown up with all the rules and customs of the Guild of Historians to keep real life at bay, and despite all he'd seen since, he could still be shocked by people like Masgard.

"I just mean it's against all the rules of Municipal Darwinism," Tom explained, looking up at the big man. He got to his feet but found that he was still looking up, for the towering Huntsman was at least a foot taller. "Fast cities eat slow ones, and strong cities eat weak ones. That's the way it's meant to work, just like in nature. Offering finders' fees and hijacking prey upsets the balance," he went on, as though Masgard were just an opponent at the Apprentice Historians' Debating Society.

Masgard's grin grew broader. He flicked his fur cloak aside and drew his sword. There were gasps and cries and a clatter of falling chairs as everyone in the vicinity tried to get as far back as possible. Hester grabbed hold of Tom and began pulling him away, always keeping her eye on that gleaming blade. "Tom, you idiot, leave it!"

Masgard stared at her a moment, then let out a roaring

laugh and sheathed his sword. "Look! The airling has a pretty girlie to keep him from harm!"

His crew laughed with him, and Hester blushed patchily and tugged up her old red scarf to hide her face.

"Come and find me later, girl!" Masgard shouted. "I'm always at home to a pretty lady! And remember, if you have a city's course to tell me of, I'll give you thirty in gold! You can buy yourself a new nose!"

"I'll remember," promised Hester, pushing Tom quickly away. Anger flapped inside her like a trapped crow. She wanted to turn and fight. She was willing to bet Masgard didn't know how to use that sword he was so proud of. . . . But the dark, murderous, revengeful part of her was something she tried to keep hidden these days, so she contented herself with slipping out her knife and quietly severing the cord of Masgard's microphone as she passed. The next time he tried to make an announcement, the laughter would be directed at him.

"Sorry," Tom said bashfully as they hurried down to the docking ring, which was crowded now with traders and sight-seers fresh in from Arkangel. "I didn't mean—I just thought—"

"It's all right," said Hester. She wanted to tell him that if he didn't do brave, foolish things like that from time to time he wouldn't be Tom, and she might not love him the way she did. But she couldn't put all that into words, so she pushed him into the space under a tier support and, after making sure that nobody was looking, wrapped her skinny arms around his neck and pulled her veil down and kissed him. "Let's leave."

"But we don't have a cargo yet. We were going to look for a fur trader or—"

"There are no fur traders here, only Old Tech, and we don't want to start carrying that sort of stuff, do we?" He looked uncertain, so she kissed him again before he could say anything. "I'm tired of Airhaven. I want to be back on the bird roads."

"All right," said Tom. He smiled, stroking her mouth, her cheek, the kink in her eyebrow where the scar cut through. "All right. We've seen enough of northern skies. Let's go."

But it was not to be that simple. When they reached Strut Seventeen, there was a man waiting beside the *Jenny Haniver*, sitting on a big leather pack. Hester, still smarting a little from Masgard's mockery, hid her face again. Tom let go of her hand and hurried to meet the stranger.

"Good day!" cried the man, standing up. "Mr. Natsworthy? Miss Shaw? I gather you are the owners of this splendid little ship? Golly, they told me at the harbor office you were young, but I didn't realize quite how young! You're barely more than children!"

"I'm almost eighteen," said Tom defensively.

"Never mind, never mind!" The stranger beamed. "Age makes no difference if the heart is great, and I'm sure you have a great heart. 'Who's that handsome young chap?' I asked my friend the harbormaster, and he told me, 'That's Tom Natsworthy, pilot of the *Jenny Haniver*.' 'Pennyroyal,' I said to myself, 'that young man may be just the fellow you're looking for!' So here I am!"

Here he was. He was a smallish man, balding and slightly overweight, and he wore a trim white beard. His clothes were the typical outfit of a northern scavenger—a long fur coat, a fur hat, a tunic with many pockets, thick breeches, and fur-lined boots—but they looked too expensive, as if they had been run up for him by a fashionable tailor as a costume for a play set in the Ice Wastes.

"Well?" he asked.

"Well what?" asked Hester, who had taken an instant dislike to this posturing stranger.

"I'm sorry, sir," said Tom, much more politely. "We don't really understand what you want. . . ."

"Oh, I do apologize, I beg your pardon," the stranger babbled. "Permit me to elucidate! My name is Pennyroyal; Nimrod Beauregard Pennyroyal. I have been exploring a little among these great horrible towering fire mountains, and now I am on my way home. I should like to book passage aboard your charming airship."

The Passenger

ENNYROYAL WAS A NAME that rang a bell with Tom, although he could not think why. He was sure he'd heard it mentioned in a lecture, back in his days as an Apprentice Historian—but what Pennyroyal had done, or said, to make him worth lecturing about he did not recall; he had spent too much time daydreaming to pay much attention to his teachers.

"We don't carry passengers," said Hester firmly. "We're bound for the south, and we travel alone."

"The south would be just fine and dandy!" Pennyroyal beamed again. "My home city is the raft resort of Brighton, and it is cruising in the Middle Sea this autumn. I am eager to be home quickly, Miss Shaw. My publishers, Fewmet and Spraint, are desperate to have a new book from me by Moon Festival, and I need the peace and quiet of my own study to begin working up my notes."

As he spoke, he glanced quickly over his shoulder, scanning the faces of the people on the docking ring. He was sweating slightly, and Hester thought he looked not so much eager to be home as downright shifty. But Tom was hooked. "You are a writer, Mr. Pennyroyal?"

"*Professor* Pennyroyal," said the man, continuing to beam and correcting him very kindly. "I am an Explorer, Adventurer, and Alternative Historian. Maybe you've come across my works: *Lost Cities of the Sands*, perhaps, or *America the Beautiful: The Truth About the Dead Continent*. . . ."

Now Tom remembered where he had heard that name before. Chudleigh Pomeroy had once mentioned Nimrod B. Pennyroyal in a lecture about Recent Trends in History. Pennyroyal (the old Historian had said) had no respect for true historical research at all. His daring expeditions were mere stunts, and he filled his books with wild theories and lurid tales of romance and adventure. Tom was rather fond of wild theories and lurid tales, and he had looked for Pennyroyal's works in the Museum Library afterward, but the stuffy Guild of Historians had refused to allow them shelf space there, so he never did find out where Pennyroyal's expeditions had taken him.

He glanced at Hester. "We do have room for a passenger, Het. And we could use the money. . . ."

Hester scowled.

"Oh, money is no object," promised Pennyroyal, pulling out a plump purse and jangling it. "Let's say five sovereigns now and five more when we dock at Brighton? It's not as sweet a deal as Piotr Masgard would offer you for betraying some poor city, but it's pretty good, and you will be doing a great service to literature."

Hester stared at a coil of hawser on the quay. She knew she had lost. This too-friendly stranger knew just how to appeal to Tom, and even she had to admit that ten sovereigns would come in handy. She made one last effort to fend off the inevitable, booting Pennyroyal's pack and asking, "What's in your baggage? We don't carry Old Tech. Seen a bit too much of what it can do."

"Heavens!" cried Pennyroyal. "I couldn't agree more! I may be Alternative, but I'm not an idiot. I too have seen what happens to people who spend their lives digging up old machines. They end up poisoned by weird radiation or blown up by malfunctioning widgets. No, all I carry is a change of undies and a few thousand pages of notes and drawings for my new book, *Fire Mountains: Natural Phenomenon or Ancient Blunder?*"

Hester kicked the pack again. It fell slowly over onto its side, but it didn't let out any metallic noises to suggest that Pennyroyal was lying. She looked down at her feet, then down again, through the perforated deck plates of Airhaven to the earth, where a town was creeping slowly westward, dragging its long shadow behind it. *Oh well,* she thought. The Middle Sea would be warm and blue, a far cry from these dismal barrens, and it should take only a week to get there. Surely she could bear to share Tom with Professor Pennyroyal for a week? She would have him to herself for the rest of their lives.

"All right," she said, and snatched the explorer's purse, counting out five gold sovereigns before he had time to change his mind. Beside her, Tom was saying, "We can make up a bed for you in the forward hold, Professor, and you can use the medical bay as a study if you wish. I was planning to stay here tonight and pull out at dawn."

"If it's all the same to you, Tom," said Pennyroyal, flashing that odd, nervous glance toward the docking ring again, "I'd rather be off right away. Mustn't keep my muse waiting. . . ."

Hester shrugged and upended the purse again. "We'll leave as soon as the harbormaster gives us clearance," she said. "There'll be a two-sovereign surcharge."

The sun went down, a red ember sinking into the haze of the western Tannhäusers. Balloons were still rising from the trading cluster below, airships and dirigibles still coming south across the basalt uplands from great Arkangel. One of them belonged to an amiable old gentleman called Widgery Blinkoe, an Old Tech antiques dealer who made ends meet by renting out rooms above his shop in Arkangel's harbor district, and by acting as an informant to anyone who would pay him.

Leaving his wives to moor the ship, Mr. Blinkoe hurried straight to the harbormaster's office and demanded, "Have you seen this man?"

The harbormaster looked at the photograph that Mr. Blinkoe pushed across his desk and said, "Why, that's Professor Pennyroyal, the historical gentleman."

"Gentleman, my hat!" cried Blinkoe angrily. "He has lodged at my home these past six weeks, and he ran off as soon as Airhaven came in sight, without paying me a penny of what he owes! Where is he? Where can I find him, the creature?"

"Too late, mate," said the harbormaster, grinning. He took a certain pleasure in delivering bad news. "He came in on one of the first balloons from Arkangel, asking after southbound ships. I put him in touch with those youngsters who fly the *Jenny Haniver*. She pulled out not ten minutes past, bound for the Middle Sea."

Blinkoe groaned, rubbing a hand wearily over his large, pale face. He could ill afford to lose the twenty sovereigns Pennyroyal had promised. Oh why, why, *why* had he not made the scoundrel pay in advance? He had been so flattered when Pennyroyal had presented him with a signed copy of *America the Beautiful* ("To my good friend Widgery, with Kindest Regards"), and so excited by the promise of a mention in the great man's next work, that he hadn't even smelled a rat when Pennyroyal started charging wine merchants' bills to his account. Hadn't even objected when he began flirting so openly with the younger Mrs. Blinkoes! Bother and blast all writers!

And then something that the harbormaster had said cut through the fog of self-pity and the incipient headache that had been clouding Blinkoe's thoughts. A name. A familiar name. A valuable name!

"Did you say the *Jenny Haniver*?"

"I did, sir."

"But that's impossible! She was lost when the gods destroyed London!"

The harbormaster shook his head. "Not so, sir; not a bit of it. Been in foreign skies these past two years, trading aboard them Nuevo-Mayan ziggurat cities, I heard."

Mr. Blinkoe thanked him and ran out onto the quay. He

was a portly man and did not often run, but this seemed worth running for. He shoved aside some children who were taking turns to peer through a telescope mounted on the handrail and used it to scan the sky. A little west of south, late sunlight flashed on an airship's stern windows, a small red airship with a clinker-built gondola and twin Jeunet-Carot engine pods.

Mr. Blinkoe hurried back to his own ship, the *Temporary Blip*, and his long-suffering wives. "Quick!" he shouted as he burst into the gondola. "Switch on the radio!"

"So Pennyroyal's slipped through his fingers again," said one wife.

"Surprise, surprise," said another.

"This is exactly what happened at Arkangel," said a third.

"Silence, wives!" Blinkoe shouted. "This is important!"

His fourth wife made a sour face. "Pennyroyal's hardly worth the bother."

"Poor, dear Professor Pennyroyal," the fifth said weepily.

"Forget Pennyroyal," bawled her husband, pulling off his hat and slipping on the radio headphones, tuning the transmitter to a secret wavelength, gesturing impatiently for wife number five to stop sniveling and turn the starting handle. "I know people who will pay me well for what I've just learned! The trader that Pennyroyal just left on was Anna Fang's old ship!"

Tom had not realized until now how much he missed the company of other historians. Hester was always happy to hear the odd facts and stories that he recalled from his Apprentice days, but she could offer little in return. She had lived by her wits since she was just a child, and although she knew how to jump aboard a speeding town, how to catch and skin a cat, and how to kick a would-be robber exactly where it hurt most, she had never bothered learning much about the history of her world.

Now here was Professor Pennyroyal, his amiable personality filling the *Jenny*'s flight deck. He had a theory or an anecdote about everything, and listening to him made Tom feel almost nostalgic for the old days in the London Museum, when he had lived surrounded by books and facts and relics and scholarly debate.

"Now, take these mountains," Pennyroyal was saying, gesturing out of the starboard window. They were following a long spur of the Tannhäusers southward, and the glow of lava in an active caldera flickered over the explorer's face. "These are to be the subject of my new book. Where did they come from? They weren't here in Ancient times, we know that from the maps that have survived. So how did they spring up so quickly? What caused them? It's just the same in far Shan Guo. Zhan Shan is the highest mountain on earth, and yet it's not mentioned at all in the Ancient records. Are these new mountains just the result of natural vulcanism, as we've always been told? Or are we looking at the results of Ancient technology gone atrociously wrong? An experimental power source, perhaps, or a terrible weapon! A volcano-maker! Think what a find that would be, Tom!"

"We're not interested in finding Old Tech," said Hester automatically. She was at the chart table, trying to plot a course, and Pennyroyal was annoying her more and more.

"Of course not, dear girl!" cried Pennyroyal, looking at the bulkhead beside her (he didn't trust himself yet to look at her awful face without wincing). "Of course not! A very noble and sensible prejudice. And yet—"

"It's not a prejudice," snapped Hester, pointing a pair of dividers at him in a way that made him fear she might do him serious mischief. "My mother was an archaeologist. An explorer and adventurer and historian, just like you. She went to the dead lands of America and dug something up and brought it home. Something called MEDUSA. The rulers of London got to hear about it and sent their man Valentine to kill her for it. He did this to my face while he was at it. He took it to London and the Engineers there got it working and *Bang!* It backfired, and that was the end of that."

"Ah, yes," said Pennyroyal, rather chastened. "Everybody knows of the MEDUSA event. Why, I can remember exactly what I was doing at the time. I was aboard Cittàmotore, in the company of a delightful young woman named Minty Bapsnack. We saw the flash light up the eastern sky from half a world away. . . ."

"Well, we were right next to it. We flew through the blast wave, and we saw what was left of London the next morning. A whole city, Tom's city, burned to ashes by something my mother dug up. That's why we steer well clear of Old Tech."

"Ah," said Pennyroyal, thoroughly uncomfortable now.

"I'm going to bed," said Hester. "I've got a headache." It was true; a few hours of Pennyroyal's lecturing had set a fierce, throbbing pain behind her blind eye. She went to the pilot's seat, meaning to kiss Tom good night, but she didn't like to with Pennyroyal looking on, so she quickly touched his ear, said, "Call me when you need a break," and headed aft to the stern cabin.

"Whoops!" said Pennyroyal when she had gone.

"She's got a bit of a temper," admitted Tom, embarrassed by Hester's outburst. "But she's lovely, really. She's just shy. Once you get to know her . . ."

"Of course, of course," said Pennyroyal. "One can see at a glance that beneath that somewhat unconventional exterior, she's absolutely, um . . ." But he couldn't think of anything good to say about the girl, so he let his voice trail away and stood looking through a window at the moonlit mountains, the lights of a small town moving on the plains below.

"She's wrong about London, you know," he said at last. "I mean, wrong about it being burned to ashes. I've spoken to people who've been there. There's a lot of wreckage left. Whole sections of the Gut lie ruined in the Out-Country west of Batmunkh Gompa. Why, an archaeologist of my acquaintance, a charming young woman by the name of Cruwys Morchard, claims to have actually been *inside* one of the larger fragments. Sounds extraordinary: charred skeletons scattered everywhere, and great chunks of half-melted build-ings and machinery. The lingering radiation from MEDUSA causes colored lights to bob among the debris like will-o'-the-wisps . . . or should that be wills-o'-the-wisp?"

It was Tom's turn to grow uncomfortable. The destruc-tion of his city was still a raw wound inside him. Two and a half years later, the afterglow of that great explosion still lit his dreams. He didn't want to talk about London's wreck, and so he steered the conversation back toward Professor Pennyroyal's favorite subject: Professor Pennyroyal.

"You must have traveled to some very interesting places, I suppose?"

"Interesting! Oh, you don't know the half of it, Tom! The things I've seen! When we touch down at Brighton air harbor, I'll go straight to a bookseller's and buy you my complete works. I'm amazed you've not come across them before, a bright young fellow like you."

Tom shrugged. "I'm afraid they didn't keep them in the London Museum Library. . . ."

"Of course not! The Guild of so-called Historians! Pah! Dusty old farts . . . Do you know, I applied to join them once. Their Head Historian, Thaddeus Valentine, turned me down flat! Just because he didn't like the findings of my trip to America!"

Tom was intrigued. He didn't like hearing his former Guild dismissed as dusty farts, but Valentine was different. Valentine had tried to kill him, and had murdered Hester's parents. Anybody Valentine had disapproved of was all right by Tom.

"What *did* you find in America, Professor?"

"Ah well, Tom, thereby hangs a tale! Should you like to hear it?"

Tom nodded. He couldn't leave the flight deck tonight, with this wind blowing up from the south, and he would be glad of a good story to keep him alert. Anyway, Pennyroyal's talk had awakened something in him, a memory of simpler times, when he had huddled under his bedclothes in the Third Class Apprentices' dorm and read by flashlight the stories of the great explorer-historians, Monkton Wylde and Chung-Mai Spofforth, Valentine and Fishacre and Compton Cark.

"Yes, please, Professor," he said.

Home
of the
Brave

NORTH AMERICA," SAID Pennyroyal, "is a Dead Continent. Everyone knows that. Discovered in the year 1924 by Christopher Columbo, the great explorer and detective, it became the homeland of an empire that once ruled the world, but that was utterly destroyed in the Sixty Minute War. It is a land of haunted red deserts, poison swamps, atomic-bomb craters, rust, and lifeless rock. Only a few daring explorers venture there: archaeologists like Valentine and your young lady friend's poor mother, out to salvage scraps of Old Tech from the ancient bunker complexes.

"And yet one hears rumors. Stories. Tales told by drunken old sky dogs in run-down air caravanserais. Yarns about airships that have been blown off course and found themselves flying over a very different sort of America: a green landscape of forests and grasslands and vast blue lakes. About fifty years ago, a flyer named Snøri Ulvaeusson was supposed to have actually landed in a green enclave he called Vineland, and made a map of it for the Lord Mayor of Reykjavik, but of course when modern researchers went looking for the map, they found no trace of it in the Reykjavik library. As for the other accounts, the punch line is always the same: The airman spends years trying to find the place again but never can. Or else he sets down his ship, only to find that the greenery that looked so inviting from above is really only toxic algae blooming on a crater lake.

"But true historians like ourselves, Tom, know that within such legends there often lurks a seed of truth. I gathered together all the stories I'd heard and decided that there was something there worth following up. Is America really dead, as wise men like Valentine have always told us? Or could there be a place, far to the north of the dead cities that the Old Tech hunters visit, where rivers of meltwater spilling from the edge of the Ice Wastes have washed away the poisons and made the Dead Continent begin to flower again?

"I, Pennyroyal, resolved to discover the truth! Back in the spring of the year 'eighty-nine, I set out to see what I could find. Myself and four companions, aboard my airship the *Allan Quatermain*. We crossed the North Atlantic and soon touched down upon the shores of America, near a place that the Ancient charts call New York. It was as dead as we'd been promised: a series of vast craters, their sides fused by the intense heat of that millennia-old conflict into the substance known as blast-glass.

"We took off again and flew west, into the very heart of the Dead Continent, and that was when disaster struck. Storms of an almost supernatural ferocity wrecked my poor

Allan Quatermain in the midst of an immense, polluted wilderness. Three of my companions perished in the smash; the fourth died a few days later, poisoned by some water from a pool that looked clear, but that must have been tainted with some ghastly Old Tech chemical—he turned blue and gave off a scent of old socks.

"Alone, I staggered on into the north, crossing the Plain of Craters, where once the legendary cities of Chicago and Milwaukee stood. I had given up all thought of finding my green America. My only hope now was that I might reach the edge of the Ice Wastes and be rescued by some wandering band of Snowmads.

"At last, even that hope faded. Weak from exhaustion and lack of water, I lay down in a dry valley between great black jagged mountains. In despair I cried out, 'Is this really to be the end of Nimrod Pennyroyal?' and the stones seemed to answer, 'Yup.' All hope was gone, d'you see? I commended my soul to the Goddess of Death and shut my eyes, expecting to open them again only as a ghost in the Sunless Country. The next thing I knew, I was wrapped in furs and laid in the bottom of a canoe, and some charming young people were paddling me north.

"These were not fellow explorers from the Hunting Ground, as I at first supposed. They were natives! Yes, there is a tribe of people actually *living* in the northernmost parts of that Dead Continent! Until then, I had accepted the traditional story—the story that I'm sure you were told by your Guild of Historians—that the few poor souls who survived the fall of America fled north onto the ice and mingled with the Inuit, producing the Snowmad race we know today. Now

I understood that some had stayed behind! Savage, uncivi-
lized descendants of a nation whose greed and selfishness
once brought the world to ruin—and yet they had enough
humanity to rescue a poor starving wretch like Pennyroyal!

"By signs and gestures I was soon able to converse with
my rescuers. They were a girl and boy, and their names were
Machine Washable and Allow Twelve Days For Delivery. It
seemed that they had been on an expedition of their own
when they found me: digging for blast-glass in the ruins of an
ancient city called Duluth. (I discovered, by the way, that the
members of their savage tribe prize a blast-glass necklace just
as much as any well-dressed lady in Paris or Traktiongrad.
Both my new friends wore armlets and earrings of the stuff.)
They were very skilled at surviving among the dreadful
deserts of America, turning over stones to catch edible grubs
and finding drinkable water by observing the growth patterns
of certain types of algae. But that wasteland was not their
home. No, they had come from farther north, and now it
seemed they were returning with me to their tribe!

"Imagine my excitement, Tom! Going up that river was
like going back to the earliest beginnings of the world. To begin
with, nothing but barren rock, pierced here and there by time-
ravaged stones or twisted girders that were all that remained of
some great building of the Ancients. Then, one day, I spied a
patch of green moss, and then another! A few more days of
northing and I began to see grass, ferns, rushes clustering on
either bank. The river itself grew clearer, and Allow Twelve
Days caught fish, which Machine Washable cooked for us over
a fire each evening on the shore. And the trees, Tom! Birches
and oaks and pines covered the landscape, and the river

opened into a broad lake, and there upon the shore were the rude dwellings of the tribe. What a sight for a historian! America alive again, after all those millennia!

"How I lived with the good people of the tribe for three years I shall not bore you with. Nor how I rescued the chief's beautiful daughter Zip Code from a ravening bear, how she fell in love with me, and how I was forced to make my escape from her angry fiancé. Nor even how I traveled north again, up onto the ice, and so returned, after many more adventures, to the Great Hunting Ground. You can read about it all in my interpolitan best-seller *America the Beautiful* when we reach Brighton."

Tom sat for a long time without speaking, his head filled with the wonderful visions that Pennyroyal's account had painted. He could hardly believe that he had never heard of the professor's great discovery before. It was world-shattering! Monumental! What fools the Guild of Historians must have been, to turn away such a man!

At last he said, "But did you never go back, Professor? Surely a second expedition, with better equipment . . ."

"Alas, Tom." Pennyroyal sighed. "I could never find anyone to fund a return trip. You must remember that my cameras and sampling equipment were all destroyed in the wreck of the *Allan Quatermain*. I took a few artifacts along with me when I left the tribe, but all were lost along my journey home. Without proof, how could I hope to fund a return expedition? The word of an Alternative Historian is not enough, I find. Why," he said sadly, "to this day, Tom, there are people who believe I never went to America at all."

The Fox Spirits

PENNYROYAL'S VOICE WAS still blaring away on the flight deck when Hester awoke the next morning. Had he been there all night? Probably not, she realized, washing her face at the small basin in the *Jenny*'s galley. He'd been to bed, unlike poor Tom, and had now come back down, lured by the smell of Tom's morning cup of coffee.

She turned to look out of the galley porthole while she cleaned her teeth—anything rather than face her own reflection in the mirror above the basin. The sky was the color of packet custard, streaked with rhubarb cloud. Three small black specks hung in the center of the view. Flecks of dirt on the glass, thought Hester, but when she tried to rub them away with her cuff, she saw that she was wrong. She frowned, then fetched her telescope and studied the specks for a while. Frowned some more.

When she reached the flight deck, Tom was preparing to turn in for a nap. The gale had not abated, but they had flown clear of the mountains now, and although the wind would slow them down, there was no longer any danger of being blown through a volcanic plume or dashed against a cliff. Tom looked tired but contented, beaming at Hester as she ducked in through the hatchway. Pennyroyal sat in the co-pilot's seat, a mug of the *Jenny*'s best coffee in his hand.

"The professor's been telling me about some of his expeditions," Tom said eagerly, standing up to let Hester take the controls. "You wouldn't believe the adventures he's had!"

"Probably not," agreed Hester. "But the only thing I want to hear about at the moment is why there's a flight of gunships closing in on us."

Pennyroyal squawked with fear, then quickly clamped a hand over his mouth. Tom went to the larboard window and looked where Hester pointed. The specks were closer now, and clearly airships: three of them, in line abreast.

"They might be traders, heading up to Airhaven," he said hopefully.

"That's not a convoy," Hester said. "It's an attack formation."

Tom took the field glasses from their hook under the main controls. The airships were about ten miles off, but he could see that they were fast and well armed. They had some sort of green insignia painted on their envelopes, but otherwise they were completely white. It made them look absurdly sinister: the ghosts of airships, racing through the daybreak.

"They're League fighters," said Hester flatly. "I recognize

those flared engine-pod cowlings. Murasaki Fox Spirits."

She sounded scared, and with good reason. She and Tom had been careful to avoid the Anti-Traction League these past two years, for the *Jenny Haniver* had once belonged to a League agent, poor dead Anna Fang, and while they had not exactly stolen her, they knew the League might not see it that way. They had expected to be safe in the north, where League forces were spread thinly since the fall of the Spitzbergen Static the year before.

"Better go about," said Hester. "Get the wind on our tail and try to outrun them, or lose them in the mountains."

Tom hesitated. The *Jenny* was much faster than her wooden gondola and scrapyard engine pods made her look, but he doubted she could outrun Fox Spirits. "Running would just make us look guilty," he said. "We've done nothing wrong. I'll talk to them, see what they want. . . ."

He reached for the radio set, but Pennyroyal grabbed his hand. "Tom, no! I've heard about these white ships. They aren't regular Anti-Traction League at all! They belong to the Green Storm, a fanatical new splinter group who operate out of secret air bases here in the north. Extremists, sworn to destroy all cities—and all city people! Great gods, if you let them catch us, we'll all be murdered in our gondola!"

The explorer's face had turned the color of expensive cheese, and pinheads of sweat gleamed on his forehead and his nose. The hand that gripped Tom's wrist was shaking. Tom couldn't imagine at first what was wrong. Surely a man who'd survived as many adventures as Professor Pennyroyal could not be *scared?*

Hester turned back to the window in time to see one of

the approaching ships fire a rocket to windward, signaling the *Jenny Haniver* to heave to and allow herself to be boarded. She wasn't sure she believed Pennyroyal, but there was something threatening about those ships. She was certain they hadn't encountered the *Jenny* just by chance. They'd been sent to find her.

She touched Tom's arm. "Go."

Tom heaved on the rudder controls, swinging the *Jenny* about until she was steering north, with the gale behind her. He pushed a sequence of brass levers forward, and the rumble of the engines rose to a higher pitch. Another lever, and small air sails unfolded, semicircles of silicone silk stretched between the pods and the flanks of the gasbag, adding a little extra thrust to help shove the *Jenny* through the sky.

"We're gaining!" he shouted, peeking into the periscope at the grainy upside-down image of the view astern. But the Fox Spirits were persistent. They altered course to match the *Jenny*'s and coaxed more power out of their own engines. Within an hour they were close enough for Tom and Hester to make out the symbol painted on their flanks—not the broken wheel of the Anti-Traction League but a jagged green lightning bolt.

Tom scanned the grayish landscape below, hoping for a town or city where he might seek sanctuary. There were none, except for a couple of slow-moving Lapp farming towns leading their herds of reindeer across the tundra far to the east, and he could not reach them without the Fox Spirits cutting him off. The Tannhäuser Mountains barred the horizon ahead, their canyons and pumice clouds offering the only hope of shelter.

"What shall we do?" he asked.

"Keep going," said Hester. "Maybe we can lose them in the mountains."

"What if they rocket us?" whimpered Pennyroyal. "They're getting terribly close! What if they start shooting at us?"

"They want the *Jenny* in one piece," Hester told him. "They won't risk using rockets."

"Want the *Jenny*? Why would anyone want this old wreck?" The tension was making Pennyroyal tetchy. When Hester explained, he shouted, "This was Anna Fang's ship? Great Clio! Almighty Poskitt! But the Green Storm worship Anna Fang! Their movement was founded amid the ashes of the Northern Air Fleet, sworn to avenge the people killed by London's agents at Batmunkh Gompa! Of course they'd want her ship back! Merciful gods, why didn't you tell me this ship was stolen? I demand a full refund!"

Hester shoved him aside and went to the chart table. "Tom?" she said, studying their maps of the Tannhäusers. "There's a gap in the volcano chain west of here: the Drachen Pass. Maybe there'll be a city there we can put down on."

They flew on, climbing into thin air above the snowy peaks and once skirting dangerously close to a plume of smoke that belched thickly from the throat of a young volcano. No pass, no city did they see, and after another hour, during which the three Fox Spirits steadily narrowed their lead, a flight of rockets came flashing past the windows and exploded just off the starboard bow.

"Oh, Quirke!" cried Tom—but Quirke had been London's god, and if he couldn't be bothered to save his own city, why would he come to the aid of a battered little airship lost in the sulfurous updrafts of the Tannhäusers?

Pennyroyal tried to hide under the chart table. "They *are* firing rockets!"

"Oh, thanks, we wondered what those big explody things were," said Hester, angry that her prediction had proved wrong.

"But you said they wouldn't!"

"They're aiming for the engine pods," said Tom. "If they disable them, we'll be dead in the sky and they'll grapple alongside and send a boarding party across. . . ."

"Well, can't you do something?" demanded Pennyroyal. "Can't you fight back?"

"We don't have any rockets," said Tom miserably. After that last terrible air battle over London, when he had shot down the *13th Floor Elevator* and watched her crew burn inside their burning gondola, he had vowed that the *Jenny* would be a peaceful ship. Her rocket projectors had been empty ever since. Now he regretted his scruples. Thanks to him, Hester and Professor Pennyroyal would soon be in the hands of the Green Storm.

Another rocket slammed past. It was time to do something desperate. He called again on Quirke, then swung the *Jenny* hard over to larboard and took her powering down into the maze of the mountains, flashing through the shadows of wind-carved basalt crags and out again into sunlight.

And below him, far below him and ahead, he saw another chase in progress. A tiny scavenger town was scurrying southward through a cleft in the mountains, and behind it, jaws agape, rolled a big, rusty three-tiered Traction City.

Tom steered the *Jenny* toward it, glancing from time to

time into his periscope, where the three Fox Spirits still hung doggedly on his tail. Pennyroyal gnawed at his fingernails and gibbered the names of obscure gods: "Oh, Great Poskitt! Oh, Deeble, preserve us!" Hester turned the radio on again and hailed the fast-approaching city, demanding permission to dock.

A pause. A rocket struck steam and splinters from a mountainside thirty yards astern. Then a woman's voice crackled out of the radio, speaking Airsperanto with a heavy Slavic accent. "This is Novaya-Nizhni Harbor Board. Your request is denied."

"What?" screamed Pennyroyal.

"But that's not—" said Tom.

"This is an emergency!" Hester told the radio. "We're being chased!"

"We know," the voice came back, regretful but firm. "We want no trouble. Novaya-Nizhni is peaceable city. Keep clear, please, or we fire upon you."

A rocket from the lead Fox Spirit came winding in to burst just off the stern. The harsh voices of the Green Storm aviators drowned out the threats from Novaya-Nizhni for a moment; then the woman was back, insisting, "Stay clear, *Jenny Haniver*, or we will fire!"

Tom had an idea.

There was no time to explain to Hester what he was about to do. He didn't think she would approve anyway, since he had borrowed this maneuver from Valentine, from an episode in *Adventures of a Practical Historian*, one of those books he had thrilled to back in his Apprentice days, before he found out what real adventures were like. Spewing gas from her dorsal vents, the *Jenny* dropped into the path of the oncoming city and went powering forward on a collision course. The voice on the radio rose to a sudden scream, and Hester and Pennyroyal screamed too as Tom steered the ship low over the rusty factories on the brim of the middle tier and drove her between two enormous supporting pillars into the shadow of the tier above. Behind him, two of the Fox Spirits pulled up short, but the leader was bolder, and followed him into the heart of the city.

This was Tom's first visit to Novaya-Nizhni, and it was rather a fleeting one. From what he could see, the city was laid out in much the same way as poor old London, with broad streets radiating out from the center of each tier. Along one of these the *Jenny Haniver* raced at lamppost height, while shocked faces gaped down at her from upper windows and pedestrians scattered for cover on the pavements. Near the tier's hub loomed a thicket of support pillars and elevator shafts, a slalom course through which the little airship slipped with inches to spare, grazing her envelope and scraping paint from her steering vanes. The pursuing Fox Spirit was not so lucky. Neither Tom nor Hester saw quite what happened, but they heard the rending crash even over the roar of the *Jenny*'s engines, and the periscope showed them the wreckage crumpling toward the deck, the gondola swinging drunkenly from an overhead tramway.

Out into sudden, blinding sunlight on the far side of the city. It seemed they had escaped, and even the petrified Pennyroyal cheered in the sudden rush of happiness that united them all. But the Green Storm did not give up so easily. The *Jenny* swung through the fog of exhaust smoke that hung behind the city, and in the clear air beyond, the two remaining Fox Spirits were waiting.

A rocket slammed into the starboard engines, the blast blowing out the flight-deck windows and flinging Hester to the floor. She scrambled up to find Tom still crouched over the controls, his hair and clothes frosted with powdered glass. Pennyroyal was slumped against the chart table with blood trickling from a gash on his bald head where one of the *Jenny*'s brass fire extinguishers had struck him a glancing blow as it fell. Hester dragged him to a window seat. He was still breathing, but his eyes had rolled up until only two half-moons of white showed under the lids. He looked as if he were studying something very interesting on the inside of his head.

More rockets struck. A buckled propeller blade hummed past, whirling down toward the snowfields like a failed boomerang. Tom was still heaving at the controls, but the *Jenny Haniver* no longer obeyed him—either the rudders were gone, or the cables that operated them had been severed. A fierce gust of wind, howling through a gap in the mountains, swung her toward the Fox Spirits. The nearer of the two made a sudden move to avoid collision, and collided with her sister ship instead.

The explosion, barely twenty yards to starboard, filled the *Jenny*'s flight deck with a lurid glare. When Hester could see again, the sky was full of tumbling litter. She could hear the rattle and crash as larger fragments of the Fox Spirits bounded away down the mountainsides into the pass below. She could hear the grumble of Novaya-Nizhni's engines a few miles astern, the squeak and thunder of its tracks as it hauled itself southward. She could hear her own heart beating, very loud and very fast, and she realized that the *Jenny*'s engines had stopped. From the increasingly frantic way that Tom tugged and hammered at the controls, it looked as if there was little hope of starting them again. A bitter wind blew in through the shattered windows, bringing with it flakes of snow and a cold, clean smell of ice.

She said a quick prayer for the souls of the Green Storm aviators, hoping that their ghosts would hurry down to the Sunless Country and not hang about up here to make more trouble. Then she went stiffly to stand beside Tom. He gave up his useless struggle with the controls and put his arms around her, and they stood there holding each other, staring at the view ahead. The *Jenny* was drifting over the shoulder of a big volcano. Beyond it there were no more mountains, just an endless blue-white plain stretching to the horizon. They were at the mercy of the wind, and it was carrying them helpless into the Ice Wastes.

6

Above
the Ice

I T'S NO GOOD," said Tom. "I can't repair the damage to the engines without setting down, and if we set down here . . ."

He didn't need to say any more. It was three days since the disaster in the Drachen Pass, and below the drifting wreck of the *Jenny Haniver* lay a landscape hostile as a frozen moon: a crosshatched waste of thick, ancient ice. Here and there a mountain peak thrust up through the whiteness, but these too were lifeless, white and inhospitable. There was no sign of towns or cities or wandering Snowmad bands, and no answer to the *Jenny's* regular distress calls. Although it was still only early afternoon, the sun was already going down, a dull red disk that gave no heat.

Hester wrapped her arms around Tom and felt him shivering inside his thick, fleece-lined aviator's coat. It was terrifyingly cold here: coldness like a living thing that pressed against your flesh, searching for a way to crawl in through your pores and smother the failing core of warmth inside your body. Hester felt as if it had already crept into her bones; she could feel it gnawing at the furrow Valentine's sword had left in her skull. But she was still warmer than poor Tom, who had been out on the starboard engine pod for the past hour, trying to chip away the ice that had formed there and make repairs.

She led him aft and sat him on the bunk in their cabin, heaping blankets and spare coats over him and snuggling in beside him to let him share her own small store of warmth.

"How's Professor Pennyroyal?" he asked.

Hester grunted. It was hard to tell. The explorer had not regained consciousness, and she was beginning to suspect he never would. At the moment, he was lying on a bed she had made up for him in the galley, covered with his own bedding roll and a few blankets that Hester felt she and Tom could ill spare. "Every time I think he's finally gone and it's time to chuck him overboard, he kind of stirs and mutters and I find I can't."

She dozed off. It was easy and pleasant to sleep. In her dreams a strange light filled the cabin: a fluttering glow that flared and shifted like the light of MEDUSA. Remembering that night, she cuddled closer to Tom and found his mouth with hers. When she opened her eye, the light from her dreams was still there, rippling across his beautiful face.

"Aurora Borealis," he whispered.

Hester sprang up. "Who? Where?"

"The Northern Lights," he explained, laughing, pointing to the window. Out in the night a shimmering veil of color swung above the ice, now green, now red, now gold, now all at once, sometimes fading almost to nothing, sometimes blazing and billowing in dazzling streamers.

"I've always wanted to see them," said Tom. "Ever since I read about them in that Chung-Mai Spofforth book, *A Season with the Snowmads*. And here they are. As if they've been ordered just for us."

"Congratulations," said Hester, and pressed her face into the soft hollow beneath his jaw so that she could not see the lights. They were beautiful, all right, but it was a huge, inhuman beauty, and she could not help thinking that they would soon become her funeral lanterns. Soon the weight of ice accumulating on the *Jenny*'s envelope and rigging would force her down, and there in the dark and the whispering cold Hester and Tom would sink into a sleep from which there would be no awakening.

She did not feel particularly frightened. It was nice, dozing there in Tom's sleepy embrace, feeling the warmth seep out of her. And everybody knew that lovers who died in each other's arms went down together to the Sunless Country, favorites of the Goddess of Death.

The only problem was, she needed to pee. The more she tried to ignore it and compose herself and wait calmly for the dark goddess's touch, the more urgent grew the pressure on her bladder. She didn't want to die distracted, but she didn't want to simply go in her breeches either: It wouldn't be nearly so romantic to go into the afterlife all soggy.

Grumbling and cursing, she wriggled out from under the covers and crept forward, slithering on the ice that had formed on the deck. The chemical toilet behind the flight deck had been smashed to pieces by one of the rocket blasts, but there was a handy hole in the floor where it had been. She crouched over it and did her business as quickly as she could, gasping at the fierce cold.

She wanted to go straight back to Tom, and later she would wish that she had, but something prompted her to go forward onto the silent flight deck instead. It was pretty up there now, with the dim glow of the instrument panels glittering through layers of frost. She knelt in front of the little shrine where the statues of the Sky Goddess and the God of Aviators stood. Most aviators decorated their flight-deck shrines with pictures of their ancestors, but neither Tom nor Hester had any images of their dead parents, so they had tacked up a photograph of Anna Fang they had unearthed from a trunk in the cabin when the *Jenny* was being repaired. Hester said a little prayer to her, hoping that she would be a friend to them down in the Sunless Country.

It was as she stood up to go back to Tom that she happened to glance out across the ice and saw the cluster of lights. At first she thought that they were just a reflection of that strange fire in the sky that Tom had been so pleased by— but these were steady points, not changing color, just twinkling a little in the frosty air. She went closer to the shattered window. The cold made her eye water, but after a while she made out a dark bulk around the lights, and a pale drift of fog or steam above them. She was looking at a small ice city, about ten miles to leeward, heading north.

Trying to ignore her strange, ungrateful sense of disappointment, she went to rouse Tom, patting his face until he groaned and stirred and said, "What is it?"

"Some god's got a soft spot for us," she said. "We're saved."

By the time he reached the flight deck, the city was closer, for the fortunate wind was blowing them almost directly toward it. It was a small, two-tiered affair, skating along on broad iron runners. Tom trained the binoculars on it and saw its curved and sloping jaws, closed to form a snowplow, and the huge hooked stern wheel that propelled it across the ice. It was an elegant city, with crescents of tall white houses on its upper tier and some sort of palace complex near the stern, but it had a faintly mournful air, and there were patches of rust and many lightless windows.

"I don't understand why we didn't pick up their beacon," Hester was saying, fumbling with the controls of the radio set.

"Maybe they don't have one," said Tom.

Hester scrolled up and down the wave bands, hunting for the warble of a homing beacon. There was nothing. It struck her as odd and faintly sinister, this lonely city creeping north in silence. But when she hailed it on the open channel, a perfectly friendly harbormaster answered her in Anglish, and after half an hour the harbormaster's nephew came buzzing up aboard a little green air tug called the *Graculus* to take the *Jenny Haniver* under tow.

They set down at an almost deserted air harbor near the front of the city's upper tier. The harbormaster and his wife, kind, round, acorn-brown people in parkas and fur bonnets, guided the *Jenny* into a domed hangar that opened like a flower, and carried Pennyroyal on a stretcher to their home behind the harbor office. There, in the warm kitchen, coffee and bacon and hot pastries awaited the newcomers, and as Tom and Hester tucked in, their hosts stood watching, beaming their approval and saying, "Welcome, travelers! Welcome, welcome, welcome to Anchorage!"

Ghost Town

I T WAS A WEDNESDAY, AND on Wednesdays Freya's chauffeur always drove her to the Temple of the Ice Gods so that she could pray to them for guidance. The temple was barely ten yards from her palace, on the same raised platform near the stern of the city, so it was not really necessary to go through the business of calling out her chauffeur, climbing into her official bug, driving the short distance, and climbing out again, but Freya went through it anyway; it would not have been seemly for the margravine to walk.

Once again she knelt in the dim candle glow of the refrigerated temple and looked up at the lovely ice statues of the Lord and Lady and asked them to tell her what she should do, or at least to send a sign to show her that the things she had already done were right. And once again there was no answer: no miraculous light, no voices whispering in her mind, no patterns of frost arranging themselves into messages on the floor, only the steady purr of the engines making the deck plates judder against her knees, the winter twilight pressing at the windows. Her mind kept drifting off, thinking about stupid, annoying things, like the stuff that had gone missing from the palace. It made her angry and a little scared that someone could come into her chambers and take her things. She tried asking the Ice Gods who the thief was, but of course they would not tell her that, either.

Finally she prayed for Mama and Papa, wondering what it was like for them down in the Sunless Country. Since their deaths she had begun to realize that she had never really known them, not in the way that other people know their parents. There had always been nannies and handmaidens to look after Freya, and she saw Mama and Papa only at dinnertime and on formal occasions. She had called them "Your Radiance" and "Sir." The closest she had been to them was on certain summer evenings when they had gone for picnics in the margravine's ice-barge—simple family affairs, just Freya and Mama and Papa and about seventy servants and courtiers. Then the plague came and she wasn't even allowed to see them, and then they were dead. Some servants laid them in the barge and set fire to it and sent it out onto the ice. Freya had stood at her window and watched the smoke going up, and it felt as if they had never existed at all.

Outside the temple, her chauffeur was waiting for her, pacing up and down and scratching patterns in the snow with the toe of his boot. "Home, Smew," she announced, and as he scurried to slide the lid of the bug open, she looked toward the bows, thinking how pathetically few lights there were in the upper city these days. She remembered issuing a proclamation about the empty houses, stating than any of the engine-district workers who wished might move out of their dingy little flats down below and take over some of the empty villas up here instead, but very few had done so. Perhaps they *liked* their dingy flats. Perhaps they needed the comfort of familiar things just as badly as she did.

Down at the air harbor a splash of red stood out gaudily amid the whites and grays.

"Smew? Whatever is that? Surely a ship has not arrived?"

The chauffeur bowed. "She put in last night, Your Radiance. A trader called the *Jenny Haniver*. Shot up by air pirates or something, and in bad need of repairs, according to Harbormaster Aakiuq."

Freya peered at the ship, hoping to make out more details. It was difficult to see much through the swirls of powder snow that were being blown off the rooftops. How odd to think of strangers walking about aboard Anchorage again after all this time!

"Why didn't you tell me before?" she asked.

"The margravine isn't normally informed about the arrival of mere merchantmen, Your Radiance."

"But who is aboard this ship? Are they interesting?"

"Two young aviators, Your Radiance. And an older man, their passenger."

"Oh," said Freya, losing interest. For a moment she had been almost excited, and had imagined inviting these new-comers to the palace, but of course it would never do for the Margravine of Anchorage to start hobnobbing with tramp aviators and a man who couldn't even afford his own airship.

"Natsworthy and Shaw were the names Mr. Aakiuq told me, Your Radiance," Smew went on, helping her into the bug. "Natsworthy and Shaw and Pennyroyal."

"Pennyroyal? Not Professor *Nimrod* Pennyroyal?"

"I believe so, Your Radiance, yes."

"Then I—then I—" Freya turned this way and that, adjusted her bonnet, shook her head. The traditions that had been her guide since everybody died had nothing to say about What To Do In The Event Of A Miracle. "Oh," she whispered. "Oh, Smew, I must welcome him! Go to the air harbor! Fetch him to the council chamber—no, to the big audience room. As soon as you've driven me home, you must go and—no, go now! I'll walk home!"

And she ran back inside the temple to thank the Gods of the Ice for sending her the sign she had been waiting for.

Even Hester had heard of Anchorage. In spite of its small size it was one of the most famous of the ice cities, for it could trace its name right back to old America. A band of refugees had fled the original Anchorage just before the Sixty Minute War broke out, and had founded a new settlement on a storm-wracked northern island. There they survived through plagues and earthquakes and ice ages until eight centuries ago, when the great Traction boom reached the north. Then every city was forced to start moving or be eaten by those that had, and the people of Anchorage rebuilt their home and set off on their endless journeyings across the ice.

It was no predator, and the small jaws at its bows were used only for gathering in salvage or gouging up freshwater ice to feed the boilers. Its people made their living by trading along the fringes of the Ice Wastes, where they would link themselves with elegant little boarding-bridges to other peaceful towns and provide a marketplace where scavengers and archaeologists could gather to sell the things they scratched up from the ice.

So what was it doing here, miles from the trade routes, heading north into the gathering winter? The question had nagged at Hester while she was helping to moor the *Jenny Haniver*, and it was nagging at her still when she woke from a long, refreshing sleep in the harbormaster's house. In the grainy dusk that passed for daylight here, she could see that the crescents of white mansions overlooking the air harbor were streaked with rust, and that many of the buildings had broken windows that opened on darkness like the eyeholes of skeletons. The harbor itself seemed to be on the verge of vanishing beneath a tide of decay: The bitter wind whipped litter and snow into drifts against the empty hangars, and a scrawny dog lifted its leg against a heap of old sky-train couplings.

"Such a pity, such a pity," said Mrs. Aakiuq, the harbormaster's wife, as she cooked up a second breakfast for her young visitors. "If you could have seen the dear place in the old days. Such riches there were, and such comings and goings. Why, when I was a girl, we often had airships stacked up twenty deep, waiting for a berth. Sky yachts and runabouts and racing sloops come up to try their luck in the Boreal Regatta, and gorgeous great liners named after old-world movie queens, the *Audrey Hepburn* and the *Gong Li*."

"So what happened?" asked Tom.

"Oh, the world changed on us," said Mrs. Aakiuq sadly.

"Prey got scarce, and the great predator cities like Arkangel, which wouldn't have spared us a second glance once, now chase us whenever they can."

Her husband nodded, pouring steaming mugs of coffee for his guests. "And then, this year, the plague came. We took aboard some Snowmad scavengers who'd just found bits of an old orbital weapons platform crashed in the ice near the pole, and it turned out to be infected with some kind of horrible engineered virus from the Sixty Minute War. Oh, don't look so worried; those old battle-viruses do their work fast and then mutate into something harmless. But it spread through the city like wildfire, killing hundreds of people. Even the old margravine and her consort died. And when it was over and the quarantine was lifted, well, a lot of folk couldn't see a future anymore for Anchorage, so they took what airships there were and went off to find a life in other cities. I doubt there's more than fifty of us left in the whole place now."

"Is that all?" Tom was amazed. "But how can so few people keep a town this size working?"

"They can't," replied Aakiuq. "Not forever. But old Mr. Scabious, the enginemaster, has done wonders—a lot of automated systems, clever Old Tech gadgets and the like—and he'll keep us moving long enough."

"Long enough for what?" asked Hester suspiciously. "Where are you going?"

The harbormaster's smile vanished. "Can't tell you that, Miss Hester. Who's to say you won't fly off and sell our course to Arkangel or some other predator? We don't want to find them lying in wait for us on the High Ice. Now eat up your seal-burgers and we'll go and see if we can't roust out some spare parts to fix that poor battered *Jenny Haniver* of yours."

They ate, and then trailed after him across the docks to a huge, whalebacked warehouse. In the dim interior, teetering stacks of old engine pods and gondola panels vied for space with spare parts ripped from the flight decks of dismantled airships and curved aluminum envelope struts like the ribs of giants. Propellers of all sizes hung overhead, swinging gently with the city's movement.

"This used to be my cousin's place," said Aakiuq, shining an electric lantern over the junk heaps. "But he went and died in the plague, so I suppose it's mine now. Never fear; there's not much goes wrong with an airship that I don't know how to fix, and there's precious little else for me to do these days."

As they followed him through the rusty dark, some small thing clattered and seemed to scrabble away among the stacked iron shelves of salvage. Hester, wary as ever, jerked her head in its direction, searching the shadows with her single eye. Nothing moved. Small things must always be falling, mustn't they, in an old storeroom of a place like this? In a building with dodgy shock absorbers that swayed and shuddered as Anchorage went plowing across the ice? And yet she could not shake off the sense that she was being watched.

"Jeunet-Carot engines, wasn't it?" Mr. Aakiuq was asking. He clearly liked Tom—people always liked Tom—and he was making great efforts to help, scurrying to and fro among the mounds of junk and checking notes in a huge, mold-speckled ledger. "I believe I have something that will suit. Your gas cells are old Tibetan jobs, by the look of 'em: Those we can't patch I'll replace with some nice RJ50s from a Zhang-Chen Hawkmoth. Yes, I believe your *Jenny Haniver* will be aloft again within three weeks."

In blue darkness far below, three pairs of keen eyes watched a small screen, staring at a grainy image of Tom and Hester and the harbormaster. Three pairs of ears as white as underground fungi strained to catch the tinny, distorted voices that came whispering down from the world above.

Back at the harbormaster's house, Mrs. Aakiuq outfitted Tom and Hester with overboots and snowshoes, thermal underwear, thick sweaters of oiled wool, mittens, scarves, and parkas. There were also cold-masks: fleece-lined leather objects with glastic eyepieces and a filter to breathe through. Mrs. Aakiuq did not say where all these things had come from, but Hester had noticed the photographs decked with mourning ribbons on the household shrine, and she guessed that she and Tom were dressing in the clothes of the Aakiuqs' dead children. She hoped those plague germs really were as dead as the harbormaster had promised. She liked the mask, though.

When they returned to the kitchen, they found Pennyroyal sitting by the stove, his feet in a bowl of steaming water and a bandage around his head. He looked pale, but otherwise he was his old self, slurping a mug of Mrs. Aakiuq's moss tea and greeting Tom and Hester cheerfully. "So glad to see you safe! What adventures we shared, eh! Something for my next book there, I suspect. . . ."

A brass telephone on the wall near the stove emitted a tinny jingle. Mrs. Aakiuq hurried to lift the earpiece, listening very carefully to the message being relayed by her friend Mrs. Umiak at the exchange. Her face broadened into a shining smile, and by the time she set the phone back on its hook and turned to her guests, she could barely speak for excitement.

"Great news, my dears! The margravine is to grant you an audience! The margravine herself! She is sending her chauffeur to carry you to the Winter Palace! Such an honor! To think, you will go straight from my own humble kitchen to the margravine's audience chamber!"

8

The Winter Palace

W HAT'S A MARGRAVINE?" Hester hissed at Tom as they
stepped outside again into the fierce cold. "It sounds like
something you spread on your toast. . . ."

"I suppose it's a sort of mayoress," Tom said.

"A margravine," Pennyroyal chipped in, "is the female version of a margrave. A lot of these small northern cities have
something similar: a hereditary ruling family, with titles
handed down from one generation to the next. Margrave.
Portreeve. Graf. The Elector Urbanus of Eisenstadt. The
Direktor of Arkangel. They're very keen on their traditions
up here."

"Well, I don't see why they can't just call her a mayoress
and have done with it," said Hester grumpily.

A bug was waiting for them at the harbor gates, an electric vehicle of the sort that Tom remembered from London,

although he didn't remember any quite as beautiful as this. It was painted bright red, with a golden letter *R* surrounded by curlicues on its flank. The single wheel at the back was larger than on a normal bug, and studded to grip snow. On the curving mudguards that arched above the two front wheels, big electric lanterns had been mounted, and snowflakes danced crazily in their twin beams.

The chauffeur saw them coming and slid open the glastic canopy as they drew near. He wore a red uniform with gold braid and epaulettes, and when he drew himself up to his full height and saluted, he just about came up to Hester's waist. A child, she thought at first, then saw that he was actually much older than her, with a grown man's head balanced on a stumpy little body. She quickly looked away, realizing that she had been staring at him in exactly the same hurtful, prying, pitiful way that people sometimes stared at her.

"Name's Smew," he said. "Her Radiance has sent me to bring you to the Winter Palace."

They climbed into the bug, squeezing into the backseat on either side of Pennyroyal, who took up a surprising amount of space for a small man. Smew slid shut the lid, and they were off. Tom looked back to wave at the Aakiuqs, who were watching from a window of their house, but the air harbor had vanished into the snow flurries and the wintry dark. The bug was driving along a broad thoroughfare, from which covered arcades opened off on either side. Shops and restaurants and grand villas flicked by, all dead, all dark. "This is Rasmussen Prospekt," Smew announced. "Very elegant street. Runs right through the middle of the upper city from bow to stern."

Tom looked out through the bug's lid. He was impressed by this beautiful, desolate place, yet the emptiness of it made him nervous. Where was it going, rushing into the dead north like this? He shivered inside his warm clothes, remembering his time aboard another town that had been in the wrong place, heading for a mysterious destination: Tunbridge Wheels, whose deranged mayor had driven it to a watery grave in the Sea of Khazak.

"Here we are," announced Smew suddenly. "The Winter Palace, home to the House of Rasmussen for eight hundred years."

They were nearing the city's stern, and the bug's electric motor griped and whinnied as it carried them up a long ramp. At the top stood the palace that Tom had glimpsed from the air the night before: a twirl of white metal with spires and balconies rimed in ice. The upper stories looked empty and abandoned, but lights showed in some of the windows on the lower floors, and gas flames danced in bronze tripods outside the circular front door.

The bug scrunched to a halt on the frosty drive, and Smew held the canopy while his passengers climbed out, then hurried up the palace steps and slid the outer door open, letting them into a small chamber called a heat-lock. He slid the door shut, and after a few seconds, when the cold air that had entered with the visitors had been warmed by heaters in the roof and walls, an inner door opened. They followed Smew into a paneled hallway, the walls hung with tapestries. Giant double doors loomed ahead, clad in priceless Old Tech alloys. Smew knocked on them, then muttered, "Wait here, please," and scurried away down a side passage.

The building creaked slightly, swaying with the motion of the city. There was a smell of mildew.

"I don't like this," said Hester, looking up at the thick veils of cobweb that swathed the chandeliers and dangled from the heating ducts. "Why has she asked us here? It could be a trap."

"Stuff and nonsense, Miss Shaw," scoffed Pennyroyal, trying not to look too alarmed by her suggestion. "A trap? Why should the margravine set a trap for us? She's a very superior sort of person, remember, a type of mayoress."

Hester shrugged. "I've come across only two mayors before, and neither of them was very superior. They were both stark, staring mad."

The doors suddenly jerked and slid sideways, grating slightly on their bearings. Beyond them stood Smew, dressed now in a long blue robe and a six-cornered hat and clutching a staff of office twice his own height. He welcomed the guests solemnly, as if he had never seen them before, and then thumped the staff three times on the metal floor. "Professor Nimrod Pennyroyal and party," he announced, and stepped aside to let them walk past him into the pillared space beyond.

A line of argon globes hung from the vaulted roof, each casting a circular glow on the floor beneath it, like stepping-stones of light leading toward the far end of the enormous chamber. Someone sat waiting there, slouched in an ornate throne on a raised dais. Hester groped for Tom's hand, and side by side they followed Pennyroyal through shadow and light, shadow and light, until they stood at the foot of the dais steps, looking up into the face of the margravine.

For some reason they had both expected someone old. Everything in this silent, rusting house spoke of age and decay, of ancient customs preserved long after their purpose had been forgotten. Yet the girl gazing haughtily down at them was even younger than they were, certainly not a day over sixteen. A large, pretty girl, dressed in an elaborate ice-blue gown and a white overmantle with a fox-fur collar. Her features had something of the Inuit look of Aakiuq and his wife, but her skin was very fair and her hair was golden. *The color of autumn leaves,* Hester thought, hiding her face. The margravine's beauty made her feel small and worthless and unneeded. She started looking for faults. *She's far too fat. And her neck needs a good wash. And the moths have been at that pretty frock, and all the buttons are done up wrong. . . .*

Beside her, Tom was thinking, *So young, and in charge of a whole city! No wonder she looks sad!*

"Your Worship," said Pennyroyal, bowing low. "May I say how very grateful I am for the kindness that you and your people have extended to myself and my young companions. . . ."

"You must call me 'Your Radiance,'" said the girl. "Or 'Light of the Ice Fields.'"

There was an awkward silence. Little scraping and clicking noises came from the fat heating ducts that snaked across the ceiling, warming the palace with recycled heat from the engines. The girl peered at her guests. At last she said, "If you're Nimrod Pennyroyal, how come you're so much fatter and balder than your picture?"

She picked up a book from a small side table and held it out to show the back cover. It bore a painting of someone who might have been Pennyroyal's hunkier younger brother.

"Ah, well, artistic license, you know," blustered the explorer. "Fool of a painter—I told him to show me as I am, paunch and high forehead and all, but you know what these artistic types are; they do love to idealize, to show the inner man. . . ."

The margravine smiled. (She looked even prettier smiling. Hester decided that she disliked her quite a lot.) "I just wanted to be sure that it was really you, Professor Pennyroyal," she said. "I quite understand about the portrait. I was always having to have mine done for plates and stamps and coins and things before the plague came, and they hardly *ever* got it right. . . ."

She stopped talking suddenly, as if some internal nanny had reminded her that a margravine does not babble in front of her guests like an excited teenager. "You may be seated," she announced, much more formally, and clapped her hands. A door behind the throne popped open and Smew came scuttling out, dragging a set of small chairs. He had taken on yet another guise: the pillbox hat and high-collared tunic of a footman. For a moment Tom wondered if there really were three identical little men in the margravine's service, but when he looked more closely, it was obvious that this was the same Smew: He was still out of breath from his quick changes, and the chamberlain's wig poked from his pocket.

"Do hurry up," said the margravine.

"Sorry, Your Radiance." Smew set the three chairs down facing the throne, then vanished into the shadows again. A moment later he was back, wheeling a heated trolley on which stood a pot of tea and a tray of almond cookies. With him came another man, tall, stern, and elderly, dressed all in black. He nodded to the newcomers, then took up a position beside the throne as Smew poured tea into tiny blast-glass cups and handed them to the guests.

"So I take it you know my work, O Light of the Ice Fields?" said Pennyroyal, simpering a little.

The margravine's mask of courtly etiquette slipped again, the excitable teenager showing through. "Oh, yes! I love history and adventures. I used to read about them all the time before . . . well, before I became margravine. I've read all the classics: Valentine, and Spofforth, and Tamarton Foliot. But yours were always my favorites, Professor Pennyroyal. That's what gave me the idea to—"

"Careful, Margravine," said the man at her side. His voice was a soft rumble, like a well-tuned engine.

"Well, anyway," said the margravine, "that's why it's so wonderful that the Ice Gods sent you here! It's a sign, you see. A sign that I made the right decision, and that we'll find what we are looking for. With you to help us, how can we possibly fail?"

"Mad as a spoon," whispered Hester to Tom, very quietly.

"I'm rather at a loss, Your Radiance," admitted Pennyroyal. "I think perhaps my intellects are still a little fuddled after that knock on the head. I'm afraid I don't quite follow."

"It's quite simple," said the margravine.

"Margravine," warned the man at her side again.

"Oh, don't be such an old gloom-bucket, Mr. Scabious!" she retorted. "This is Professor Pennyroyal! We can trust him!"

"I don't doubt it, Your Radiance," said Scabious. "It is his young friends I am concerned about. If they get wind of our course, there is a danger they may be off to sell us to Arkangel as soon as their ship is repaired. Direktor Masgard would dearly love to get his hands on my engines."

"We'd never do anything like that!" cried Tom, and would have sprung forward to confront the old man if Hester had not held him back.

"I think I can vouch for my crew, Your Radiance," said Pennyroyal. "Captain Natsworthy is a historian like myself, trained at the London Museum."

The margravine turned to study Tom for the first time, with a look of such admiration that he blushed and stared down at his feet. "Then welcome, Mr. Natsworthy," she said softly. "I hope that you will stay here and help us too."

"Help you with what?" asked Hester bluntly.

"With our journey to America, of course," the girl replied. She turned the book that she was holding to display the front cover. It showed a muscly, too-handsome Pennyroyal fighting a bear, egged on by a girl in a fur bikini. It was a first edition of *America the Beautiful*.

"This one was always my favorite," the margravine explained. "I expect that's why the Ice Gods put the idea of America into my head. We're going to find our way across the ice to the new green wilderness that Professor Pennyroyal discovered. There we'll swap our skids for wheels, and chop down the trees for fuel, and trade with the savages, and introduce them to the benefits of Municipal Darwinism."

"But, but, but . . ." Pennyroyal gripped the handrests of his chair as if he were riding a roller coaster. "But I mean to say, the Canadian Ice Sheet— West of Greenland— No city has ever attempted to—"

"I know, Professor," the girl agreed. "It will be a long and dangerous journey for us, just as it was for you when you came on foot out of America, up onto the ice. But the gods are with us. They must be. Otherwise they would not have sent you to us. I am going to appoint you Honorary Chief Navigator, and with your help I know we will come safely into our new hunting ground."

Tom, thrilled by the boldness of the margravine's vision, turned to Pennyroyal. "What wonderful luck, Professor!" he said happily. "You'll be able to return to America after all!"

Pennyroyal made a gurgling sound, and his eyes bulged. "I . . . chief navigator, eh? You are too kind, Light of the Ice Fields, too kind. . . ." His blast-glass cup dropped from his fingers as he fainted, shattering on the iron floor. Smew tutted, because the set was an old heirloom of the House of Rasmussen, but Freya did not care. "Professor Pennyroyal is still weak from his adventures," she said. "Put him to bed! Air out rooms in the guest quarters for him and his friends. We must nurse him back to health as soon as possible. And do stop fretting about that silly little cup, Smew. Once the professor has led us to America, we shall be able to dig up all the blast-glass we could possibly desire!"

9

Welcome to the Facility

FAR TO THE SOUTH, BEYOND the margins of the ice, an island rose from a cold sea. Black it was, and jagged, streaked with the droppings of the gulls and skuas that made their homes upon its ledges. The noise of the birds could be heard from miles away as they clanged and shrieked and squabbled, diving into the surf for fish or wheeling in great flocks about the high summit, sometimes perching on the roofs of the squat buildings that clung there, or on the rusting handrails of the precarious metal walkways that jutted from the sheer cliffs like bracket fungus on a dead tree stump. For although the place looked uninhabitable, people lived there: Airship hangars had been blasted out of the rock, and clusters of spherical fuel tanks huddled like spiders' eggs in narrow crevices. This was Rogues' Roost, where Red Loki and his legendary band of air pirates had built their aerie.

Loki was gone now, and there were still the scars of rocket explosions on some of the buildings to show that he had not gone willingly. A Green Storm assault unit had come down upon this place one calm night, butchered the pirates, and taken control of the Roost, establishing a base that no hungry city could come at.

The sun was setting, the red and purple and smoky orange smeared across the western sky, making the island look even more sinister than usual as the *Temporary Blip* came chugging in from windward. Gun emplacements swiveled like armored heads, tracking the plump old airship. As she edged in toward the main hangar, her escort of Fox Spirits flew circles around her, like farm dogs chivying a reluctant ewe into a fold.

"What a dump!" complained one of Widgery Blinkoe's wives, peering out through the gondola windows.

"You told us reporting that old airship would bring us luck and money," agreed another. "You said we'd be sunning ourselves on a raft resort, not trailing out here off the edge of the world."

"You promised new dresses, and slaves!"

"Silence, wives!" shouted Blinkoe, trying to concentrate on his steering levers while the ground crew guided him into the hangar with colored flags. "Show some respect! This is a Green Storm base! It is an honor to be asked here: a sign that they value my services!" But in truth he was as dismayed as they at being summoned to Rogues' Roost. After he radioed his sighting of the *Jenny Haniver* to the Storm's base in the Tannhäusers, he'd expected a thank-you, and perhaps a nice payment. He had certainly not expected to be jumped by a flight of Fox Spirits as soon as he left

Airhaven and dragged all the way out here.

"Well, really!" grumbled his wives, nudging one another.

"It's a pity the Green Storm don't respect him as much as he respects them!"

"Value his services, indeed!"

"Think of the business we're losing, trailing out here!"

"My mother warned me not to marry him."

"So did mine!"

"Mine too!"

"He knows this is a fool's errand! See how worried he looks!"

Mr. Blinkoe was still looking worried as he stepped out of the *Temporary Blip* in the chaotic, echoey hangar, but his expression changed to an indulgent smile when a pretty subaltern came hurrying up to salute him. Widgery Blinkoe had a weakness for pretty young women, which was how he had ended up marrying five of them, and although those five had all turned out to be rather shrill and headstrong and tended to gang up on him, he could not help toying with the thought of asking the subaltern to become number six.

"Mr. Blinkoe?" she asked. "Welcome to the Facility."

"I thought it was called Rogues' Roost, my dear?"

"The commander prefers us to call it the Facility."

"Oh."

"I'm here to take you to her."

"Her, eh? I hadn't realized there were so many ladies in your organization."

The girl's smile vanished. "The Green Storm believes that both men and women must play their part in the coming war to defeat the Tractionist barbarians and make the Earth green again."

"Oh, of course, of course," said Mr. Blinkoe quickly. "I couldn't agree more. . . ." He didn't like that sort of talk: War was so terribly bad for business. But the past few years had been bad for the Anti-Traction League: London had rolled almost to the gates of Batmunkh Gompa, and its agents had burned the Northern Air Fleet. That had meant that there were no spare ships to come to the aid of the Spitzbergen Static when Arkangel attacked it last winter, and so the last great Anti-Tractionist city of the north had been swallowed into the predator's gut. It was only natural that some of the League's younger officers had grown impatient with the dithering of the High Council, and itchy for revenge. Hopefully it would all come to nothing.

Trailing after the subaltern, he tried to judge the strength of this little base. There were a couple of well-armed Fox Spirits standing ready on docking pans, and a lot of soldiers in white uniforms and bronze crab-shell helmets, all wearing armbands with the lightning-flash symbol of the Green Storm. *Heavy security*, he thought, his gaze slipping quickly over their steam-powered machine guns. But why? What was going on out here at the back end of nowhere that warranted all this? A line of troops tramped past, carrying big metal cases stenciled FRAGILE and TOP SECRET, tightly locked. A little bald-headed man wearing a transparent plastic coat over his uniform was fussing at the soldiers. "Do go carefully now! Don't jostle! Those are sensitive instruments!" Sensing Blinkoe's gaze, he glanced toward him. There was a small tattoo between his eyebrows, in the shape of a red wheel.

"What exactly is it you're doing here?" Blinkoe asked his escort, following her out of the hangar and along damp tunnels and stairways, climbing up and up through the heart of the rock.

"It's secret," she said.

"But surely you can tell me?"

The subaltern shook her head. She was a rude, officious, military sort of girl, Blinkoe decided; not sixth–Mrs. Blinkoe material at all. He turned his attention to the posters tacked to the passage walls. They showed League airships raining down rockets on mobile towns, beneath angry slogans that exhorted the reader to DESTROY ALL CITIES. Between the posters were stenciled signs pointing the way to cellblocks, barracks, various gun platforms, and a laboratory. That seemed strange too. The Anti-Traction League had always been sniffy about science; they thought any technology more complicated than an airship or a rocket projector was barbaric, and best ignored. Clearly the Green Storm had different ideas.

Mr. Blinkoe began to feel a little afraid.

The commander's office was in one of the old buildings on the summit of the island. It had once been Red Loki's private quarters, and the walls had been decorated with saucy murals that the commander had primly whitewashed over. The whitewash was thin, though, and here and there faint painted faces were beginning to show through, like the ghosts of dead pirates looking on in disapproval at the Roost's new tenants. In the far wall a big circular window looked out at nothing much.

"You're Blinkoe? Welcome to the Facility."

The commander was very young. Mr. Blinkoe had hoped she'd be pretty, but she turned out to be a stern-looking little minx, all cropped black hair and a hard, peat-colored face. "You are the agent who sighted the *Jenny Haniver* at Airhaven?" she asked. Her hands kept clenching and flexing, like fidgety brown spiders. And the way she stared at him with those great dark eyes! Blinkoe wondered if she was slightly mad.

"Yes, Your Honor," he said nervously.

"And you're sure it was her? There is no mistake? This is not some story you cooked up to defraud the Green Storm of money?"

"No, no!" said Blinkoe hastily. "Gods, no; it was the Wind-Flower's ship, as clear as day!"

The commander turned away from him and walked to the window, peering out through the salt-frosted glass at the swiftly darkening sky. After a moment she said, "A wing of Fox Spirits was scrambled from one of our secret bases to intercept the *Jenny*. None of them returned."

Widgery Blinkoe was uncertain what to say. "Oh, dear," he ventured.

She turned toward him again, but he couldn't see her expression, standing as she was against that luminous window. "The two barbarian infiltrators who stole the *Jenny Haniver* from Batmunkh Gompa may have looked like Out-Country urchins, but they were really highly trained agents in the pay of London. No doubt they used their infernal cunning to outwit and destroy our ships, then fled north into the Ice Wastes."

"It's, um, perfectly possible, Commander," agreed

Widgery Blinkoe, thinking how unlikely it sounded.

She came close to him, a short, slight girl, her eyes burning into his. "We have many Fox Spirits. The Green Storm grows stronger every day. A great many League commanders are on our side, and are prepared to send soldiers and ships to strengthen our bases. What we lack is an intelligence network. That is why we need you, Blinkoe. I want you to find me the *Jenny Haniver*, and the barbarians who fly her."

"That's, um, well, that might, yes," said Blinkoe.

"You will be paid well for your services."

"How well? I don't want to seem mercenary, but I do have five wives to support. . . ."

"Ten thousand when you deliver the ship here."

"Ten thou—!"

"The Green Storm rewards its servants well," the commander assured him. "But we punish those who betray us too. If you breathe a word of this, or of what you have seen at the Facility, to anyone, we will find you, and kill you. Quite painfully. Do you understand?"

"Eep!" squeaked Blinkoe, turning his hat around and around in his hands. "Um, may I ask why? I mean, why this ship is so important? I thought she might have sentimental value, as a sort of symbol for the League, but she hardly seems worth—"

"She is worth what I am offering you." The commander smiled for the first time, a thin, cold, pained little smile, like someone thanking a distant relative for attending a funeral. "The *Jenny Haniver* and the barbarians who stole her could be vital to our work here," she said. "That is all you need to know. Find her and bring her to me, Mr. Blinkoe."

10

The Wunderkammer

ALL ANCHORAGE'S DOCTORS were dead. The best nurse who could be found for Professor Pennyroyal was Windolene Pye of the Steering Committee, who had once done a first-aid course. Sitting by his bed in a luxurious guest room high in the Winter Palace, she held his wrist between her thin fingers, checking his pulse against her pocket watch.

"I believe he has simply fainted," she announced. "Perhaps it was exhaustion, or delayed shock after his terrible adventures, poor gentleman."

"How come we haven't keeled over, then?" Hester wanted to know. "We went through terrible adventures too, and you don't see us swooning all over the place like maiden aunts."

Miss Pye, who was a maiden aunt herself, gave Hester a hard stare. "I think you should leave the professor in peace.

He requires silence and round-the-clock care. Shoo, now, all of you. . . ."

Hester, Tom, and Smew retreated into the corridor, and Windolene Pye closed the door firmly behind them. Tom said, "I expect he was just overcome. He spent years trying to get somebody to fund a second expedition to America, and to find out so suddenly that the margravine's taking her whole city there . . ."

Hester laughed. "It's impossible! She's mad!"

"Miss Shaw!" gasped Smew. "How can you say such things? The margravine is our ruler and the Ice Gods' representative on Earth. It was her ancestor, Dolly Rasmussen, who led the survivors of the first Anchorage out of America to safety. It's only natural that it should fall to a Rasmussen to lead us home again."

"I don't know why you're defending her," Hester grumbled. "She treats you like something she found clinging to the sole of her shoe. And I hope you know you aren't fooling anybody with all these costume changes. We can tell there's only one of you."

"I am not trying to fool anybody," Smew replied with immense dignity. "The margravine must be attended by certain servants and officials: chauffeurs, chefs, chamberlains, footmen, et cetera. Unfortunately, they are all dead. So I have had to step into the breach. I do my bit to keep the old traditions going."

"And what were you before? A chauffeur or a chamberlain?"

"I was the margravine's dwarf."

"What did she need a dwarf for?"

"The margravine's household has *always* had a dwarf. To amuse the margravine."

"How?"

Smew shrugged. "By being short, I suppose."

"Is that amusing?"

"It's tradition, Miss Shaw. We have been glad of our traditions in Anchorage, since the plague came. Here are your rooms."

He flung open the doors of two rooms a little farther along the corridor from Pennyroyal's. Each had long windows, a big bed, fat heating ducts. Each was about the size of the *Jenny Haniver*'s entire gondola.

"They look lovely," said Tom gratefully. "But we just need the one."

"Out of the question," said Smew, bustling into the first room to adjust the controls on the ducts. "It would be unheard-of for unmarried young persons of the opposite gender to share a room in the Winter Palace. All manner of canoodling might occur. Quite out of the question." A rattling inside one of the ducts distracted him for an instant; then he turned to Hester and Tom with a sly wink. "However, there's a connecting door between these rooms, and if someone wished to slip through, why, nobody would ever know. . . ."

But somebody knew almost everything that happened in Anchorage. Peering at their screens in the blue dark, the watchers saw a grainy, fish-eye view of Tom and Hester following the dwarf into the second room.

"She's so ugly!"

"She doesn't look too happy."

"Who would, with a face like that?"

"No, it's not that. She's jealous. Didn't you see the way Freya looked at her boyfriend?"

"I'm bored with this lot. Let's hop."

The picture changed, jumping to other views: the Aakiuqs in their living room, Scabious in his lonely house, the steady, patient work of the engine district and the agricultural quarter. . . .

"Shouldn't we send word to the Aakiuqs?" asked Tom as Smew made his adjustments to the ducts in the second room and prepared to leave. "They might be expecting us back."

"It's already been done, sir," said Smew. "You are guests of the House of Rasmussen now."

"Mr. Scabious won't be too happy about that," said Hester. "He didn't seem to like us one bit."

"Mr. Scabious is a pessimistic man," said Smew. "It is not his fault. He is a widower, and his only son, Axel, died in the plague. He has not borne the loss well. But he has no power to stop the margravine from offering you her hospitality. You are both very welcome here in the Winter Palace. Just ring for a servant—oh, all right, me—if you need anything. Dinner will be at seven, but if you would please come down a little earlier, the margravine wishes to show you her Wunderkammer."

Her what? thought Hester, but she was sick of looking stupid and ignorant in front of Tom, so she kept quiet. When Smew had gone, they opened the connecting door and sat on Tom's bed, bouncing up and down to test the springs.

"America!" said Tom. "Just think of it! She's very brave,

this Freya Rasmussen. Hardly any cities venture west of Greenland, and none have ever tried to reach the Dead Continent."

"No, because it's *dead*," said Hester sourly. "I don't think I'd risk a whole city on one of Pennyroyal's books."

"Professor Pennyroyal knows what he's talking about," said Tom loyally. "Anyway, he's not the only one to report green places in America."

"All those old airmen's legends, you mean?"

"Well, yes. And Snøri Ulvaeusson's map."

"The one you told me about? The one that conveniently vanished before anybody could check it out?"

"Are you saying the professor's lying?" asked Tom.

Hester shook her head. She wasn't sure what she was saying, only that she found it hard to accept Pennyroyal's tale of virgin forests and noble savages. But who was she to doubt him? Pennyroyal was a famous explorer who'd written books, and Hester had never even *read* a book. Tom and Freya believed in him, and they knew much more about these things than she did. It was just that she couldn't equate the timid little man who had quivered and whined each time a rocket came near the *Jenny Haniver* with the brave explorer who fought off bears and befriended savage Americans.

"I'll go and see Aakiuq tomorrow," she said. "See if he can speed up work on the *Jenny*."

Tom nodded, but he wouldn't look at her. "I like it here," he said. "This city, I mean. It's sad, but it's lovely. It reminds me of the nicer bits of London. And it doesn't go about eating other towns, like London did."

Hester imagined a gap opening between the two of them,

like a crack in ice, very thin at the moment but likely to widen. She said, "It's just another Traction City, Tom. Traders or predators, they're all the same. Very nice up top, but down below it'll be slaves and dirt and suffering and corruption. The sooner we leave, the better for both of us."

Smew returned for them at six and led them down by long, spiraling staircases to a receiving room where Freya Rasmussen was waiting.

The margravine seemed to have made an attempt to do something interesting with her hair but given up halfway through. She blinked at her guests through her overgrown bangs and said, "I'm afraid Professor Pennyroyal is still indisposed, but I'm sure he'll be all right. The Gods of the Ice would hardly have sent him here if they were just going to let him die, would they? It wouldn't be fair. But you'll be interested in my Wunderkammer, Tom, a London Historian like you."

"All right, what's a Wunderkammer?" asked Hester, tired of being ignored by this spoiled teenager.

"It's my private museum," said Freya. "My Cabinet of Wonders." She sneezed, waited a moment for a handmaiden to come and wipe her nose, then remembered they were all dead and wiped it on her cuff. "I love history, Tom. All those old things people dig up. Just ordinary things that were once used by ordinary people, but made special by time." Tom nodded eagerly, and she laughed, sensing that she'd met a kindred spirit. "When I was little, I didn't want to be margravine at all. I wanted to be a historian like you and Professor Pennyroyal. So I started my own museum. Come and see."

Smew led the way, and the margravine kept up her flow of bright chatter as they passed through more corridors, across a vast ballroom where chandeliers lay mothballed under dust sheets, out into a glass-walled cloister. Lights shone in the dark outside, illuminating whirling snow, an iced-up fountain. Hester stuck her hands into her pockets and made them into fists, stalking along behind Tom. *So she's not just pretty*, she thought. *She's read all the same books as he has, and she knows all about history, and she still expects the gods to play fair. She's like Tom's mirror image. How am I sup-posed to compete with that?*

The journey ended in a circular lobby, at a door guarded by two Stalkers. As he recognized their angular shapes, Tom flinched backward and almost cried out in terror, for one of those ancient armored fighting machines had once chased him and Hester halfway across the Hunting Ground. Then Smew lit an argon globe and he saw that these Stalkers were only relics, rusted metal exoskeletons hacked out of the ice and placed here at the entrance to Freya Rasmussen's Wunderkammer by way of decoration. He glanced at Hester to see if she shared his fear, but she was looking away, and before he could attract her attention, Smew had unlocked the door and the margravine was leading them all through it into her museum.

Tom followed her into the dust and dimness with a strange sensation of coming home. True, the single big room looked more like a junk shop than the careful displays he had been used to back in London, but it was a cave of treasures all the same. The Ice Wastes had seen the rise and fall of at least two civilizations since the Sixty Minute War, and Freya owned important relics of each. There was also a model of Anchorage as it might have looked back in its static days, a shelf of vases from the Blue Metal Culture, and some photographs of Ice Circles, a mysterious phenomenon encountered sometimes on the High Ice.

Wandering like a sleepwalker among the exhibits, Tom didn't notice how reluctant Hester was to follow. "Look!" he called, glancing back delightedly over his shoulder. "Hester! Look!"

Hester looked—and saw things she hadn't the education to understand, and her own grisly face reflected in the glass fronts of display cases. She saw Tom drifting away from her, exclaiming over some beat-up old stone statue, and he looked so *right* that she thought her heart was going to break.

One of Freya's favorite treasures hung in a case near the back of the room. It was an almost perfect sheet of the thin, silvery metal that turned up in American Empire landfill sites all over the world, and that the Ancients had called "tinfoil." The margravine stood beside Tom and gazed at it, enjoying the sight of their faces reflected side by side in its ripply surface. "They had so much *stuff*, those Ancients."

"It's amazing," agreed Tom, whispering because the thing in the case was so old and precious that it felt sacred, fingered by the Goddess of History. "To think that there were ever people so rich that they could throw away things like this! Even the poorest of them lived like Lord Mayors."

They moved on to the next display: a collection of those strange metal rings so often found in Ancient rubbish heaps, some still with a teardrop-shaped pendant attached bearing the word PULL.

"Professor Pennyroyal doesn't accept that these things *were* thrown away," said Freya. "He says that the sites that modern archaeologists call rubbish heaps were really religious centers, where the Ancients sacrificed precious objects to their Consumer Gods. Haven't you read his book about it? It's called *Rubbish? Rubbish!* I'll lend you a copy. . . ."

"Thank you," said Tom.

"Thank you, *Your Radiance*," Freya corrected, but she smiled so sweetly, it was hard to feel offended.

"Of course," she went on, running her fingers through the dust on a vitrine, "what this place really needs is a curator. There used to be one, but he died in the plague, or left; I forget which. Now everything's getting dusty, and stuff's been stolen; some nice old jewelry, and a couple of machines—though I can't imagine who would want them, or how they got in here. But it will be important to remember the past, once we reach America." She looked at him again, smiling. "You could stay, Tom. I'd like to think I had a proper London Historian running my little museum. You could expand it, open it to the public. We'll call it the Rasmussen Institute. . . ."

Tom breathed the museum air more deeply, inhaling the fusty scents of dust and floor polish and moth-eaten stuffed animals. When he was an Apprentice Historian, he had longed to escape and have adventures, but now that his whole life was an adventure, the idea of working in a museum again seemed strangely tempting. Then he looked past Freya and saw Hester watching him, a thin, lonely figure half hidden in the shadows near the door, one hand holding her old red scarf across her face. For the first time, he felt annoyed by her. If only she were prettier, and more sociable!

"I'm sorry," he said. "Hester wouldn't want to stay here. She's happiest in the sky."

Freya glared at the other girl. She wasn't used to having people turn her down when she offered them positions. She had been starting to like this handsome young historian. She had even been starting to wonder if the Ice Gods had sent him to her to make up for the fact that there were no suitable boys left aboard Anchorage. But why, oh why, had they decided to send Hester Shaw along with him? The girl wasn't just ugly, she was downright horrible, and she stood between Freya and this nice young man like a demon guarding an enchanted prince.

"Oh well," she said, as if his refusal had not disappointed her at all. "I gather it will take Aakiuq a few weeks to repair your ship. So you will have plenty of time to think it over." *And plenty of time*, she added silently, *to dump that horrid girlfriend.*

Restless Spirits

TOM SLEPT WELL THAT NIGHT, and dreamed of museums. Hester, lying next to him, barely slept at all. The bed was so big that she might as well have stayed in the other room. The way she liked sleeping was cuddled against Tom on the *Jenny Haniver*'s narrow bunk, her face in his hair, her knees against the backs of his knees, their two bodies fitting together like bits of a jigsaw. On this big, soft mattress he rolled sleepily away from her and left her all alone in a sweaty tangle of sheets. And the room was too hot; the dry air hurt her sinuses, and metallic rattlings came from the ducts on the ceiling, a faint, horrid noise, like rats in the walls.

At last she pulled on her coat and boots and went out of the palace into the searing cold of the three-in-the-morning streets. A twining staircase led down through a heat-lock into Anchorage's engine district, a region of steady, pounding noise where bulbous boilers and fuel holds clustered in the dark between the tier supports like fungi. She headed sternward, thinking, *Now we'll see how the little Snow Queen treats her workers*. She looked forward to shocking Tom out of his liking for this place. She would spoil his breakfast with her report of conditions on the lower tier.

She crossed an iron footbridge where huge cogwheels creaked and whirred on either side of her, like the innards of some colossal clock. She followed an enormous segmented duct down into a sunken sublevel where pistons rose and fell, powered by a set of kludged-together Old Tech engines of a type she'd never seen before: armored spheres that hummed and warbled, shooting out shafts of violet light. Men and women strode purposefully about, carrying toolboxes or driving big, multiarmed laboring machines, but there were none of the shackled slave gangs or swaggering overseers Hester had expected. Freya Rasmussen's insipid face gazed down from posters on the tier supports, and the workers bobbed their heads respectfully as they passed beneath it.

Maybe Tom was right, thought Hester, prowling unseen along the edges of the engine well. Maybe Anchorage really was as civilized and peaceful as it seemed. Maybe he could be happy here. The city might even survive its journey to America, and he could stay aboard as Freya Rasmussen's museum keeper and teach the savage tribes about the world their distant ancestors had made. He could keep the *Jenny* on as his private sky yacht, and go prospecting for Old Tech in the haunted deserts on his days off. . . .

He's not going to need you, though, is he? asked a bitter little voice inside her. *And what are you going to do without him?*

She tried to imagine a life for herself without Tom, but she couldn't. She had always known that it wouldn't last forever, but now that the end was in sight, she wanted to shout, *Not yet! I want more! Just another year of being happy. Or maybe two . . .*

She wiped away the tears that kept fogging her eye and hurried aft, sensing cold and open air somewhere beyond the city's vast heat-recycling plant. The beat of the strange engines faded behind her, replaced by a steady, skirling hiss that grew louder as she neared the stern. After a few more minutes she emerged onto a covered walkway that ran the whole width of the city. There was a protective screen made out of panels of steel grille, and beyond it the Northern Lights glimmered in the ceaselessly rolling bulk of Anchorage's great stern wheel.

Hester crossed the walkway and pushed her face against the cold grille and looked through. The wheel had been burnished mirror-bright, and in the cascade of reflections she could see the metal spurs that studded it falling endlessly past her and past her to dig into the ice and shove Anchorage on its way. A fine, cold rain of meltwater flew from it, and fragments of upflung ice dinned and rattled at the screen. Some of the chunks were very large. A few feet from where Hester stood, a section of grille had been beaten loose and swung inward each time an ice block struck it, opening a gap through which sleet and smaller pieces of ice splattered onto the walkway.

How easy it would be to slip through that gap! There would be a moment of falling, and then the wheel would roll over her, leaving only a red smear on the ice, quickly forgotten.

Wouldn't that be better than watching Tom drift away from her? Wouldn't it be better to be dead than alone again?

She reached out for the flapping edge of the grille, but suddenly a hand grabbed her arm, and a voice was shouting in her ear: "Axel?"

Hester swung around, reaching for her knife. Søren Scabious stood behind her. His eyes, as she turned, seemed to be shining with hope and unshed tears; then he recognized her, and his face settled back into its habitual look of deep unhappiness. "Miss Shaw," he growled. "In the dark, I thought you were—"

Hester backed away from him, hiding her face. She wondered how long he had been watching her. "What are you doing here?" she asked. "What do you want?"

Scabious, embarrassed, took refuge in anger. "I could ask you the same thing, aviatrix! Come to spy on my engine district, have you? I trust you had a good look."

"I'm not interested in your engines," Hester said.

"No?" Scabious reached out again, gripping her by the wrist. "I find that hard to believe. The Scabious Spheres have been perfected by my family over twenty generations. One of the most efficient engine systems in the world. I'm sure you'll want to go and tell Arkangel or Ragnaroll all about the riches they'll find if they devour us."

"Don't be stupid," Hester spat. "I wouldn't take predator's gold!" A thought struck her suddenly, hard and cold like one of the ice splinters drumming at the grille behind her. "Anyway, who's Axel? Wasn't he your son? The one Smew talked about? The dead one? Did you think I was his ghost or something?"

Scabious let go of her arm. His anger faded quickly, like a fire damped down. His eyes darted toward the drive wheel, up toward the lights in the sky, looking anywhere but at Hester. "His spirit walks," he muttered.

Hester let out a short, ugly laugh, then stopped. The old man was perfectly serious. He glanced quickly at her and away. His face, lit by that fluttering, uncertain light, was suddenly gentle. "The Snowmads believe that the souls of the dead inhabit the Aurora, Miss Shaw. They say that on nights when it is at its brightest, they come down to walk upon the High Ice."

Hester said nothing, just hunched her shoulders, uneasy in the presence of his madness and sorrow. She said awkwardly, "Nobody returns from the Sunless Country, Mr. Scabious."

"But they do, Miss Shaw." Scabious nodded earnestly. "Since our journey to America began, there have been sightings. Movements. Things go missing from locked rooms. People hear footsteps and voices in parts of the district that have been closed up and abandoned since the plague. That's why I come down here, whenever my work allows and the Aurora is bright. I've glimpsed him twice now: a fair-haired lad, looking out at me from shadows, vanishing as soon as I see him. There are no fair-haired boys left alive in this city. It is Axel, I know it is."

He stared a moment longer at the luminous sky, then turned and walked away. Hester watched him until his tall silhouette disappeared around the corner at the far end of the gallery. Watched, and wondered. Did Scabious really believe that this city could reach America? Did he even care?

Or had he simply gone along with the margravine's crazy plans because he hoped to find his son's ghost waiting for him on the High Ice?

She shivered. She had not realized until now how cold it was here on the city's stern. Although Scabious was gone, she still had the feeling of being watched. The hair at the nape of her neck began to prickle. She glanced behind her, and there in the mouth of an access passageway she saw—or thought she saw—the pale smudge of a face fade quickly into the dark, leaving only the afterimage of a white-blond head.

No one returns from the Sunless Country. Hester knew that, but it did not stop every ghost story she'd ever heard from waking and stirring in her brain. She turned away and ran, ran as fast as she could through the suddenly threatening shadows, back to busier streets.

Behind her, among the tangle of pipes and ducts that overhung the stern gallery, something metallic scuttled and clattered and fell still.

Uninvited Guests

M R. SCABIOUS WAS BOTH RIGHT and wrong about the ghosts. His city was haunted, all right, but not by the spirits of the dead.

The haunting had begun almost a month before, and not in Anchorage but in Grimsby, a very strange and secret city indeed. It had begun with a small sound: a hollow click, like a fingernail flicked once against the taut skin of a toy balloon. Then a sigh of static, the crackle of a microphone being picked up, and the ear on Caul's ceiling started talking to him.

"Up, boy. Wake. This is Uncle calling. Got a job for you, Caul, boy. Yes."

Caul, surfacing through a flotsam of dreams, realized with a sudden shock that this was real. He rolled off his bunk and stood up groggily. His room was little bigger than a cupboard, and apart from the shelf-wide bunk and some spectacular water stains, the only thing in it was the tangle of wires in the center of the ceiling, where a camera and a microphone huddled. The Eyes and Ears of Uncle, the boys called these fixtures. Nothing about the Mouth of Uncle. And yet it was talking to him all the same.

"You awake, boy?"

"Yes, Uncle!" said Caul, trying not to let the words sound slurred. He had been working hard in the Burglarium yesterday, trying to catch out a gaggle of younger boys as they crept through the maze of corridors and stairways that Uncle had designed to train them in the arts of subtle, unseen thieving. He'd gone to bed dead tired, and must have slept for hours, but he felt as if it were only a few minutes since the lights went out. He jerked his head, trying to shake the thickness of sleep out of his thoughts. "I'm awake, Uncle!"

"Good."

The camera stretched down toward Caul: a long, gleaming snake made up of metal segments, mesmerizing him with its one unblinking eye. He knew that in Uncle's quarters, high in the old Town Hall, his face was coming into focus on a surveillance screen. On an impulse he grabbed the coverlet off his bed and used it to hide his bare body. "What do you want of me, Uncle?" he asked.

"I've got a city for you," the voice replied. "Anchorage. A sweet little ice city, down on its luck, heading north. You'll take the limpet *Screw Worm* and burgle it."

Caul tried to think of something sensible to say, standing there dressed in a coverlet in the unwavering gaze of the camera.

"Well, boy," Uncle snapped. "Don't you want the job? Don't you feel you're ready to command a limpet?"

"Oh, of course! Yes! Yes!" cried Caul eagerly. "It's just—I thought the *Screw Worm* was Wrasse's ship. Shouldn't he be going, or one of the older boys?"

"Don't question my orders, boy. Uncle Knows Best. It happens I'm sending Wrasse away south on another job, and that leaves us shorthanded. Ordinarily I wouldn't put a youngster in charge of a burgling trip, but I think you're ready, and Anchorage is too pretty a prize to miss."

"Yes, Uncle." Caul had heard talk about this mysterious job down south, which more and more of the older boys and better limpets were being transferred to. The rumor was that Uncle was planning the most daring robbery of his long career, but nobody knew what it was. Not that it mattered to Caul. Not if Wrasse's absence meant that he got to command his own limpet!

At fourteen, Caul had crewed on a dozen limpet missions, but he had been expecting to wait at least two more seasons before he was offered his own command. Limpet commanders were usually older boys, glamorous figures with homes of their own on the upper floors, a far cry from the little hutches Caul had always lived in, here in the damp stories above the Burglarium where brine seeped in around the rusting rivets and stressed metal filled the nights with its gloomy song; where whole rooms had been known to implode without warning, killing the boys inside. If he could just make a success of this mission and bring home stuff that Uncle liked, he would be able to bid good-bye to these dingy quarters forever!

"You'll take Skewer with you," Uncle said. "And a newbie, Gargle."

"Gargle!" exclaimed Caul, trying too late not to sound incredulous. Gargle was the dunce of his whole class, nervous and clumsy, and with a personality that seemed to attract bullying from the older boys. He had never made it past level two of the Burglarium without getting caught. Usually it was Caul who did the catching, dragging him out quickly before he could fall victim to one of the other trainers, like Skewer, who took a delight in beating failed pupils. Caul had lost track of the times he had led the boy, white-faced and snivel-ing, back to the newbies' dorm. And now Uncle expected him to take the poor kid on a live job!

"Gargle is clumsy, but he's bright," said Uncle. (Uncle always knew what you were thinking, even if you didn't say anything.) "He's good with machines. Good at operating cameras. I've had him working in the archives, and I'm think-ing of moving him up here full-time, but first I want you to take him out and show him what the life of a Lost Boy is all about. I'm asking you because you're more patient than Wrasse and Turtle and the rest."

"Yes, Uncle," said Caul. "You Know Best."

"Damn right I do. You'll go aboard the *Screw Worm* as soon as the day shift begins. Bring me home some pretty things, Caul. And stories. Lots and lots of stories."

"Yes, Uncle!"

"And Caul—"

"Yes, Uncle?"

"Don't get caught."

✿ ✿ ✿

And here was Caul, a month later and hundreds of miles from Grimsby, crouching breathless in the shadows while he waited for the beat of Hester's running feet to fade away. What had come over him since he'd arrived here, to make him keep taking these risks? A good burglar never let himself be seen, but Caul was almost sure that young aviatrix had spotted him, and as for Scabious . . . He shivered, imagining what would happen if Uncle heard of this.

When he was sure he was alone, he slipped out of his hiding place and went quickly and almost soundlessly down by a secret way into the *Screw Worm*, which hung hidden in the oily shadows of Anchorage's underbelly, not far from the drive wheel. It was a rusty, ramshackle old limpet, but Caul was proud of it, and proud of the way its hold was already filling with the things he and his crew had pilfered from the abandoned workshops and villas of the city above. He dumped his latest bag of plunder with the rest and slid between the stacked bales and bundles into the forward compartment. There, amid the soft buzz of machinery and the steady blue flutter of the screens, the rest of the *Screw Worm*'s three-boy crew were waiting for him. They had seen everything, of course. While Caul had been following Hester quietly through the engine district, they had been tracking her with their secret cameras, and they were still chuckling over her conversation with the enginemaster.

"Wooooh! Ghostie!" said Skewer, grinning.

"Caul, Caul," chirped Gargle. "Old Scabious thinks you're a ghost! His dead son come back to say hello!"

"I know," said Caul. "I heard." He shoved past Skewer and settled himself into one of the creaky leather seats, suddenly annoyed at how cluttered and stuffy the *Screw Worm* felt after the clean chill of the city above. He glanced at his companions, who were still watching him with foolish grins, expecting him to join in their mockery of old Scabious. They too seemed smaller and less vital, compared to the people he had just been watching.

Skewer was the same age as Caul, but bigger and stronger and more sure of himself. Sometimes it seemed strange to Caul that Uncle had not put Skewer in charge of this trip, and sometimes there was an edge to Skewer's jokes that made him suspect Skewer thought the same thing. Gargle, ten years old and permanently wide-eyed with the rush of his first burgling mission, seemed unaware of the tension between them. He had turned out as clumsy and useless as Caul had feared: Inept at burglary, freezing with terror whenever a Dry came near him, he came back from most of his expeditions into the city with his hands shaking and his trousers sodden. Skewer, who was always quick to make the most of another's weakness, would have bullied and mocked him mercilessly, but Caul held him back. He still remembered his own first job, stuck with a couple of unfriendly older boys in a limpet under Zeestadt Gdansk. All burglars had to start somewhere.

Skewer was still grinning. "You're slipping, Caul! Letting people see you. Lucky for you the old man's mad. A ghost, eh! Wait till we get home and tell the others! Caul the ghoul! Whooooo!"

"It's not funny, Skew," said Caul. What Mr. Scabious said had made him feel edgy and strange. He was not sure why. He checked his reflection in the cabin window. There wasn't much resemblance to the portraits of Axel he'd seen when he was casing Scabious's office. The Scabious boy had been much older, tall and handsome and blue-eyed. Caul had a burglar's build, skinny as a skeleton key, and his eyes were black. But they both had the same untidy white-blond hair. An old man whose heart was broken, glimpsing a fair head through darkness or mist, might jump to conclusions, mightn't he?

He realized with a start that Skewer was talking to him, and had been talking to him for some time. ". . . And you know what Uncle says. The First Rule of Burgling—Don't Get Caught."

"I'm not going to get caught, Skew. I'm careful."

"Well, how come you've been seen, then?"

"Everybody gets unlucky sometimes. Big Spadger off the *Burglar Bill* had to knife a Dry who spotted him in the underdecks of Arkangel last season."

"That's different. You spend too much time watching the Drys. It's all right if it's just on-screen, but you hang around up there watching them for real."

"He does," agreed Gargle, eager to please. "I've seen him."

"Shut up," said Skewer, absentmindedly kicking the smaller boy.

"They're interesting," said Caul.

"They're Drys!" said Skewer impatiently. "You know what Uncle says about Drys. They're like cattle. Their brains don't move as fast as ours. That's why it's right for us to take their stuff."

"I know!" said Caul. Like Skewer, he'd had all this drummed into him when he was just a newbie, back in the Burglarium. "We're the Lost Boys. We're the best burglars in the world. Everything that ain't nailed down is ours." But he knew Skewer was right. Sometimes he felt as if he wasn't meant to be a Lost Boy at all. He liked watching people better than burgling them.

He swung himself out of his seat and snatched his latest report from a shelf above the camera controls: thirteen pages of Freya Rasmussen's best official notepaper covered in his big, grubby handwriting. He waved them in Skewer's face as he headed aft. "I'm sending this back to base. Uncle gets angry if he doesn't get an update once a week."

"That's nothing to how angry he'll be if you go and get us caught," Skewer muttered.

The *Screw Worm*'s fish bay was beneath the boys' sleeping cabin, and had taken on the same smell of stale sweat and unwashed socks. There were racks for ten message-fish, but three were already empty. Caul felt a pang of regret as he started prepping number four for launch. In just six more weeks the last fish would be gone. Then it would be time for the *Screw Worm* to decouple from Anchorage and head for home. He would miss Freya and her people. But that was stupid, wasn't it? They were only stupid Drys. Only pictures on a stupid screen.

The message-fish looked like a sleek silver torpedo, and if it had been standing upright it would have been taller than Caul. As always, a slight sense of awe overcame him as he checked the fish's fuel tank and placed his rolled-up report in the watertight compartment near its nose. All over the north, limpet captains just like him were sending fish home to Uncle so that Uncle would know everything that was going on everywhere and be able to plan ever-more-daring burglaries. It made Caul feel even more guilty about his liking for the Drys. He was so lucky to be a Lost Boy. He was so lucky to be working for Uncle. Uncle Knew Best.

A few minutes later the message-fish slid from the *Screw Worm*'s belly and dropped unnoticed out of the complex shadows on Anchorage's underside, down onto the ice. As the city swept on into the north, the fish began drilling its way down through the snow, down through the ice, patiently down and down and down until it broke through at last into the black waters beneath the ice cap. Its Old Tech computer brain ticked and grumbled. It wasn't bright, but it knew its way home. It extended stubby fins and a small propeller and went purring quickly away toward the south.

13

The Wheelhouse

HESTER DID NOT TELL TOM about her strange encounter. She did not want him to think her silly, babbling about ghosts. The shape she had seen watching her from the shadows had been a trick of her imagination, and as for Mr. Scabious, he was mad. The whole town was mad, if they believed Freya and Pennyroyal and their promises of a new green hunting ground beyond the ice, and Tom was mad along with them. There was no point in arguing, or in trying to make him see sense. Better just to concentrate on getting him safely away.

Days and then weeks went by, with Anchorage running north across broad plains of sea ice as it skirted the mountainous shield of Greenland. Hester began to spend most of her time at the air harbor, watching Mr. Aakiuq work on the *Jenny Haniver*. There was not much she could do to help him, for she was no mechanic, but she could pass him tools and fetch things from his workshop and pour him cups of scalding purple-dark cocoa from his old thermos flask, and she felt that just by being there, she might help to hasten the day when the *Jenny* would be ready to take her away from this haunted city.

Sometimes Tom joined her in the hangar, but mostly he stayed away. "Mr. Aakiuq doesn't want both of us hanging about," he told Hester. "We'd just get in his way." But they both knew the real reason: He was enjoying his new life in Anchorage too much. He hadn't realized until now how much he'd missed living aboard a moving city. It was the engines, he told himself: that faint, comfortable vibration that made the buildings feel alive, that sense that you were going somewhere and would wake up each morning to a new view from your bedroom window—even if it was just another view of darkness and of ice.

And perhaps, although he didn't like to admit it to himself, it had something to do with Freya. He often met her in the Wunderkammer or the palace library, and although the meetings were rather formal, with Smew or Miss Pye always waiting in the background, Tom felt that he was coming to know the margravine. She intrigued him. She was so unlike Hester, and so like the girls he used to daydream about as a lonely Apprentice back in London: pretty and sophisticated. It was true that she was a bit of a snob and obsessed with ritual and etiquette, but that seemed understandable when you remembered how she had been brought up, and what she'd lived through. He liked her more and more.

Professor Pennyroyal had made a full recovery, and had moved into the chief navigator's official residence, in a tall, blade-shaped tower called the Wheelhouse that stood in the precincts of the Winter Palace, near the temple. Its top floor housed the city's control bridge, but below was a luxurious apartment, into which Pennyroyal settled with an air of satisfaction. He had always thought himself a rather grand person, and it was pleasant to be aboard a city where everybody else thought so too.

Of course, he had no idea how to actually steer an ice city, so the practical day-to-day work of guiding Anchorage was still done by Windolene Pye. She and Pennyroyal spent an hour together each morning, poring over the city's few, vague charts of the western ice. The rest of the time he relaxed in his sauna, or put his feet up in his drawing room, or went scavenging in the abandoned boutiques of Rasmussen Prospekt and the Ultima Arcade, picking out expensive clothes to suit his new position.

"We certainly fell on our feet when we landed on Anchorage, Tom, dear boy!" he said when Tom came visiting one night-dark Arctic afternoon. He waved a bejeweled hand around his huge sitting room, with its ornate carpets and framed paintings, its fires aglow in bronze tripods, its big windows with their views across the rooftops to the passing ice. Outside, a fierce wind was rising, driving snow across the city, but in the chief navigator's quarters all was warmth and peace.

"How is that airship of yours coming along, by the way?" Pennyroyal asked.

"Oh, slowly," said Tom. In truth he had not been near the air harbor for several days and did not know how the work on the *Jenny Haniver* was progressing. He didn't like to think about it too much, for when the repairs were complete, Hester would want to leave, dragging him away from this lovely city and from Freya. *Still*, he thought, *it's kind of the professor to show an interest.*

"And what about the journey to America?" he asked. "Is everything going well, Professor?"

"Absolutely!" cried Pennyroyal, settling himself on a sofa and rearranging his quilted silicone-silk robes. He poured himself another beaker of wine and offered one to Tom. "There are some excellent vintages in the chief navigator's cellar, and it seems a waste not to get through as much as we can before . . . well . . ."

"You should keep the best to toast your arrival in America," Tom said, sitting down on a small chair near the great man's feet. "Have you decided on a course yet?"

"Well, yes and no," Pennyroyal said airily, gesturing with his beaker and slopping wine over the fur throws on his sofa. "Yes and no, Tom. Once we get west of Greenland, it'll be plain skating all the way. Windolene and Scabious had planned something very complicated, wiggling between a lot of islands that might not even be there anymore, then running down the west coast of America. Luckily, I was able to show them a much easier route." He indicated a map on the wall. "We'll nip across Baffin Island into Hudson Bay. It's good, thick, solid sea ice, and it stretches right into the heart of the North American continent. That's the way I came on my journey home. We'll whiz across that, hoist up the stern wheel, and simply roll on our caterpillar tracks into the green country. It'll be a cinch."

"I wish I was coming with you," sighed Tom.

"No, no, dear boy!" the explorer said sharply. "Your place is on the bird roads. As soon as that ship of yours is better, you and your, ah, lovely companion must return to the sky. By the way, I hear Her Heftiness the margravine has lent you a few of my books?"

Tom blushed at the mention of Freya.

"So what do you make of them, eh?" Pennyroyal went on, pouring himself more wine. "Good stuff?"

Tom wasn't quite sure what to say. Pennyroyal's books were certainly exciting. The trouble was, some of the Alternative Historian's history was a little *too* alternative for Tom's London-trained mind. In *America the Beautiful* he reported seeing the girders of ancient skyscrapers jutting from the dust of the Dead Continent—but no other explorer had described such sights, which would surely have been eaten away by wind and rust aeons ago. Had Pennyroyal been hallucinating when he saw them? And then, in *Rubbish? Rubbish!* Pennyroyal claimed that the tiny toy trains and ground cars sometimes found at Ancient sites weren't toys at all. *Undoubtedly,* he wrote, *these machines were piloted by minute human beings, genetically engineered by the Ancients for unknown reasons of their own.*

Tom didn't doubt that Pennyroyal was a great explorer. It was just that when he sat down at a typewriting machine, his imagination seemed to run away with him.

"Well, Tom?" asked Pennyroyal. "Don't be shy. A good writer never objects to constrictive crusticism. I mean consumptive cretinism. . . ."

"Oh, Professor Pennyroyal!" cried the voice of Windolene Pye, blaring from a brass speaking tube on the wall. "Come quickly! The lookouts are reporting something on the ice ahead!"

Tom felt himself grow cold, imagining a predator city lurking out there on the ice, but Pennyroyal just shrugged. "What does the silly old moo expect me to do about it?" he asked.

"Well, you *are* chief navigator now, Professor," Tom reminded him. "Perhaps you're supposed to be on the bridge at a time like this."

"*Honorararary* Chief Nagivator, Tim," said Pennyroyal, and Tom realized that he was drunk.

Patiently he helped the tipsy explorer to his feet and led him to a small private elevator, which whisked them up to the top floor of the Wheelhouse. They stepped out into a glass-walled room where Miss Pye stood nervously beside the engine-district telegraph while her small staff spread charts out on the navigation table. A burly helmsman waited at the city's huge steering wheel for instructions.

Pennyroyal collapsed on the first chair they passed, but Tom hurried to the glass wall and waited for the wiper blade to sweep across so that he could catch a glimpse of the view ahead. Thick flurries of snow were driving across the city, hiding all but the nearest buildings. "I can't see—" he began to say. And then a momentary break in the storm showed him a glitter of lights away to the north.

In the emptiness ahead of Anchorage, a hunter-killer suburb had appeared.

The Suburb

FREYA WAS TRYING TO SORT OUT a guest list for dinner. It was
a difficult business, for by long tradition only citizens of the
highest rank could dine with the margravine, and these days
that meant just Mr. Scabious, who was nobody's idea of good
company. The arrival of Professor Pennyroyal had cheered
things up no end, of course—it was quite acceptable for the
city's chief navigator to sit at the table with her—but even
the professor's fascinating stories were beginning to wear a
little thin, and he had a tendency to drink too much.

What she really wanted (although she tried not to admit
it to herself as she sat there at her desk in the study) was to
invite Tom. Just Tom alone, so that he could gaze at her in
the candlelight and tell her how beautiful she was; she was
sure he wanted to. The trouble was, he was only a common
aviator. And even if she broke with all tradition and asked

him, he would bring his nasty girlfriend, and that wasn't the sort of evening she wanted at all.

She slumped back in her chair with a sigh. Portraits of earlier margravines gazed down kindly at her from the study walls, and she wondered what they would have done in a situation like this. But of course there had never been a situation like this before. For them the ancient traditions of the city had always worked, providing a simple, infallible guide to what could and could not be done—their lives had ticked along like clockwork. *Just my luck to be left in charge when the spring breaks*, thought Freya gloomily. *Just my luck to be left with a load of rules and traditions that don't quite fit anymore.*

But she knew that if she took off the armor of tradition, she would have to face all sorts of new problems. The people who had stayed aboard her city after the plague had done so only because they revered the margravine. If Freya stopped behaving like a margravine, would they still be prepared to go along with her plans?

She went back to her guest list, and had just finished doodling a small dog in the bottom left corner when Smew burst in, then burst out again and gave the traditional triple knock.

"You may enter, Chamberlain."

He came in again, breathless, his hat back to front. "Sorry, Your Radiance. Bad news from the Wheelhouse, Radiance. Predator, dead ahead."

By the time she reached the bridge, the weather had closed in completely and nothing could be seen outside but the swarming snow.

"Well?" she asked, stepping out of the elevator before

Smew could announce her.

Windolene Pye bobbed a frightened little curtsy. "Oh, Light of the Ice Fields! I am almost sure it's Wolverinehampton! I saw those three metal tower blocks behind its jaws quite clearly, just as the storm struck. It must have been lying in wait up here, hoping to snap up whaling towns on the Greenland run. . . ."

"What is Wolverinehampton?" asked Freya, wishing she had paid more attention to all her expensive tutors.

"Here, Your Radiance . . ."

She had not noticed Tom until he spoke. Now, seeing him, she felt a little warm glow inside her. He held out a dog-eared book and said, "I looked it up in *Cade's Almanack of Traction Cities.*"

She took the book from him, smiling, but her smile faded as she opened it at the page he had marked and saw Ms. Cade's diagram and the legend underneath:

WOLVERINEHAMPTON: *An Anglish-speaking suburb which migrated north in 768 T.E. to become one of the most feared small predators on the High Ice. Its enormous jaws, and its tradition of staffing its engine districts with shamefully ill-treated slaves, make it a town best avoided.*

The deck beneath Freya's feet juddered and shook. She snapped the book shut, imagining Wolverinehampton's great jaws already closing on her city—but it was only the Scabious Spheres shutting down. Anchorage slowed, and in the eerie quiet she could hear sleet pecking at the glass walls.

"What's happening?" asked Tom. "Is something wrong with the engines?"

"We're stopping," said Windolene Pye. "Because of the storm."

"But there's a predator out there!"

"I know, Tom. It's terrible timing. But we always stop and anchor when a really big storm blows in. It's too dangerous not to. The wind on the High Ice can gust up to five hundred miles per hour. It's been known to overturn small cities. Poor old Skraelingshavn was flipped onto its back like a beetle in the winter of 'sixty-nine."

"We could lower the cats," suggested Freya.

"Cats?" cried Pennyroyal. "What cats? I have allergies. . . ."

"Her Radiance is referring to our caterpillar tracks, Professor," Miss Pye explained. "They would provide extra traction, but it might not be enough, not in this storm."

The wind howled agreement, and the glass walls bowed inward, creaking.

"What about this Wolverinetonham place?" asked Pennyroyal, still flopped in his seat. "They'll be stopping too, will they?"

Everyone looked at Windolene Pye. She shook her head. "I'm sorry to say they won't, Professor Pennyroyal. They are lower and heavier than we. They should be able to run right through this storm."

"Yikes!" whimpered Pennyroyal. "Then we'll be eaten for sure! They must have got a bearing on our position before the weather closed in! They'll just follow their noses and *gollop*!"

Tipsy as he was, the explorer seemed to Tom to be the only person on the bridge talking sense. "We can't just sit here and wait to get eaten!" he agreed.

Miss Pye glanced at the whirling needles of her wind-speed

indicators. "Anchorage has never moved in a wind this strong—"

"Then maybe it's time to start!" Tom shouted. He turned to Freya. "Talk to Scabious! Tell him to turn out the lights, alter course, and run on as fast as he can through the storm. It would be better to capsize than get eaten, wouldn't it?"

"How dare you talk to Her Radiance like that!" cried Smew, but Freya felt touched and pleased that Tom should care so much about her city. Still, there was tradition to consider. She said, "I'm not sure if I can, Tom. No margravine has ever ordered such a thing before."

"But no margravine has ever set out for America either," Tom pointed out.

Behind him, Pennyroyal heaved himself upright. Before Smew or any of the others could stop him, he shoved Tom aside and lunged at Freya, grabbing her by her plump shoulders and shaking her until all her jewelry rattled. "Just do as Tim says!" he shouted. "Do as he says, you silly little ninny, before we all end up as slaves in the belly of Wolverteeningham!"

"Oh, Professor Pennyroyal!" shrieked Miss Pye.

"Get your filthy paws off Her Radiance!" shouted Smew, drawing his sword and leveling it at the explorer's knees.

Freya shook herself free, startled, indignant, furious, wiping Pennyroyal's spittle from her face. No one had ever talked to her in that way before, and for a moment she thought, *This is what happens when I break with custom and appoint a commoner to high office!* Then she remembered Wolverinehampton, racing toward her city through the storm, its massive jaws probably open by now, the furnaces of its gut alight. She turned to her navigators and said, "We will do as Tom says! Don't stand there staring! Alert Mr. Scabious! Change course! Full speed ahead!"

❄ ❄ ❄

The city's anchors tugged free of the snow-swept ice, and the strange turbines in the hearts of the Scabious Spheres began to whirl again. The fat banks of caterpillar tracks that jutted from Anchorage's skirts on hydraulic arms jerked into motion amid a spray of vapor and antifreeze. They were lowered until the studded tracks gripped the ice. Wobbling slightly as the wind hammered at its superstructure, Anchorage swung onto a new course. If the Ice Gods were kind, Wolverinehampton would not detect the maneuver— but what Wolverinehampton's own course was, what it was doing out there in the swirling murk, only the Ice Gods knew, for the storm had settled in now, a wild Arctic tempest that ripped shutters and roof panels from the abandoned buildings of the upper tier and sent them whirling high into the sky while Anchorage put out its lights and ran on blindly into the blind dark.

Caul was filling his burglar's bag with machine parts from an empty workshop in the engine district when the city changed course. The sudden movement almost made him overbalance. He clutched his bag tight against him so the booty inside would not rattle and crept outside and moved quickly along the maze of now-familiar streets toward the heart of the district and the pit where the Scabious Spheres were housed. Crouching between two empty fuel hoppers, he heard the workers shouting to one another as they hurried to their stations and slowly understood what was happening. He hunched himself deeper into the shadows, wondering what to do.

He knew what he *should* do; Uncle's rules were very

clear. When a host city was in danger of being eaten, any limpet attached to it must decouple and escape at once. It was part of the big rule: Don't Get Caught. If even one limpet were to be found, and the cities of the north learned how they had been preyed on and robbed these many years, they would start posting guards and taking security measures. The life the Lost Boys led would become impossible.

And yet Caul did not start back toward the *Screw Worm*. He didn't want to leave Anchorage: not yet, and not like this. He tried telling himself it was because this city was his territory: There were still good pickings to be had, and no stupid predator suburb was going to snatch that from him. No way was he going to take his first command home early and defeated, with her holds barely half full!

But that wasn't the real reason, and he knew it in the depths of his mind even as the surface seethed with anger at the impertinence of Wolverinehampton.

Caul had a secret. It was a secret so deep and dark that he could never begin to tell Skewer or Gargle about it. The terrible truth was, he *liked* the people he was burgling. He knew it was wrong, but he couldn't help himself. He cared about Windolene Pye, and sympathized with her secret fear that she was not good enough to steer the city to America. He worried about Mr. Scabious, and was moved by the courage of Smew and the Aakiuqs and the men and women who staffed the engine district and the livestock and algae farms. He felt drawn to Tom, because of his kindness and the life he had led in the sky. (It seemed to Caul that if Uncle hadn't taken him to be a Lost Boy, he might have been a lot like Tom himself.)

As for Freya, he had no word to describe the mixture of new feelings she stirred up in him.

The howl of the Scabious Spheres rose in pitch. The city lurched and jittered, heavy objects crashing to the deck and rolling somewhere in the streets behind Caul's hiding place, but he knew he couldn't leave. He couldn't abandon these people, now that he had come to know them so well. He would take his chances and wait out the chase. Skewer and Gargle wouldn't decouple without him, and even if they could see him hiding here, they couldn't know what he was thinking. He'd tell them he hadn't dared try to get back to the *Screw Worm* through all this chaos. It would be all right. Anchorage would survive. He trusted Miss Pye and Scabious and Freya to see it through.

Tom had often watched town-hunts from the observation decks on London's second tier, cheering his city on as it raced after small industrials and heavy, lumbering trading towns, but he had never experienced a chase from the prey's point of view before, and he was not enjoying it. He wished he had a job to do, like Windolene Pye and her staff, who were busily laying out more charts and weighting the curly corners down with coffee mugs. They had been drinking endless mugs of coffee since the chase began, and kept darting prayerful glances at the statuettes of the Ice Gods on the Wheelhouse shrine.

"Why are they all so nervous?" Tom asked, turning to Freya, who stood nearby with just as little to do as him. "I mean, the wind's not that bad, is it? It couldn't really flip us over?"

Freya pursed her lips and nodded. She knew her city better than Tom did, and she could feel the uneasy quiver that ran through the deck plates as the gale slid its fingers under the hull and tried to lift it. And it wasn't only the wind they had to fear. "Most of the High Ice is safe," she said. "Most of the ice cap is a thousand feet thick, and in some places it goes right down to the ocean floor. But there are patches where it's thinner. And then there are the polynyas—like lakes of unfrozen water in the midst of all the ice—and the Ice Circles, which are smaller, but could still turn us over if one of the skids plunged in. Polynyas shouldn't be too hard to avoid, because they're more or less permanent and they'll be marked on Miss Pye's charts. But the circles just appear on the ice at random."

Tom remembered the photos in the Wunderkammer. "What causes them?"

"Nobody knows," said Freya. "Currents in the ice, maybe, or the vibration from passing cities. You often see them where a city has passed by. They're very odd. Perfectly round, with smooth edges. The Snowmads say they're made by ghosts cutting fishing holes." She laughed, glad to be talking about the mysteries of the High Ice instead of thinking about the all-too-real predator out there in the storm. "There are all sorts of tales about the High Ice. Like the ghost crabs—giant spider-crab things, as big as icebergs, that people have seen scuttling about in the light of the Aurora. I used to have nightmares about them when I was little. . . ."

She moved closer to Tom until her arm brushed the sleeve of his tunic. She felt very daring. It had been scary at first, going against the old ways, but now that they were racing through the storm, defying both Wolverinehampton and all the traditions of Anchorage, it felt more than scary. *Exhilarating*, that was the word. She was glad Tom was here with her. If they survived this, she decided, she would break another tradition and invite him to dine with her, all alone.

"Tom . . ." she said.

"Look out!" shouted Tom. "Miss Pye! What's that?"

Beyond the dim outlines of Anchorage's roofs, a row of lights blazed suddenly through the darkness, then gigantic claw-toothed wheels and the bright windows of buildings, all rushing past at right angles to Anchorage's new course. It was the stern of Wolverinehampton. The heavy wheels spun into reverse as its lookouts sighted Anchorage, but the suburb's massive jaws made it slow to turn, and already the storm was clamping down again, thick, furious snow hiding the predator from its prey.

"Thank Quirke!" Tom whispered, and laughed with relief. Freya squeezed his fingers, and he found that in the shock of seeing the predator, they had reached for each other, and her warm, plump hand was nestled in his. He let go quickly, embarrassed. He had not thought of Hester since the chase began.

Miss Pye ordered course change after course change, steering the city deep into the labyrinths of the blizzard. An hour passed, and then another, and slowly a feeling of reprieve seeped into the Wheelhouse. Wolverinehampton would not waste more fuel trying to follow them through the night, and by the time dawn came, the storm would have erased their tracks. Miss Pye hugged her colleagues, then the helmsman, then Tom. "We've done it!" she said. "We've escaped!" Freya was beaming. Professor Pennyroyal, sensing that the danger had passed, had fallen asleep in a corner.

Tom returned the navigator's hug and laughed, happy to be alive and very, very happy to be aboard this city, among these good and friendly people. He would talk to Hester as soon as the storm was over, and make her see that there was no need for them to go flying off as soon as the *Jenny Haniver* was repaired. He put his hand flat on the chart table and let the steady throb of Anchorage's engines beat against his palm, and it felt like home.

In a cheap hotel behind Wolverinehampton's air quay, Widgery Blinkoe's five wives turned five unbecoming shades of green. "Ooooh!" they groaned, clutching their delicate stomachs as the suburb tilted and veered, angrily scouring the blizzard for its vanished prey.

"I've never been aboard such a *horrid* little town!"

"Does this hotel have no shock absorbers at all?"

"What were you *thinking* of, husband, setting us down here?"

"You should have known you'd find no trace of the *Jenny Haniver* aboard a mere suburb!"

"I wish I'd flown away with dear Professor Pennyroyal. He was madly in love with me, you know."

"I wish I'd listened to my mother!"

"I *wish* we were back in Arkangel!"

Widgery Blinkoe carefully stoppered his ears against their complaints with small balls of wax, but he too was sick and scared and missing his home comforts. Bother and blast the Green Storm, for sending him on this wild-goose chase! For weeks now he'd been trailing across the Ice Wastes like some

Snowmad sky-tramp, setting down on every town he saw to ask for news of the *Jenny Haniver*. People he had questioned in Novaya-Nizhni said they had seen her fly off northward after wrecking the Green Storm's fighters, but there had not been a sighting since. It was as if the wretched airship had simply vanished!

Dimly, he wondered about the city Wolverinehampton had just tried to snaffle: Anchorage. If he took off when the storm ended, he could probably spot the place and catch up with it . . . but what was the point? He was sure those two young aviators could not have brought their old ship this far west. Besides, he was beginning to think that he would rather face the assassins of the Green Storm than tell his wives they had to land at yet another dingy little harbor.

It was definitely time for a change of plan.

He took out his earplugs, just in time to hear wife number three say plaintively, ". . . and now they've lost their catch, the ruffians who run this town will grow angry and wild! We shall be murdered, and it will all be Blinkoe's fault!"

"Nonsense, wives!" boomed Blinkoe, standing up to show them that he was the head of the household and that a break-neck chase through a blizzard aboard a savage suburb couldn't upset him. "Nobody is going to be murdered! As soon as this storm ends, we shall fetch the *Temporary Blip* out of her hangar and fly home to Arkangel. I shall sell details of a few of the towns we've touched at to the Huntsmen so our trip won't leave us out of pocket, and as for the Green Storm . . . well, all manner of aviators pass through the Arkangel Air Exchange. I shall question them all. One of them must know something about the *Jenny Haniver*."

Hester
Alone

STILL THE STORM BLEW, THE shrill voice of the wind rising higher and higher. In the upper city several empty buildings were blown down, and many more lost roofs and windows. Two of Mr. Scabious's workers, venturing out onto the bow to lash down a loose deck plate, were lifted clear off the city with it and vanished into the darkness off the leeward side, clinging to their trailing cables like the owners of an unwieldy kite.

Hester had been at work with Mr. Aakiuq in the *Jenny*'s hangar when his nephew came bursting in with news of the chase. Her first instinct had been to run to the Winter Palace to be with Tom, but when she stepped outside, the wind hit her like a well-aimed mattress, flattening her against the side of the hangar. A glance at the snow driving across the empty docking pans told her that she could go no farther than the harbormaster's house. She sat out the storm in his kitchen while the Aakiuqs fed her algae stew and told her about other storms, far worse than this, which dear old Anchorage had come through quite unscathed.

Hester felt grateful to them for trying to reassure her, but she was not a child, and she could tell that behind their smiles they were just as scared as her. It wasn't just this unnatural, unexpected pressing on into the teeth of the storm; it was the thought of that predator, waiting to swallow them all. *Not now!* thought Hester, gnawing the sides of her thumbs till the blood came. *We can't be eaten now. Just another week, another few days . . .*

For the *Jenny Haniver* was almost airworthy again: her rudders and engine pods repaired, her envelope patched, her gas cells filled, she awaited only a new coat of paint and a few small repairs to the gondola electrical system. It would be a horrible irony if she were to be eaten before she could take off.

At last the telephone clattered. Mrs. Aakiuq ran to answer it and came back beaming. "That was Mrs. Umiak! She's heard from the Wheelhouse, and they say we've escaped Wolverinehampton. We shall run on just a little longer and then anchor and let the tempest blow over. Apparently it was dear Professor Pennyroyal who advised Her Radiance to keep going despite the storm. That good gentleman! We must all give thanks to the Ice Gods, who sent him here. And Hester, dear, I am to tell you that your young man is safe. He has returned to the Winter Palace."

A little later Tom himself called to say much the same things. His voice sounded tinny and unnatural as it came filtering through the tangled yards of wiring all the way from the palace. He might as well have been speaking from some other dimension. He and Hester exchanged little flat bits of news. "I wish I was with you," she said, putting her face very near the mouthpiece and speaking low, for fear Mrs. Aakiuq might overhear.

"What? Pardon? No, we'd best stay put. Freya told me people sometimes freeze to death in the streets in storms like this. When Smew drove us back here from the Wheelhouse, the bug almost blew away!"

"Freya now, is it?"

"What?"

"The *Jenny*'s nearly ready. We can leave by the end of the week."

"Oh! Good!" She could hear the hesitation in his voice, and behind him other voices talking happily, as if there were a lot of people at the palace, all celebrating. "But maybe we can stay a bit longer," he said hopefully. "I'd like to stay aboard until we get to America, and then, well, we'll see. . . ."

Hester smiled and sniffed and tried to speak, but couldn't for a moment. He sounded so sweet, and so full of love for this place, that it seemed unfair to be angry with him, or to point out that she'd rather go anywhere but the Dead Continent.

"Hester?" he said.

"I love you, Tom."

"I can't hear you very well."

"It's all right. I'll see you soon. I'll see you as soon as the storm ends."

But the storm showed no sign of ending. Anchorage slid slowly westward for a few more hours, keen to put as much ice as possible between itself and Wolverinehampton. There were not only polynyas and thin ice to be wary of now. The city was nearing the northeastern fringes of Greenland, where mountains jutted through the ice sheet to rip the bottoms out of unsuspecting towns. Mr. Scabious cut power by half, then half again. Searchlights probed ahead, like long white fingers trying to part the curtains of snow, and survey teams were sent out on motorized sleds to sound the ice. Miss Pye checked and rechecked her charts and prayed for a glimpse of the stars to confirm her position. At last, with the navigator's prayers unanswered, Anchorage was forced to halt.

A lightless day limped by. Hester sat by the Aakiuqs' stove and looked at the photos of their dead children propped on the household shrine and the collection of souvenir plates on the wall, commemorating the births, marriages, and jubilees of the House of Rasmussen. All the faces looked like Freya, who must even now be sitting snugly with Tom in the Winter Palace. They were probably drinking mulled wine and talking about history and their favorite books.

Tears filled Hester's eye. She excused herself before the Aakiuqs started asking what was wrong and ran upstairs to the storeroom, where they had made up a bed for her. *Why keep on with something that makes me feel this bad?* she asked herself. It would be easy to put an end to it. She could go and find Tom when the storm quieted down and say, *It's over, stay here with your Snow Queen if you want, see if I care. . . .*

She wouldn't, though. He was the only good thing she had ever had. It was different for Freya and Tom; they were nice and sweet-natured and good-looking and would have many, many chances to find love. For Hester there would never be anyone else. "I wish Wolverinehampton *had* eaten us," she said to herself, drifting into headachy sleep. At least in the slave holds Tom would have needed her again.

When she awoke it was midnight, and the storm had stopped.

Hester pulled on her mittens, cold-mask, and outdoor clothes and went quickly downstairs. Faint snoring came from the Aakiuqs' bedroom as she crept past the open door. She slid the kitchen heat-lock open and stepped out into the cold. The moon was up, lying on the southern horizon like a lost coin, and by its light Hester could see that all the buildings of the upper tier were covered in a glaze of ice, teased out by the wind into wild, trailing spines and filaments. Icicles dangled from overhead cables and the gantries and cranes of the air harbor, tapping together in the faint breeze to fill the city with an eerie music, the only sound to break the perfect silence of the snow.

She wanted Tom. She wanted to share this cold beauty with him. Alone with him in these deserted streets, she would be able to tell him how she felt. She ran and ran, scrambling in her borrowed snowshoes over drifts that were sometimes more than shoulder deep even in the lee of the buildings, while the cold burned through her mask and sawed at the back of her throat. Up the stairways from the lower city came sudden gusts of laughter and snatches of music as the engine district celebrated Anchorage's deliverance. Dizzy with cold, Hester climbed the long ramp to the Winter Palace.

When she had tugged at the bellpull for about five minutes, Smew opened the door. "I'm sorry," Hester said, pushing straight through the heat-lock and letting a blast of cold air into the hallway. "I know it's late. I've got to see Tom. I know my way, so you needn't bother—"

"He's not in his room," said Smew grumpily, wrapping his robe tighter and fussing with the wheels of the heat-lock. "He's in the Wunderkammer, with Her Radiance."

"At this hour?"

Smew nodded sullenly. "Her Radiance does not wish to be disturbed."

"Well, she's going to get disturbed, whether she wishes it or not," muttered Hester, shoving him aside and setting off through the corridors of the palace at a run. As she went, she tried to tell herself that it was all perfectly innocent. Tom and the Rasmussen girl had probably just gone to peer at her unrivaled collection of weird old garbage, and lost track of the time. She would find him deep in some conversation about forty-third-century ceramics or the rune-stones of the Raffia Hat Era. . . .

Light spilled from the open doorway of the Wunderkammer, and Hester slowed as she approached it. It would be best to stride straight in with a cheery "hello," but she wasn't the cheery sort; she was more the lurking-in-dark-corners sort. She found a dark corner, behind one of the Stalker skeletons, and lurked. She could hear Tom and Freya talking, but not clearly enough to make out what about. Tom laughed, and her heart seemed to open and shut. There had been a time, after the fall of London, when *she* had been the only person who could make him laugh.

She slid out of her hiding place and crept into the Wunderkammer. Tom and Freya were over on the far side, half a dozen dusty cabinets between them and Hester. Through the many sheets of thick glass she saw them vaguely, rippling like reflections in a distorting mirror. They were standing very close together, and their voices had grown soft. Hester opened her mouth to speak, longing to make some noise that would distract them from each other, but nothing came out. And as she stood there watching, Freya reached toward Tom and they were suddenly in each other's arms, and kissing. Still she could make no sound, only stand and stare at Freya's white fingers moving in Tom's dark hair, his hands on her shoulders.

She had not felt such a fierce urge to kill somebody since she had hunted Valentine. She tensed, ready to snatch one of the old weapons down from the wall and hack and hack at those two, those two, at Tom—at *Tom!* Appalled, she turned and flung herself blindly out of the museum. There was a heat-lock in the cloister, and she pushed out through it into the frigid night.

She flung herself down into a drift and lay there helpless, sobbing. More dreadful than the kiss itself was the fierce thing that it had stirred inside her. How could she even have thought of harming Tom? It wasn't his fault! It was that girl, that girl, she had bewitched him; he had never even looked at another girl this way until this podgy margravine came along, Hester was sure of it. She imagined killing Freya. But what good would that do? Tom would hate her then, and besides, it wasn't just Freya, it was this whole city that had won his heart. It was over. He was lost to her. She would lie here in the cold and die, and he would find her frozen body when daylight came, and be sorry. . . .

But she had spent too long surviving to die as easily as that. After a few moments she lifted herself on her hands and knees and tried to calm her ragged, painful gasps. The cold was in her throat, and gnawing at her lips and the tips of her ears, and an idea was coiled in her skull like a red snake.

It was an idea so terrible that for a little while she could not believe it was really she who had thought of it. She rubbed frost from a window and stared at her own dim reflection, wondering. Could it work? Did she dare? But she had no choice but to try; it was her only hope. She tugged up her hood, pulled her cold-mask into place, and set off through snow and moonlight to the air harbor.

It had been a strange day for Tom, trapped in the Winter Palace with the blizzard battering at the windows and Hester lost on the other side of town. A strange day, and a stranger evening. He had been sitting in the library, trying to concentrate on another of Pennyroyal's books, when Smew appeared in full chamberlain's garb to tell him that the margravine wanted him to join her for dinner.

From the look on Smew's face, Tom could tell that this invitation was a huge honor. Formal robes had been found for him, newly laundered and neatly pressed. "They belonged to the old chamberlain," Smew told him, helping him into them. "They're about your size, I reckon."

Tom had never worn robes before, and when he glanced in the mirror, he saw someone who looked handsome and sophisticated and nothing at all like him. He felt very nervous, following Smew toward the margravine's private dining room. The wind seemed to be shoving at the shutters with less urgency than before, so perhaps the storm was lifting. He would eat as quickly as he could, and then go and find Hester.

But it wasn't really possible to eat quickly; not a formal dinner like this, with Smew in footman's garb bringing in dish after dish and then hurrying back to the kitchens to put on his chef's hat and cook up more, or running to the wine cellars for another bottle of vintage red from the vineyard city of Bordeaux-Mobile. And after a few courses Tom found that he didn't want to make his excuses and go out into the dying blizzard, for Freya was good company, and it felt nice to be alone with her. There was something shiny about her tonight, as if she thought she had done a very daring thing by asking him to eat with her, and she spoke more easily than before about her family and Anchorage's history, right back to her long-ago ancestress Dolly Rasmussen, a high school girl who had had visions of the Sixty Minute War before it started and had led her little band of followers out of the first Anchorage just before it was vaporized.

Tom watched her talk and noticed that she had tried to do something really impressive with her hair, and that she was wearing the most glittery and least moth-eaten of her gowns. Had she gone to all that trouble for him? The idea made him feel thrilled and guilty; he looked away from her and met Smew's disapproving gaze as he cleared the dessert things and poured coffee.

"Will there be anything else, Your Radiance?"

Freya drank, watching Tom over the rim of her cup. "No, thank you, Smew. You can turn in. I thought Tom and I might go down to the Wunderkammer."

"Certainly, Your Radiance. I shall accompany you."

Freya looked up sharply at him. "There's no need, Smew. You can go."

Tom sensed the servant's unease. He felt a little uneasy himself, but maybe that was just the margravine's wine going to his head. He said, "Well, perhaps another day . . ."

"No, Tom," said Freya, reaching out to touch his hand with her fingertips. "Now. Tonight. Listen, the storm is over. The Wunderkammer will be beautiful by moonlight. . . ."

The Wunderkammer was beautiful by moonlight, but not as beautiful as Freya. As she led him into the little museum, Tom understood why the people of Anchorage loved and followed her. If only Hester could be more like her! He kept finding himself making excuses for Hester these days, explaining that she was only the way she was because of the awful things that had happened to her, but Freya had been through awful things too, and she wasn't all bitter and angry.

The moon gazed down through snow-veiled glass, transforming the familiar artifacts with its light. The sheet of foil shone inside its case like a window into another world, and when Freya turned in its dim reflected light to face him, Tom knew that she wanted him to kiss her. It was as if some strange gravity were drawing their faces together, and as their lips touched, Freya made a soft little contented noise. She pushed closer to him, and his arms went around her without his meaning them to. She had a slightly sweaty, unwashed odor, which seemed strange at first and then very sweet. Her gown crinkled under his hands, and her mouth tasted of cinnamon.

Then something—a faint noise from the doorway, a breath of cold air from the corridor beyond—made her glance up, and Tom forced himself to push her gently away.

"What was that?" asked Freya, whispering. "I thought I heard someone. . . ."

Glad of an excuse to move away from her warmth and her luring smell, Tom backed to the door. "Nobody. Just the heating ducts, I expect. They're always rattling and scratching."

"Yes, I know; it's an awful bore. I'm sure they never used to before we came to the High Ice. . . ." She came close again, holding out her hands. "Tom . . ."

"I must go," he said. "It's late. I'm sorry. Thank you."

Hurrying up the stairs to his room, he tried to ignore the warm cinnamon taste of Freya in his mouth and think of Hester. Poor Het! She had sounded so lonely when he spoke to her on the telephone. He should go to her. He would just lie down for a bit and gather his thoughts, and then he would pull on cold-weather gear and head down to the harbor. How soft this bed was! He closed his eyes and felt the room revolving. Too much wine. It was only the wine that had made him kiss Freya; it was Hester he was in love with. So why could he not stop thinking about Freya? "You idiot!" he said aloud.

Above his head the heating duct rattled, as if something inside it was agreeing, but Tom didn't notice, for he had already drifted off to sleep.

Hester was not the only one who had seen Tom and Freya's kiss. Caul, sitting alone in the forward cabin of the limpet while Skewer and Gargle were off housebreaking, had been flipping idly through the spy channels when he was brought up short by the sight of them embracing. "Tom, you fool," he whispered.

What Caul liked most about Tom was his kindness. Kindness was not valued back in Grimsby, where the older boys were encouraged to torment the younger ones, who would grow up to torment another batch of youngsters in their turn. "Good practice for life," Uncle said. "Hard knocks, that's all the world's about!" But maybe Uncle had never met anyone like Tom, who was kind to other people and seemed to expect nothing more than kindness in return. And what could be kinder than going out with Hester Shaw, making that ugly, useless girl feel loved and wanted? To Caul it seemed almost saintly. It was horrible to see Tom kissing Freya like that, betraying Hester, betraying himself, ready to throw everything away.

And maybe, too, he was a little jealous.

He glimpsed a blurred face in the open doorway behind the couple and zoomed in just in time to recognize Hester as she turned and ran. When he pulled back, the other two had broken away from each other; they looked uncertainly toward the door, talking in low, embarrassed voices. "*I must go. It's late.*"

"Oh, Hester!" He flipped away from the Wunderkammer, checking other channels, searching for her. He didn't know why it should upset him so, the thought of her in pain, but it did. Perhaps it was partly envy—and the knowledge that if she did something stupid, Tom would end up with Freya. Whatever it was, it made his hands shake as he fumbled with the controls.

There was no sign of her on the other palace cameras. He moved a spare into a position on the roof and swung it around, checking the grounds and the surrounding streets. Her blundering feet had jotted a long, illegible sentence on the white page of Rasmussen Prospekt. Caul leaned closer to his screens, perspiring slightly as he started scuttling cameras into positions at the air harbor. Where *was* she?

Night
Flight

THE AAKIUQS WERE STILL asleep. Hester crept back to her room and took the money Pennyroyal had given her at Airhaven from its hiding place under her mattress, then went straight to the *Jenny*'s hangar. Scrabbling away the snow that had drifted against the door, she dragged it open. She lit the work lamps. The *Jenny Haniver*'s red bulk loomed over her, ladders propped against half-painted engine pods, raw new panels covering the holes in the gondola like fresh skin over a recent wound. She went aboard and turned the heaters on. Then, leaving everything to warm up, she trudged back out into the snow, heading for the fuel tanks.

Up in the hangar's shadowy dome, something scuttled and clanked.

It was not hard to guess what she was planning. Caul thumped the control desk in front of him and groaned,

"Hester, no! He was drunk! He didn't mean it!" He perched on the brink of his chair, feeling like some impotent god who could watch events unfold but was powerless to alter them.

Except that he could. If Tom knew what was happening, Caul was sure he would go straight to the harbor, reason with Hester, apologize, make her understand. Caul had seen couples making up before, and he felt sure this silly rift need not be final—if only Tom *knew*.

But the only person who could tell him was Caul.

"Don't be stupid," he told himself angrily, pulling his hands back from the camera controls. "What do a couple of Drys mean to you? Nothing! Not worth risking the *Screw Worm* for. Not worth disobeying Uncle."

He reached for the controls again. He couldn't help it. He had a responsibility.

He switched to the camera inside Tom's bedchamber at the palace and made it rattle its legs against the inside of the duct it was hiding in. Tom just lay there, fast asleep with his stupid mouth open and no idea that his life was falling apart.

Leave it, thought Caul. *You tried, you couldn't wake him, it's over. It doesn't matter.*

He checked on Hester, then sent a camera racing through the heating ducts of the upper-city villa where Skewer and Gargle were working, peering into each room in turn until he found them in the kitchen, slipping silver plate into their carryalls. The cam tapped the inside of the duct: three taps, then a pause, then another three. *Return at once.* The blurred figures on the screen leaped up, recognizing the code, clownish in their clumsy haste to stow the last of the loot and get back to the limpet.

Caul hesitated for one moment longer, cursing his soft

heart and reminding himself what Uncle would do to him if word of this got out. Then he ran, scrabbling up the ladder, through the hatchway, out into the silent city.

She had been afraid that the fuel tanks would be frozen, but she had reckoned without the ingenuity of eight hundred years of Anchorage harbormasters, who had found ways of adapting to the arctic cold. The fuel was mixed with antifreeze, and the pump controls were housed in a heated building next to the main tank. She unhooked the fuel hose and heaved the big nozzle up onto her shoulder, stomping back to the hangar with it uncoiling across the snow behind her. Inside the hangar she attached the nozzle to a valve in the airship's underside, then returned to the pump house to switch it on. The hose began to shudder slightly as the fuel started gurgling through it. While the tanks were filling, she went aboard and started to make ready. The gondola lights weren't yet working, but she found her way around by the work lamps outside. As she began flicking switches on the control panels, the instruments sprang to life, their illuminated dials filling the flight deck with a firefly glow.

Tom woke up, surprised to find that he had been asleep. There was a thick, silty feeling in his head, and somebody was in the room with him, leaning over his bed, touching his face with cold fingers.

"Freya?" he said.

It was not the margravine. A bluish flashlight flicked on, lighting up the pale face of a total stranger. Tom thought he knew everybody aboard Anchorage by sight, but he did not recognize this white face, this pale fire of white-blond hair.

The voice was strange too, with a soft accent that was not the accent of Anchorage. "No time to explain, Tom! You've got to come with me. Hester's at the air harbor. She's leaving without you!"

"What?" Tom shook his head, trying to shake the remnants of his dreams away, half hoping that this was one of them. Who was this boy, and what was he talking about? "Why would she do that?"

"Because of you, you idiot!" the boy shouted. He ripped Tom's bedcovers away and flung his outdoor clothes at him. "How do you think she felt, watching you snog Freya Rasmussen?"

"I didn't!" said Tom, appalled. "It was just— And Hester couldn't have— Anyway, how do you know about—?" But the stranger's urgency was beginning to infect him. He pulled off his borrowed robe, fumbled his boots and cold-mask on, pulled on his old aviator's coat, and followed the boy out of the room, then out of the palace by a side entrance he had never even noticed before. The night was wrenchingly cold, the city a dream of winter. Off the western side the mountains of Greenland hunched themselves up out of the ice, looking crisp edged in the moonlight and close enough to touch. The Aurora flared above the rooftops, and in the silence Tom thought he could hear it crackling and buzzing like a power line on a frosty morning.

The stranger led him down a stairway on Rasmussen Prospekt, along a maintenance walkway under the belly of the tier, up another stairway to the air harbor. As they emerged into the open again, Tom saw he had been wrong about the noise. The crackling was the sound of ice falling from the *Jenny's* hangar as the domed roof opened, and the buzzing was her engine pods swiveling into takeoff position.

"Hester!" Tom shouted, pushing himself through the snow. In the open hangar the *Jenny*'s running lights snapped on, reflections flaring across the drifts. He heard a ladder that had been propped against her side fall with a crash, heard the triple clang as the docking clamps released. It couldn't really be Hester, could it, moving about behind the darkened flight-deck windows? He scrabbled and swam through an ocean of snow. "Hester! Hester!" he shouted, and still didn't really believe that she would take off. She couldn't know about that stupid kiss, could she? She had been upset when he told her he wanted to stay here; she was teaching him a lesson, that was all. He kicked and struggled his way through the drifts, faster now, but when he was still twenty yards from the hangar, the *Jenny Haniver* lifted into the sky and turned southeast, sweeping away very quickly over the rooftops and out across the endless ice.

"Hester!" he shouted, suddenly angry. Why couldn't she just tell him how she felt, like a normal person, instead of storming off like this? The west wind was rising, carrying the airship swiftly away from him, flinging powder snow into his face as he turned to look for his mysterious companion. The boy was gone. He was alone except for Mr. Aakiuq, who was stumbling toward him and shouting, "Tom? What's happened?"

"Hester!" said Tom in a tiny voice, and sat down in the snow. He could feel tears soaking into the fleece inside his cold-mask as the *Jenny*'s stern lantern, a tiny flake of warmth in that great cold, dwindled and dwindled, and merged at last with the Aurora.

After Hester

OM MADE HIS WAY BACK ALONG the undertier walkway with a horrible, empty, kicked-in-the-stomach feeling. It was several hours since the *Jenny Haniver* had taken off. Mr. Aakiuq had tried to contact Hester by radio, but there had been no reply. "Perhaps she's not switched it on," the harbormaster said. "Or perhaps it's not working: I never had a chance to test all the valves. And there is not nearly enough gas in the envelope—I only filled it to check the cells were sound. Oh, why did the poor child have to take off so suddenly?"

"I don't know," Tom had replied, but he did. If only he had understood sooner how much she hated it here. If only he had spared a thought for how she must feel, before he started to fall in love with this city. If only he hadn't kissed Freya. But his guilt kept twisting around and turning into anger. After all, *she* hadn't thought about *his* feelings. Why shouldn't he stay here if he wanted to? She was so selfish. Just because she hated city life didn't mean that he wanted to be a homeless sky-tramp forever.

Still, he had to find her again. He didn't know if she would take him back, or if he even wanted her to, but he couldn't let it end in this horrible, messy, broken way.

The city's engines were purring into life as he hurried up into the cold of the upper tier. He went toward the Winter Palace, stumbling along in the same flailing track that he had made earlier. He didn't want to see Freya—his insides curled up like burning paper when he thought about what had passed between them in the Wunderkammer—but only Freya had the power to order the city to turn back and pursue the *Jenny Haniver*.

He was passing through the long shadow of the Wheelhouse when the door slammed open and a frantic silk-robed apparition came blundering at him through the snow. "Tim! Tim, is it true?" Pennyroyal's eyes were wide and bulging, his grip on Tom's arm sharp as frostbite. "They're saying that girl of yours has left! Flown off!"

Tom nodded, feeling ashamed.

"But without the *Jenny Haniver* . . ."

Tom shrugged. "Maybe I'll have to come with you to America after all, Professor."

He pushed past the explorer and ran on, leaving Pennyroyal to wander back toward his apartments muttering, "America! Ha-ha! Of course! America!" In the Winter Palace he found Freya waiting for him. She was perched on a chaise longue in the smallest of her receiving rooms, a chamber no larger than a football field and lined with so many mirrors that there seemed to be a thousand Freyas sitting there, and a thousand Toms bursting in wet and disheveled to drip melted snow onto her marble floor.

"Your Radiance," he said, "we must turn back."

"Turn back?" Freya had been expecting all sorts of things, but not this. Flushed with delight at the news of Hester's leaving, she had imagined herself comforting Tom, reassuring him that it was all for the best, making him understand that he was far better off without his hideous girlfriend and that it was clearly the Ice Gods' will that he remain here, in Anchorage, with her. She had put on her prettiest gown to help him understand, and she had left the top button undone in a way that revealed a tiny triangle of soft white flesh below the hollow of her throat. It made her feel shiveringly bold and grown-up. She had been expecting all sorts of things, but she had not expected this.

"How can we turn back?" she demanded, half laughing, in the hope that he was making some sort of joke. "Why should we turn back?"

"But Hester . . ."

"We can't catch up with an airship, Tom! And why would we want to? I mean, with Wolverinehampton out there behind us somewhere . . ." But he wasn't even looking at her; his eyes were shiny and sliding with tears. She fumbled the top of her gown closed, feeling embarrassed and then quickly cross. "Why should I risk my whole city for the sake of a mad girl in an airship?"

"She's not mad."

"She acts mad."

"She's upset!"

"Well, I'm upset!" shouted Freya. "I thought you cared about me! Doesn't what happened earlier mean anything? I thought you'd forgotten Hester! She's nothing! She's nothing but air trash, and I'm glad she's dumped you! I want you to be my, my, *my* boyfriend! I hope you understand just what an honor that is!"

Tom stared at her and could think of nothing to say. He saw her suddenly as Hester must: a plump, spoiled, petulant girl who expected the world to arrange itself to suit her. He knew that she was right to refuse his request, that it would be madness to turn the city around, but somehow her rightness made her seem even more unreasonable. He mumbled something and turned away.

"Where are you going?" demanded Freya shrilly. "Who said you could go? I have not given you permission to leave my presence!"

But Tom did not wait for permission. He ran from the room, the door crashing shut behind him, and left her there alone with all her reflections, which turned their heads this way and that in the trembling mirrors, looking blank-faced at each other as if to ask, *What did we do wrong?*

He ran through the long corridors of the Winter Palace with no idea where he was going, barely noticing the rooms he passed or the faint scratching and scrabbling noises that came sometimes from the ducts and ventilation shafts. Ever since he'd fallen out of London, Hester had been beside him, looking after him, telling him what to do, loving him in that fierce, shy way of hers. Now he had driven her away. He wouldn't even have known that she was gone if it hadn't been for that boy. . . .

For the first time since the *Jenny Haniver* took off, Tom thought of his strange visitor. Who had he been? Someone from the engine district, judging by the way he'd been dressed (Tom remembered layers and layers of dark clothes, a tunic smeared with oil and grease, black paint crackling off its brass buttons). And how had he known what Hester was about to do? Had she confided in him? Told him things she had not told Tom? He felt an odd jab of jealousy at the thought of Het sharing her secrets with someone else.

But what if the boy knew where she had been going? Tom had to find him, talk to him. He ran out of the palace to the nearest stairway and down to the engine district, hurrying through the thunder and fog of the Scabious Spheres to the enginemaster's office.

Skewer and Gargle were waiting for Caul when he came scurrying back from the air harbor, breathless and jumpy from running. They were ready inside the hatchway with guns and knives in case the Drys were on his tail, and they bundled him through and would not let him speak until they were quite sure no one had followed him.

"What were you thinking of?" asked Skewer angrily. "What did you think you were doing? You *know* it's forbidden to leave the limpet unguarded. And as for talking to a Dry! Didn't you learn nothing in the Burglarium?" He put on a strange, whining voice that Caul guessed was supposed to be an impression of him. "'Tom! Tom! Quickly, Tom! She's leaving you!' You fool!"

Caul sat on the floor of the hold, his back to a bale of stolen clothes, failure sluicing over him like meltwater.

"You've blown it, Caul," said Skewer with a sudden smile.

"I mean, you've *really* blown it. I'm taking charge of this ship. Uncle will understand. When he hears what you've done, he'll be sorry he didn't put me in command right from the start. I'm sending a message-fish away, tonight, to let him know all about it. No more snooping for you, you Dry-lover. No more midnight expeditions. No more mooning over margravines—oh, don't think I haven't seen you going gooey-eyed each time her face comes on the screens."

"But Skewer—" whined Gargle.

"Quiet!" said Skewer, cuffing him hard around the head, turning to kick Caul down as he started up to protect the smaller boy. He looked flushed and pleased with himself. "You can stay quiet too, Caul. From now on, we'll run this limpet my way."

Mr. Scabious, whose home on the upper tier held too many unhappy memories, spent almost all his spare time in his office, a narrow hut squeezed into a gap between two tier supports at the heart of the engine district. It contained a desk, a filing cabinet, a bunk, a Primus stove, a small hand-basin, a calendar, an enamel mug, and not much else. Scabious's mourning robes hung from a hook on the back of the door, flapping like a black wing when Tom pushed it open. The man himself sat at his desk, a statue of melancholy. The furnace flicker of the engine district sliced in between the slats of the blinds on the window, striping him with bars of light and shadow. Only his eyes moved, spiking the new-comer with a chilly stare.

"Mr. Scabious," panted Tom, "Hester's gone! She's taken the *Jenny* and gone!"

The enginemaster nodded, staring at the wall behind Tom's head as if a film were being projected there that only he could see. "Then she is gone. Why come to me?"

Tom sat down heavily on the bunk. "There was a boy. I've not seen him before. A pale sort of fair-haired boy from the engine districts, a bit younger than me. He seemed to know all about Hester."

Scabious moved for the first time, springing up and coming quickly toward Tom. There was a strange look on his face. "You've seen him too?"

Tom flinched, surprised by the enginemaster's sudden show of passion. "I thought he might be able to tell me where she was going."

"There is no one like the boy you describe aboard this city. No one *living*."

"But—it sounded like he'd talked to her. If you could just tell me where to find him . . ."

"You cannot find Axel. He will find you, when he wishes to. Even I have seen him only from a distance. What did he say to you? Did he mention me? Did he give you any message for his father?"

"His father? No."

Scabious barely seemed to listen. He fumbled in a pocket of his overalls and pulled out a small silver book, a little photo frame. Tom knew a lot of people who carried these portable shrines, and as Scabious opened his, he sneaked a look at the picture inside. He saw a heavy, thick-set young man, like a younger version of Scabious himself. "Oh," he said, "that's not the boy I saw. He was younger, and thin. . . ."

That shook the enginemaster, but only for a moment.

"Don't be a fool, Tom!" he snapped. "The ghosts of the dead can take on any form they wish. My Axel was as slender as you once. It is only natural that he would appear as he was in those days, young and handsome and filled with hope."

Tom didn't believe in ghosts. At least he didn't think he did. *No one comes back from the Sunless Country*. That was what Hester always said, and he muttered it under his breath several times for reassurance as he walked away from Mr. Scabious's office and climbed the suddenly dark and shadowy stairways to the upper tier. The boy could not have been a ghost: Tom had felt him, smelled him, sensed the warmth of his body. He had left footprints as he led the way toward the hangar. The footprints would prove it.

But when he reached the air harbor, the wind had risen, and powder snow was pouring over the surface of the drifts like smoke. The prints around the hangar were already so faint that it was impossible to say how many feet had made them, and whether the strange boy had been real, or a ghost, or only a fragment of a dream.

18

Predator's Gold

HESTER WAS GRATEFUL FOR the wind. It hurried her away from Anchorage, but it was fickle and blustery, sometimes veering around into the north, sometimes gusting fiercely, sometimes dropping away to nothing. She had to concentrate to keep the *Jenny Haniver* on course, and that was good because it left her no time to think about Tom, or the things she was planning to do. She knew that if she thought too hard about either, she would end up losing her nerve, putting the airship about and flying back to Anchorage.

But sometimes, as she snatched catnaps at the controls, she could not help wondering what Tom was doing. Was he sorry she had left? Had he even noticed? Was Freya Rasmussen comforting him? "It doesn't matter," she told herself. Soon she would make everything just as it had been before, and he would be hers again.

On the second day out she sighted Wolverinehampton. The suburb had turned south after failing to catch Anchorage, and its luck had turned with it, for it had found prey: a cluster of whaling towns driven off course by the storm. There were three of them, each much larger than Wolverinehampton, but the suburb had sped quickly from one to the next, biting away drive wheels and skid supports, and when Hester saw it, it was turning back to devour them where they lay crippled. It looked to her as if it would be busy with its feast for several weeks, and she was glad that it would not be ranging west to menace Anchorage again and interfere with her own plans.

She flew on and on, through brief days and long, dark, bitter nights, and at last her nightly search of the radio dial was greeted by the wavering howl of a city's homing beacon. She altered course, the signal growing clearer, and a few hours later she saw Arkangel squatting over its own prey on the ice ahead.

The predator city's big, noisy, closed-in air harbor made her feel strangely homesick for the peace of Anchorage, and the easy rudeness of its ground crew and customs men made her think wistfully of Mr. Aakiuq. She spent half of Pennyroyal's sovereigns on fuel and lifting gas and hid the rest in one of the secret compartments that Anna Fang had installed under the *Jenny*'s deck. Then, feeling sick and guilty at what she was about to do, she made her way to the Air Exchange, a big building behind the fuelworks where traders met with the city's merchants. When she began asking where she might find Piotr Masgard, the aviators glared at her disapprovingly, and one woman spat on the deck at her feet, but after a while an amiable old merchant seemed to take pity on her and called her gently aside.

"Arkangel's not like other cities, my dear," he explained, leading her toward an elevator station. "The rich here don't live up on top but in the middle, where it's warmest, a district called the Core. Young Masgard has a mansion there. Get off at Kael Station and ask again from there."

He watched her carefully as she paid her fare and stepped aboard a Core-bound elevator. Then he hitched up his robes and went hurrying back to his shop on the far side of the harbor, a large, tatty, cluttered establishment called Blinkoe's Old Tech and Antiquities.

"Quickly, wives!" he blustered, bursting into the narrow parlor behind the shop. He waved his arms in urgent semaphore as the five Mrs. Blinkoes looked up from their novels and embroideries. "She's here! That girl! The ugly one! To think, all these weeks spent searching and questioning, and she walks into our own Air Exchange bold as brass! Quickly now, we must make ready!"

He rubbed his hands together in glee, already imagining ways to spend the bounty that the Green Storm would pay him when he brought them Hester and the *Jenny Haniver.*

The Core was a perplexing place: a great booming cavern, filled with the thunder of the city's engines, hazy with smoke and drifting steam, crisscrossed by hundreds of walkways and railways and elevator shafts. The buildings sat crammed together on ledges and stilt platforms, or clung underneath like the nests of house martins. Slaves in iron collars swept the pavements, while others were whipped past in gangs by fur-clad foremen, off to perform unpleasant chores in chilly outer districts. Hester tried not to see them, or the rich ladies leading little boys on leashes, or the man who kicked and kicked and kicked a slave who accidentally brushed against him. It was none of her business. Arkangel was a city where the strong did as they liked.

Iron statues of the wolf-god Eisengrim guarded the gates of Masgard's mansion. Inside, gas jets burned on iron tripods, filling the big reception room with patterns of jittery light and slashing, knife-edged shadow. A willowy young woman wearing a jeweled slave collar looked Hester up and down and asked her business. Hester gave her the same answer she had given to the guards outside: "I have information to sell to the Huntsmen of Arkangel."

There was a buzz of engines in the shadows under the barn-high roof, and Masgard came swooping down on her, riding a leather chair that swung beneath a small gasbag, midget engine pods sprouting from the headrest. It was a chairship, a rich man's toy, and he steered it close to Hester and hovered in front of her, relishing her surprise. His slave girl rubbed her head against the toe of his boot like a cat.

"Well," he said. "I know you! You're that scar-faced quail from Airhaven. Come to take up my offer, have you?"

"I've come to tell you where you can find prey," said Hester, trying not to let her voice shake.

Masgard steered the chairship a little closer, keeping her waiting, studying the play of guilt and fear on her ruined face. His city was too big to survive anymore without the help of scum like this girl, and he hated her for it.

"So?" he asked at last. "What town do you wish to betray?"

"Not just a town," said Hester. "A city. Anchorage."

Masgard tried to go on looking bored, but Hester saw sparks of interest in his eyes. She did her best to fan them into flame. "You must have heard of Anchorage, Mr. Masgard. A great big ice city. Apartments full of rich furnishings, the biggest drive wheel on the ice, and a nice Old Tech engine array called the Scabious Spheres. They're heading around the top of Greenland, bound for the western ice."

"Why?"

Hester shrugged. (Better not mention the journey to America; too hard to explain and too hard to believe.) "Who knows? Perhaps they've learned about some Old Tech site and they're off to dig it up. I'm sure you'd find a way to pry the details out of their beautiful young margravine. . . ."

Masgard grinned. "Julianna here was a margrave's daughter, before great Arkangel ate her daddy's town."

"Then think what a pretty addition Freya Rasmussen will make to your collection," said Hester. She seemed to be standing outside herself; she felt nothing except a faint pride at just how heartless she could be. "And if you want a snack to keep you going on the way, I can give you the coordinates of Wolverinehampton, a predator suburb with a fat new catch."

Masgard was hooked. He'd had word of Anchorage and Wolverinehampton from Widgery Blinkoe a few days earlier, but the oily antiquarian had not known Wolverinehampton's present course. As for Anchorage, Masgard was not sure whether to believe a sighting of an ice city so far west. Yet this mangy sky-urchin sounded like she knew her stuff, and with Blinkoe's report to back it up, her information would be enough to persuade the Council to change course. He let her wait a moment, so that she could appreciate just how despicable she was. Then he opened a compartment in the armrest of his flying chair and pulled out a thick sheet of parchment, which he signed with a fountain pen. His slave girl passed the paper to Hester. There were words printed on it in Gothic script, and seals with the names of the gods of Arkangel: Eisengrim and the Thatcher.

"A promissory note," explained Masgard, revving his chair's engines and lifting away from her. "If your information proves correct, you can come and collect your fee when we eat Anchorage. Give the details to my clerk."

Hester shook her head. "I'm not doing this for predator's gold."

"Then what?"

"There's somebody aboard Anchorage. Tom Natsworthy, the boy you saw me with in Airhaven. When you eat the city, you'll let me have him. But he's not to know it's been arranged. I want him to think I'm rescuing him. Everything else aboard the stinking place is yours, but not Tom. He's mine. My price."

Masgard stared down at her for a moment, genuinely surprised. Then he flung back his head, and his laughter filled the room with echoes.

Waiting at the station for an elevator that would take her back to the air harbor, she felt the deck plates shiver as great Arkangel began to move. She patted her pocket, checking again that she had Masgard's revised promissory note safe. How glad Tom would be when she came to rescue him from the predator city's gut! How easily she would make him forget his infatuation with the margravine, once they were together again on the bird roads!

She had done what she had to, for Tom's sake, and there was no going back. She would fetch a few bits and pieces from the *Jenny Haniver* and find a room somewhere to wait out the journey.

It was night again by the time she reached the air harbor, and snowflakes were fluttering around the landing lights at the harbor mouth. The noise of raucous laughter and cheap music drifted from taverns behind the docking pans, gusting louder whenever someone opened a door. Dim lamplight made puddles of shadow under the big moored traders: ships with northern names, the *Fram* and the *Froud* and the *Smaug*. She began to feel nervous as she walked toward the low-rent docking pan where the *Jenny* waited. This was a dangerous city, and she had lost the habit of being alone.

"Miss Shaw?" The man surprised her, coming up on her blind side. She reached for her knife, then recognized the nice old merchant who had helped her earlier. "I'll walk you to your ship, Miss Shaw. There are some Snowmad traders aboard, ruffianly types. It's not safe for a young woman alone. Your vessel's the *Jenny Haniver*, isn't she?"

"That's right," said Hester, wondering how he knew her name and that of her ship. She supposed he must have asked around earlier, or looked it up in the new-arrivals ledger at the harbor office.

"You've seen Masgard, then?" her new friend asked. "I suppose that has something to do with this sudden move to the west? You've sold him a town?"

Hester nodded.

"I'm in a similar line of work myself," the merchant said, and slammed her against a metal stanchion beneath a trader called the *Temporary Blip*. She gasped, hurt and surprised, trying to gulp in enough air to scream for help. Something stung the side of her neck like a hornet. The merchant stepped away from her, breathing hard. A brass syringe flashed in the light from the distant taverns as he slid it back into his pocket.

Hester tried to put her hand to her neck, but the drug was taking effect quickly and her limbs no longer obeyed her. She tried to call out, but all that emerged was a wordless hoot. She took a step forward and fell, her face a few inches from the man's boots. "Terribly sorry," she heard him say, his voice wavery and far away, like Tom's voice the last time she'd heard it, seeping out of the telephone in the Aakiuqs' parlor. "I have five wives to support, you see, and they all have expensive tastes and nag me something rotten."

Hester hooted again, drooling onto the deck plate.

"Don't worry!" the voice went on. "I'm just taking you and your ship down to Rogues' Roost. You're wanted for questioning. That's all."

"But Tom—" Hester managed to moan.

More boots appeared: expensive, fashionable ladies' boots, with tassels. New voices babbled overhead. "You're sure it's her, Blinkoe?"

"Eugh! She's so ugly!"

"She can't be worth anything to anyone!"

"Ten thousand in cash when I get her to the Roost," said Blinkoe smugly. "I'll take her there aboard her own ship and tow the *Blip*'s tender to bring me home again. Be back in no time, with bags full of money. Look after the shop while I'm gone, dears."

"No!" Hester tried to say, because if he took her away, she wouldn't be there to rescue Tom; he would be eaten along with the rest of Anchorage, and all her schemes would come to nothing. . . . But although she tried to struggle as they rummaged for her keys, she could not move or make a sound or even blink. It took her a long time to lose consciousness, however, and that was the worst of it, for she understood everything that was happening as the merchant and his wives dragged her aboard the *Jenny Haniver* and began the preparations for takeoff.

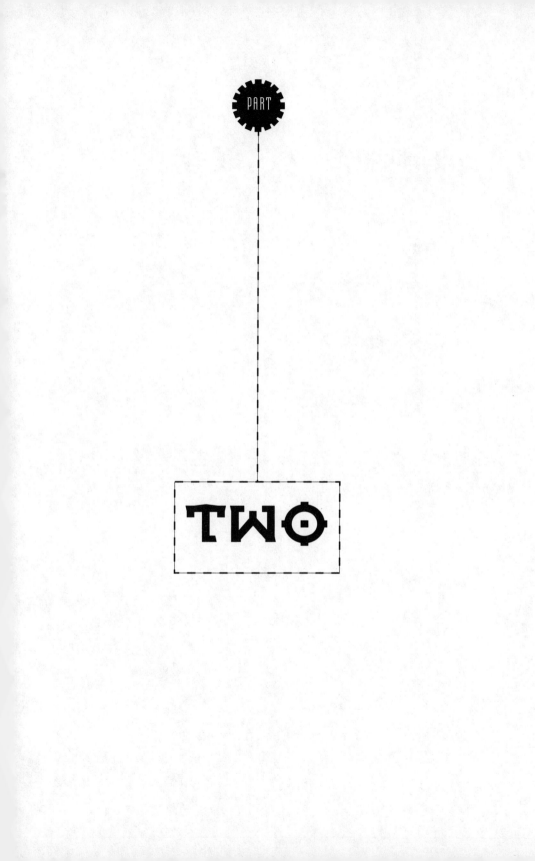

PART

TWO

The Memory Chamber

ICE WATER WOKE HER: A STORM of it, driving her sideways across a cold stone floor and thrusting her against a wall of white tiles. She gasped and screamed and gurgled. Water filled her mouth. Water plastered draggled hair across her face so that she couldn't see, and when she raked it aside, there was not much to see anyway, only a chill white room lit by a single argon globe, and men in white uniforms aiming hoses at her.

"Enough!" shouted a female voice, and the storm ceased, the men turning away to hook the hoses' dribbling snouts over a metal frame bolted to the wall. Hester choked and cursed and spewed water out onto the floor, where it swirled away into a central drain. Dim flickers of memory came back to her, of Arkangel, and a merchant; of surfacing from sleep in the cold, rattly hold of the *Jenny* and finding that she was tied up. She had struggled and tried to shout, and the merchant had come, all apologetic, and there had been that hornet sting on her neck again, and darkness. He had drugged her and kept her drugged, and while she was under, he had flown her from Arkangel to whatever this place was. . . .

"Tom!" she moaned.

Booted feet came sloshing toward her. She looked up snarling, expecting the merchant, but this wasn't him. This was a young woman in white, with a bronze badge on her breast that marked her out as a subaltern in the Anti-Traction League and an armband embroidered with green lightning.

"Dress her," barked the subaltern, and the men dragged Hester upright by her wet hair. They didn't bother toweling her, just forced her weak limbs into the arms and legs of a shapeless gray overall. Hester could barely stand, let alone resist. They pushed her barefoot out of the shower room and along a dank corridor, the subaltern leading the way. There were posters on the walls with pictures of airships attacking cities and handsome young men and women in white uniforms gazing at a sunrise beyond a green hill. Other soldiers passed, their boots loud under the low roof. Most were not much older than Hester, but all wore swords at their sides, and lightning-bolt armbands, and the shiny, smug expressions of people who know they are right.

At the end of the passage was a metal door, and behind the door was a cell: a tall, narrow tomb of a room with a single window very high up. Heating ducts snaked across the crumbling concrete ceiling but gave out no warmth. Hester shivered, drying slowly in her scratchy overalls. Someone flung a heavy coat at her, and she realized that it was her own and pulled it on gratefully. "Where are the rest?" she asked, and had trouble making them understand, what with her teeth chattering and the aftereffects of the merchant's drugs numbing her already-clumsy mouth. "The rest of my clothes?"

"Boots," said the subaltern, taking them from one of her men and throwing them at Hester. "The rest we burned. Don't worry, barbarian; you won't need them again."

The door closed; a key turned in the lock; booted feet marched away. Hester could hear the sea somewhere far below, hissing and sighing against a stony shore. She hugged herself against the cold and started to cry. Not for herself, or even for Tom, but for her burned clothes: her waistcoat with Tom's photograph in the pocket, and the dear red scarf he had bought for her in Peripatetiapolis. Now she had nothing left of him at all.

The darkness beyond the high, small window faded slowly to a washed-out gray. The door rattled and opened, and a man looked in and said, "Up, barbarian; the commander's waiting."

The commander was waiting in a big, clean room where the vague forms of dolphins and sea nymphs showed faintly through the whitewash on the walls and a circular window looked out over a cheese-grater sea. She sat behind her big steel desk, brown fingers drumming out manic little patterns on a manila folder. She stood up only when Hester's guards saluted. "You may leave us," she told them.

"But Commander—" said one.

"I think I can handle one scrawny barbarian." She waited

till they were gone, then came slowly around the desk, staring at Hester the whole way.

Hester had met that fierce, dark stare before, for the commander was none other than the girl Sathya, Anna Fang's fierce young protégée from Batmunkh Gompa. She did not feel particularly surprised. Ever since she had reached Anchorage, her life had taken on the strange logic of a dream, and it seemed only right that she should meet a familiar, unfriendly face here at the end of it. Two and a half years had passed since their last meeting, but Sathya seemed to have aged much more than that; her face was gaunt and stern, and in her dark eyes there was an expression that Hester couldn't read, as if rage and guilt and pride and fear had all got mixed up inside her and turned into something new.

"Welcome to the Facility," she said coldly.

Hester stared at her. "What is this place? Where is it? I didn't think your lot had any bases left in the north, not since Spitzbergen got scoffed."

Sathya only smiled. "You don't know much about my lot, Miss Shaw. The High Council may have withdrawn League forces from the Arctic theater, but some of us do not accept defeat so calmly. The Green Storm maintain several bases in the north. Since you will not be leaving here alive, I can tell you that this Facility is on Rogues' Roost, an island some two hundred miles from the southern tip of Greenland."

"Nice," said Hester. "Come here for the weather, did you?"

Sathya slapped her hard, leaving her dazed and gasping. "These were the skies where Anna Fang grew up," she said. "Her parents traded in these regions, before they were enslaved by Arkangel."

"Right. Sentimental reasons, then," muttered Hester. She tensed, expecting another blow, but it did not come. Sathya turned away from her toward the window.

"You destroyed one of our units over the Drachen Pass three weeks ago," she said.

"Only because they attacked my ship," Hester replied.

"She is not your ship," the other girl snapped. "She is . . . She was Anna's. You stole her the night Anna died, you and your barbarian lover, Tom Natsworthy. Where is he, by the way? Don't tell me he has abandoned you?"

Hester shrugged.

"So what were you doing alone aboard Arkangel?"

"Just betraying a few cities to the Huntsmen," said Hester.

"I can believe that. Treachery is in your blood."

Hester frowned. Had Sathya dragged her all the way here just to be rude about her parents? "If you mean I take after my mother, well, she was pretty stupid digging up MEDUSA, but I don't think she actually betrayed anybody."

"No," Sathya agreed. "But your father . . ."

"My dad was a farmer!" cried Hester, feeling suddenly and strangely angry that this girl could stand there and insult the memory of her poor dead dad, who had never done anything but good.

"You are a liar," said Sathya. "Your father was Thaddeus Valentine."

Outside, snow fell like sifted confectioners' sugar. Hester could see icebergs plowing through the comfortless gray of the winter sea. In a tiny voice she said, "That isn't true."

Sathya pulled a sheet of writing paper from the folder on her desk. "This is the report that Anna wrote for the League's

High Council, that day she brought you to Batmunkh Gompa. What does she say about you . . . ? Ah, yes: *Two young people: one an adorable young Apprentice Historian from London, quite harmless, the other a poor, disfigured girl who I am sure is the lost daughter of Pandora Rae and Thaddeus Valentine.*"

Hester said, "My dad was David Shaw, of Oak Island. . . ."

"Your mother had many lovers before she married Shaw," said Sathya, in a voice crisp with disapproval. "Valentine was one of them. You are his child. Anna would never have written such a thing if she had not been certain."

"My dad was David Shaw," sniveled Hester, but she knew it wasn't true. She had known it in her heart these two years past, ever since her gaze had met Valentine's over the body of his dying daughter Katherine. Some sort of understanding had crackled between them then like electricity, a half recognition that she had crushed as quick and as hard as she could, because she didn't want him for a father. She had understood, though, deep down. No wonder she couldn't bring herself to kill him!

"Anna was wrong about you, wasn't she?" Sathya said, turning away, going to stand at the window. The snow had passed; patches of sunlight dappled the gray sea a lighter gray. She said, "You weren't lost, and Tom wasn't harmless. You were both in league with Valentine all along. You used Anna's kindness to get inside Batmunkh Gompa and help him burn our Air Fleet."

"No!" said Hester.

"Yes. You lured Anna to a place where he could murder her, and then you stole her ship."

Hester shook her head. "You're so wrong!"

"Stop lying!" shouted Sathya, rounding on her again. There were tears in her eyes.

Hester tried to remember that night at Batmunkh Gompa. It had mostly been a blur of flames and running, but she had a feeling that Sathya had not acted very well. For all her fighting talk, Sathya had let her beloved Anna run off to tackle Valentine alone, and Valentine had killed her. Hester knew quite well that you didn't forgive yourself for things like that. Instead, you blotted out the memories or sank into despair.

Or you found someone else to blame. Like Valentine's daughter.

Sathya said, "You will pay for what you did. But first, perhaps, you can help to make amends." She took a gun from her desk and gestured to a small door on the far side of her office. Hester walked toward it, not really caring where she went or whether Sathya was going to shoot her. *Valentine's daughter,* she kept thinking. *Valentine's daughter goes through a doorway. Valentine's daughter goes down some iron steps. Valentine's daughter.* No wonder she had such a temper. No wonder she had been able to sell a city full of good people to Arkangel with barely a squeak from her conscience. She was Valentine's daughter, and she took after Daddy.

The steps led to a tunnel, then a sort of antechamber. Two guards watched Hester coldly through the tinted glastic visors of their crab-shell helmets. A third man stood waiting beside a heavy steel door: a twitchy little pink-eyed rabbit of a man, gnawing nervously at his fingernails. The argon lamps on the walls bounced bright reflections off his bald scalp. Between his eyebrows was a red wheel.

"He's an Engineer!" said Hester. "A London Engineer! I

thought they were all dead. . . ."

"A few survived," said Sathya. "After London exploded, I was put in charge of the squadron sent out to round up survivors escaping from the wreck. Most were sent to slave-labor camps deep in League territory, but when I interrogated Dr. Popjoy and learned what his work had been, I realized he might be able to help us."

"Help you with what? I thought the League hated Old Tech?"

"There have always been some in the League who believed that to defeat the cities, we should use their own infernal devices against them," said Sathya. "After what you and your father did at Batmunkh Gompa, their voices began to be heard more loudly. A secret society of young officers was formed: the Green Storm. When I told them about Popjoy, they saw his potential at once and agreed to let me set up this Facility."

The Engineer bared big yellow teeth in a nervous grin and said, "So this is Hester Shaw, is it? She may be helpful. Yes, yes. Someone who was 'in at the kill,' so to speak. Her presence in the Mnemonic Environment may provide just the trigger we've been seeking."

"Get on with it," snapped Sathya, and Hester saw that she too was extremely nervous.

Popjoy pulled a series of levers on the door, and the massive electromagnetic locks released with hollow thuds and clangs, like docking clamps disengaging. The guards tensed, wraiths of steam scrolling from the funnels of their bulky machine guns as they flipped the safety catches off. All this security wasn't designed to keep people out, Hester realized.

It was meant to keep something *in*.

The door swung open.

Later Hester would learn that the Memory Chamber was a decommissioned fuel tank, one of dozens of steel globes clumped in the corries of Rogues' Roost, but at first sight it seemed just an insanely huge room, with rusty walls curving up to form a dome above her and down to make a bowl below. All over the walls big pictures had been fixed: grainy blowups of people's faces, photographs of London and Arkangel and Marseilles, a silk painting of Batmunkh Gompa in an ebony frame. Loops of scratchy film repeated endlessly on whitewashed panels: a little golden girl with pigtails laughing in a meadow; a young woman drawing on a long-stemmed pipe and blowing smoke at the camera.

Hester felt suddenly sick with fear, and did not know why.

A walkway ran around the edge of this spherical vault, and a narrow footbridge stretched from it to a platform in the center, where a monklike figure stood robed in gray. Hester tried to hang back as Sathya and Popjoy started along the bridge, but one of the guards was behind her, pushing her firmly forward. Ahead, Sathya reached the central platform and touched the arm of the one who waited there. She was crying silently, her face shining with tears in the dim light. "I've brought you a present, dearest," she said softly. "A visitor. Someone you're sure to remember!"

And the robed figure turned, the gray cowl fell aside, and Hester saw that it was—no, that it *had once been*—Anna Fang.

20

The New Model

D R. POPJOY HAD DONE GOOD work for his new masters. Of course he and his fellow Engineers had spent many years studying Stalker technology. They had learned much from Grike, the mechanized bounty killer who had once adopted Hester. They had even made Stalkers of their own: Hester had seen squads of the Resurrected Men marching through the streets of London on the night MEDUSA went off. But comparing those lurching, mindless creatures to the thing that stood before her now was like comparing a tatty old cargo balloon to a brand-new Serapis Cloud Yacht.

It was slender and almost graceful, and not very much taller than Miss Fang had been in life. Its face was hidden by a bronze death mask of the aviatrix, and the ducts and electrical cords that sprouted from its skullpiece were gathered neatly behind its head. The faint, curious twitchings of its head and hands as it peered at Hester seemed so human that for a moment she almost imagined the Engineer had succeeded in bringing Anna back.

Sathya started talking, quick and brittle. "She doesn't remember yet, but she will. This place acts as her memory, until her own memories come back to her. We've collected photographs of everyone she ever knew, everywhere she went, the cities she fought against, her lovers and her enemies. It will all come back to her. She's been resurrected for only a few months, and . . ."

She stopped suddenly, as if understanding that her stream of hopeful chatter was only making the horror of what she had done more horrible. Echoes of her words went whispering off around the inside of the old fuel tank: "And, and, and, and, and . . ."

"Oh, Gods and Goddesses," said Hester. "Why couldn't you let her rest in peace?"

"Because we need her!" yelled Sathya. "The League has lost its way! We need new leaders. Anna was the best of us. She will show us the path to victory!"

The Stalker flexed its clever hands, and a slender blade slid from each fingertip, snick, snick, snick.

"This isn't Anna," Hester said. "Nobody comes back from the Sunless Country. Your tame Engineer may have managed to get her corpse up and about, but it isn't her. I knew a Stalker once: They don't remember who they were in life. They aren't the same person; that person's *dead*, and when you stick one of those Old Tech machines in their head, you make a new person, like a new tenant moving into an empty house. . . ."

Popjoy began to chuckle.

"I hadn't realized that you were an expert, Miss Shaw. Of course you would be referring to the old Grike model, a very inferior piece of work. Before I installed the Stalker machinery in Miss Fang's brain, I programmed it to seek out her memory centers. I have every confidence that we will be able to reignite the memories that lie buried there. That's what this chamber is for: to stimulate the subject with constant reminders of her former life. It's all a question of finding the right mnemonic trigger—a smell, an object, a face. That's where you come in."

Sathya shoved Hester forward until she was standing only a few inches from the new Stalker. "Look, dear!" she said brightly. "Look! This is Hester Shaw! Valentine's daughter! You remember how you found her in the Out-Country and brought her to Batmunkh Gompa? She was there when you died!"

The Stalker leaned close. In the shadows behind its bronze mask a dead black tongue licked withered lips. Its voice was a dry whisper, a night wind blowing through valleys of stone. "I do not know this girl."

"You *do*, Anna!" urged Sathya, with awful patience. "You *must!* Try and remember!"

The Stalker glanced up, scanning the hundreds of portraits on the walls and floor and ceiling of its spherical prison. Anna Fang's parents were there, and Stilton Kael, who had been Anna's master when she was a slave in the salvage yards of Arkangel. Valentine was there, and Captain Khora, and Pandora Rae, but there was no picture of Hester's disfigured face. It focused its mechanical eyes on her again, and its long claws twitched. "I do not know this girl. I am not Anna Fang. You are wasting my time, little Once-Born. I wish to leave this place."

"Of course, Anna, but you must try to remember. You must be yourself again before we take you home. Everyone in the League's lands loved you; when they hear you have returned, they will rise up and follow you."

"Ah, Commander," muttered Popjoy, backing toward the bridge. "I think we should withdraw now. . . ."

"I am not Anna Fang," said the Stalker.

"Commander, I definitely think . . ."

"Anna, please!"

Instinctively, Hester grabbed Sathya and dragged her backward. The claws scythed past, an inch from her throat. The guard leveled his machine gun, and the Stalker hesitated just long enough for them all to scurry back across the bridge. As they reached the door, the man stationed outside pulled a heavy red-handled lever. Red warning lights came on amid a rising buzz of electricity. "I am not Anna Fang!" Hester heard the Stalker shout as she bundled out after the others into the antechamber. Glancing back in the instant before the guards slammed and locked the door, she saw it watching her, its claws jerking and glinting.

"Fascinating," said Popjoy, making notes on his clipboard. "Fascinating. With hindsight, it may have been a tad unwise to install the finger-glaives so early. . . ."

"What's wrong with her?" Sathya demanded.

"It's hard to be entirely sure," admitted Popjoy. "I imagine the new memory-seeking components that I added to the basic Stalker brain are clashing with its tactical and aggressive instincts."

"You mean it's mad?" asked Hester.

"Really, Miss Shaw, 'mad' is such an unhelpful term. I would prefer to say that the former Miss Fang is 'differently sane.'"

"Poor Anna," whispered Sathya, stroking her throat with the tips of her fingers.

"Don't worry about Anna," said Hester. "Anna's dead. Poor *you* is what you mean. You've got a mad killing machine in there, and your stupid guns aren't going to keep it penned in forever. It could climb down off that platform! It could reach the door and—"

"The bridge is electrified, Miss Shaw," said Popjoy firmly. "The girders under the platform are electrified. The inside of the door is also electrified. Even Stalkers dislike massive electric shocks. As for the guns, I am pretty sure the former Miss Fang does not yet understand her new strength; she is still wary of them. That may well be a sign that she does indeed possess lingering memories of her earlier, human incarnation."

Sathya glanced at him, a flicker of hope in her eyes. "Yes. Yes, doctor. We must not give up. We will bring Hester here again."

She turned away smiling, but Hester had seen the panicky look behind Popjoy's spectacles. He had no idea at all of how to restore the dead aviatrix's memories. Surely even Sathya must soon realize that this attempt to bring her friend back from the Sunless Country was doomed. And when she did, there would be no more reason for her to keep Hester around.

I'm going to die here, she thought as guards took her back to her cell and locked her in. *Either Sathya or that mad thing will kill me, and I'll never see Tom again, and I'll never rescue him, and he'll die too, in the slave pits of Arkangel, cursing me.*

She leaned against the wall and slid slowly down until she was kneeling, curled into a little miserable knot. She could hear the sea hissing between the rocks of Rogues' Roost, as cold as the voice of the new Stalker. She could hear small bits of paint and cement falling from the damp-rotted roof of her cell, and faint, scratchy noises in the old heating duct that reminded her of Anchorage. She thought about Mr. Scabious, and Sathya, and about the desperate, hopeless things that people did to try and hold on to the people they loved.

"Oh, Tom! Oh, oh, Tom!" she sobbed, imagining him safe and happy in Anchorage, with no idea that she had set great Arkangel on his tail.

21

Lies and Spiders

A WEEK WENT BY, AND THEN another and another. Anchorage swung west, creeping along the northern edge of Greenland with survey sleds sent out ahead to sound the ice. No city had come this way before, and Miss Pye did not trust her charts.

Freya felt as if she had wandered into unmapped territory too. Why was she so unhappy? How had everything gone so wrong, when it had all seemed to be going so right? She could not understand why Tom didn't want her. *Surely*, she thought, wiping a hole in the dust on her dressing-room mirror to study her reflection, *surely he cannot still be missing Hester? Surely he can't prefer her to me?*

Sometimes, sniffling with self-pity, she concocted elaborate schemes to win him back. Sometimes she grew angry and stomped along the dusty corridors muttering all the things she *should* have said during their argument. Once or twice she found herself wondering whether she could order him to be beheaded for high treason, but Anchorage's executioner (a very ancient gentleman whose post had been purely ceremonial) was dead, and Freya doubted that Smew could lift the axe.

Tom had moved out of his suite in the Winter Palace into an abandoned apartment in a big, empty building on Rasmussen Prospekt, not far from the air harbor. Without the Wunderkammer or the margravine's library to distract him, he devoted his days to feeling sorry for himself and wondering how to get Hester back, or at least find out where she had gone.

There was no way off Anchorage—that much was certain. He had pestered Mr. Aakiuq about fitting out the *Graculus* for long-range travel, but the *Graculus* was just a tug; she had never flown more than half a mile from the air harbor before, and Mr. Aakiuq claimed it would be impossible to give her the bigger fuel tanks she would need if Tom were to take her back east. "Besides," the harbormaster added, "what would you fill them with? I've been checking fuel levels in the harbor tanks. There's almost nothing left. I don't understand it. The gauges still read full, but the tanks are nearly empty."

Fuel was not the only thing that had been going missing. Unconvinced by Scabious's talk of ghosts, Tom had been asking around in the engine district for anyone who might know something of Hester's mysterious friend. Nobody did, but they all seemed to have their own tales of figures glimpsed in corners of the district where no one should be, and of tools set down at a shift's end and never seen again. Things vanished from lockers and bolted rooms, and an oil tank on Heat Exchange Street had run dry, even though the gauges showed it nearly full.

"What's going on?" asked Tom. "Who would take all these things? Do you think there's somebody aboard we don't know about? Someone who stayed on in secret after the plague, to line their pockets?"

"Bless you, young man." The engine-district workers chuckled. "Who'd stay aboard a city like this unless they wanted to help Her Radiance take it to America? There's no way off, no way to sell the things they've stolen."

"Then who—?"

"Ghosts" was all they'd say, shaking their heads, fingering the amulets they all wore around their necks. "The High Ice has always been haunted. The ghosts come aboard and play tricks on the living. Everyone knows that."

Tom was not so sure. There *was* something spooky about the engine district, and sometimes when he was by himself in the dingy streets, he had the strangest feeling that he was being watched, but he couldn't see what ghosts would want with oil, and tools, and airship fuel, and trinkets from the margravine's museum.

"He's onto us," said Skewer darkly, watching the screens one evening as Tom poked about among some deserted buildings on the edge of the engine district. "He knows."

"He doesn't *know*," said Caul wearily. "He suspects, that's all. And he doesn't even know *what* he suspects, he's just got an idea that something's going on."

Skewer looked at him in surprise, then laughed. "You know what he thinks pretty well, don't you?"

"I'm just saying you haven't got to worry about him, that's all," muttered Caul.

"And I'm just saying we have, and maybe we ought to do him in. Make it look like an accident. How'd you like that?"

Caul said nothing, refusing to rise to the bait. It was true that the burglars had had to be a lot more careful since Tom started his investigations, and it was delaying them. Skewer was keen to prove that he'd been right to take command, and determined that when he took the *Screw Worm* home to Uncle she'd be bulging with loot, but although he and Caul went upstairs nearly every night, they dared not steal anything too obvious for fear of arousing Tom's suspicions further. They'd had to remove their lamprey hoses from the fuel tanks at the air harbor too, and that would become a problem soon, since the message-fish and most of the *Screw Worm*'s systems ran on stolen aviation fuel.

The Lost Boy part of Caul knew Skewer was right. A knife between Tom's ribs on a lonely street, the body heaved off the stern gallery, and normal burglary could be resumed. But the other part of him, the kinder part, couldn't bear that idea. He wished Skewer would just give up and go back to Grimsby, leaving him here alone to watch Tom and Freya and the others. Sometimes he even wondered about giving himself up, throwing himself on the mercy of the people of Anchorage. Except that, for as long as he could remember, he had been told that the Drys *had* no mercy. His trainers in the Burglarium, his comrades, Uncle's voice whispering out of the speakers in the Grimsby canteen, all agreed that however civilized the Drys might seem, however comfortable their cities, however pretty the girls, they would do horrible things to a Lost Boy if they caught him.

Caul wasn't sure anymore that that was true, but he hadn't the courage to go up and find out. How could he? *Hello, I'm Caul. I've been burgling you. . . .*

The telegraph machine at the rear of the cabin began to chatter excitedly, breaking in on Caul's thoughts. He and Skewer both started at the sudden noise, and Gargle, who had grown jumpier than ever under Skewer's harsh leadership, squealed with fright. The little machine jerked its brass limbs up and down like a mechanical cricket, and a long ribbon of punched white paper began to spew out of a slot in its glastic dome. Somewhere far beneath Anchorage a message-fish from Grimsby was swimming, beaming a signal up through the ice.

The three boys looked at one another. This was rare. Neither Caul nor Skewer had ever been aboard a limpet that had received a message from Uncle. In his surprise, Skewer forgot his new role for a moment and looked worriedly at Caul.

"What do you think it is? You think something's gone wrong at home?"

"You're the captain now, Skew," Caul replied. "Better check."

Skewer crossed the cabin, shoved Gargle aside, and grabbed the curling ribbon of tape, his eyes narrowing as he studied the patterns of holes. His smile faded.

"What is it, Skew?" asked Gargle eagerly. "Is it from Uncle?"

Skewer nodded, looked up, then back at the tape, as if he could not quite believe what he had read there. "Of course it's from Uncle, you gowk. He says he's read our reports. We're to return to Grimsby at once. And he says we're to bring Tom Natsworthy with us."

"Professor Pennyroyal!"

The great explorer had become a rare sight in Anchorage these past few weeks, keeping to his quarters and not even showing up for meetings of the Steering Committee. "I have a cold!" he had explained, in a muffled voice, when Freya sent Smew to knock upon his door. But as Tom emerged from the engine-district stairway onto Rasmussen Prospekt that night, he saw Pennyroyal's familiar turbaned figure stumbling through the snow ahead of him.

"Professor Pennyroyal!" he shouted again, breaking into a run, and caught up with him near the foot of the Wheelhouse.

"Ah, Tim!" said Pennyroyal with a pallid smile. His voice was slurred, and his arms were full of bottles of cheap red wine that he had just borrowed from an abandoned restaurant called Nosh o' the North. "So glad to see you again. No luck with that airship, I suppose?"

"Airship?"

"A little bird told me you were asking Aakiuq about his air tug. The *Crapulous*, or whatever he calls it. About using it to escape these boreal realms and flit back to civilization."

"That was weeks ago, Professor."

"Oh?"

"It didn't work out."

"Ah. Pity."

They stood in awkward silence, Pennyroyal swaying slightly.

"I've been looking for you for ages," Tom said at last. "There's something I wanted to ask you. As an explorer and historian."

"Ah!" said Pennyroyal wisely. "Ah. You'd better come up."

The Honorary Chief Navigator's official residence had gone to seed since Tom last saw it. Piles of papers and dirty crockery had sprouted like fungus from every flat surface, expensive clothes lay crumpled on the floor, and ranks of empty bottles ringed the sofa, flotsam washed up on a spring tide of pilfered wine.

"Welcome, welcome," said Pennyroyal vaguely, waving Tom toward a chair and rummaging in the debris on his desk for a corkscrew. "Now, what can I help you with?"

Tom shook his head. It sounded silly, now that he came to say it aloud. "It's only," he said, "well, during your travels, have you ever come across stories of intruders aboard ice cities?"

Pennyroyal almost dropped the bottle he was holding. "Intruders? No! Why? You don't mean there's someone aboard—"

"No. I'm not sure. Maybe. Someone's been stealing stuff, and I don't see why it would be one of Freya's people—they can have anything they want; they've no reason to steal."

Pennyroyal opened the wine and took a long drink straight from the bottle. It seemed to steady his nerves. "Maybe we've picked up a parasite," he said.

"What do you mean?"

"Haven't you read *Ziggurat Cities of the Serpent-God*, my

breathtaking account of a journey through Nuevo-Maya?" asked Pennyroyal. "There's a whole chapter on parasite towns: '*Las Ciudades Vampiras.*'"

"I've never heard of a parasite town," said Tom doubtfully. "Do you mean some sort of scavenger?"

"Oh, no!" Pennyroyal took a seat close to him, breathing hot gusts of wine fumes into his face. "There's more than one way to prey on a city. These vampire towns conceal themselves in the litter of the Out-Country until one passes over them. Then they spring up and attach themselves to its underside with gigantic suction cups. The poor city goes trundling on with no idea what's clinging to its belly, but all the while the parasite people are sneaking aboard, draining fuel tanks, stealing equipment, murdering the menfolk one by one, carrying off beautiful young women to sell in the slave markets of Itzal as sacrifices to the volcano gods. Eventually the host city comes shuddering to a halt, an empty shell, a husk, its engines stripped out, its people dead or captured, and the fat vampire town crawls off in search of fresh prey."

Tom thought about that for a while. "But that's impossible!" he said at last. "How would a city not know it had an entire town hanging underneath it? How would they not spot all these people running around pinching stuff? It doesn't make sense! And . . . *suction cups?*"

Pennyroyal looked shocked. "What are you saying, Tom?"

"I'm saying that you . . . you made it up! Just like the stuff in *Rubbish? Rubbish!* and the old buildings you said you saw in America. . . . Oh, Great Quirke!" Tom felt cold suddenly, even though the apartment was warm and stuffy. "Did you ever even *go* to America? Or was that all made up too?"

"Course I did!" said Pennyroyal angrily.

"I don't believe you!" The old Tom, brought up to honor his elders and respect all historians, would never have dared to say such things, even to think them. Three weeks without Hester had changed him more than he realized. Standing, he looked down into Pennyroyal's puffy, sweating face and knew that he was lying. "It was just a fantasy, wasn't it?" he said. "Your whole trip to America was a story spun out of aviators' yarns and the legend of old Snøri Ulvaeusson's disappearing map, which probably never existed in the first place!"

"How dare you, sir!" Pennyroyal heaved himself heavily upright, gesturing with his empty wine bottle. "How dare you, a mere former Apprentice Historian, insult me! I'll have you know my books have sold over a hundred thousand copies! Been translated into a dozen different languages! I'm very highly thought of, me. 'Brilliant, Breathtaking, and Believable'—*The Shuddersfield Gazette*. 'A rattling good yarn'—*The Panzerstadt Coblenz Advertiser*. 'Pennyroyal's works are a breath of fresh air in the dull world of practical History'—*The Wantage Weekly Waffle . . .*"

A breath of fresh air was what Tom needed, but not the sort that Pennyroyal could provide. He pushed past the hectoring historian and ran down the stairs and out into the street. No wonder Pennyroyal had been so keen to see the *Jenny Haniver* repaired, and so distraught when Hester flew away. His talk of green places was all a lie! He knew full well that Freya Rasmussen was driving her city to its doom!

He began running to the Winter Palace, but had not gone far before he changed his mind. Freya was the wrong person to tell about this. She had invested everything in the journey west. If he burst in on her claiming that Pennyroyal had been wrong all along, her pride would be dented, and Freya had a lot of pride to dent. Worse, she might think that this was just some ruse on Tom's part to make her turn the city around so he could go looking for Hester.

"Mr. Scabious!" he said aloud. Scabious had never wholly believed in Professor Pennyroyal. Scabious would listen. He turned and ran as fast as he could back to the stairway. As he passed the Wheelhouse, Pennyroyal leaned over a balcony to watch, shouting after him, "'A Startling Talent!'—*The Wheel-Tapper's Weekly*!"

Down in the hot dark of the engine district everything thrummed and thundered with the beat of the engines as they drove the city on toward disaster. Tom stopped the first men he saw and asked where he could find Scabious. They nodded toward the stern, fingering their amulets. "Gone to look for his son, like every night."

Tom ran on, into quiet, rusty streets where nothing moved. Or almost nothing. As he passed beneath one of the dangling argon lamps, a faint movement in the mouth of a ventilation shaft flicked a sliver of reflected light into the corner of his eye. He stopped, breathing hard, his heart thumping, hairs prickling on his wrists and the back of his neck. In his panic over Pennyroyal he had all but forgotten the intruders. Now all his half-formed theories about them flooded his mind again. The ventilator looked empty and innocent enough now, but he was sure there had been something there, something that had darted guiltily back into the shadows just as his eye caught it. And he was sure that it was still in there, watching him.

"Oh, Hester," he whispered, suddenly very frightened, wishing she were here to help. Hester would have been able to cope with this, but he wasn't at all sure he could, not alone. Trying to imagine what she would do, he forced himself to walk on, one step after another, not looking toward the ventilator until he was sure he was out of sight of whatever hid there.

"I think he saw us," said Caul.

"Never!" sneered Skewer.

Caul shrugged unhappily. They had been tracking Tom with their cameras all evening, waiting for him to reach a place that was quiet enough and close enough to the *Screw Worm* for them to carry out Uncle's mysterious command. They'd never watched a Dry this closely for this long, and something in Tom's face as he glanced toward the camera made Caul uneasy. "Come on, Skew," he said. "It must all build up after a while, mustn't it? The noises, and the feeling you're being watched. And he was suspicious even before. . . ."

"They never see!" said Skewer firmly. The strange message from Uncle had made him nervous, and faced with the task of tracking Tom, he'd been forced to admit that Gargle was the best cam operator aboard and hand over the controls to him. He clung to the idea of his superiority over the Drys as if it were the last certain thing in the world. "They might look, but they never see. They're not as observant as us. There, what did I tell you? He's walked past. Stupid Dry."

It wasn't a rat. All the rats of Anchorage were dead, and anyway, this thing looked mechanical. As he crept back through shadows toward the ventilator, Tom could see the light jinking on segmented metal. A bulbous, fist-sized body, supported on too many legs. A single camera-lens eye.

He thought of the mysterious boy who had come for him on the night Hester left, and how he seemed to know everything that went on at the air harbor and the Winter Palace. How many of these things were there, scuttling and spying in the city's ducts? And why was this one watching him?

"Where is he, Gargle? Find him. . . ."

"I think he's gone," said Gargle, panning to and fro.

"Careful!" warned Caul, resting his hand on the younger boy's shoulder. "Tom's still around there somewhere, I'm sure of it."

"What, psychic as well now, are you?" asked Skewer.

Tom took three deep breaths, then flung himself at the ventilator. The metal thing scrabbled, trying to retreat into the dark shaft. Glad that he was still wearing his heavy outdoor mittens, Tom grabbed its thrashing legs and pulled.

"He's got us!"

"Reel in! Reel in!"

Eight steel legs. Magnets for feet. An armored body warted with rivets. That cyclops lens whirring as it struggled to focus on him. It was so like a gigantic spider that Tom dropped it and flinched away as it lay there on its back on the deck, writhing its legs helplessly. Then the thin cable that trailed from its rear end went suddenly taut, dragging it backward against the ventilator with a clang. Tom lunged after it, but he was too slow. The crab-thing was tugged quickly into the shaft and vanished, leaving him listening to the fading clatter as it was hauled away into the city's depths.

Tom scrambled up, his heart beating quickly. Who would own such a thing? Who would want to spy on the people of Anchorage? He thought of Pennyroyal's tale of the vampire towns, and suddenly it did not seem quite so unlikely after all. He leaned against the wall to catch his breath and then started to run again. "Mr. Scabious!" he shouted, the echoes rolling ahead of him down the tubular streets or vanishing upward into great, dark, dripping, haunted vaults. "Mr. Scabious!"

"Lost him again! No, there—camera twelve . . ." Gargle flipped wildly from camera to camera. Tinnily, through the cabin speakers, Tom's voice was shouting, *"Mr. Scabious! He's not a ghost! I know where he comes from!"*

"I think he's heading for the stern gallery."

"Gotta get him quick!" wailed Skewer, rummaging through lockers for a gun, a net. "He'll blow our cover! Uncle'll kill us! I mean really, really kill us! Gods, I hate this! We're burglars, not kidnappers! What's Uncle thinking? We've never been asked to kidnap Drys before; not full-grown ones. . . ."

"Uncle Knows Best," Gargle reminded him.

"Oh, shut up!"

"I'll go," said Caul. The emergency had made him calm; he knew what had to be done, and he knew how he would do it.

"Not without me!" Skewer shouted. "I don't trust you up there alone, Dry-lover!"

"All right." Caul was already halfway to the hatch. "But let me handle him. He knows me, remember?"

"Mr. Scabious?"

Tom burst out onto the stern gallery. The moon was up, hanging low in the sky behind the city, and the drive wheel flung its reflection across the deck plates. The boy stood waiting there in the flash and flicker like a gray ghost.

"How are you doing, Tom?" Caul asked. He looked nervous and a little shy, but friendly, as if it were the most natural thing in the world for them to meet like this.

Tom swallowed his yelp of surprise. "Who are you?" he said, backing away. "Those crab-things—you must have loads of them, creeping all over the city, watching everything. Why? Who are you?"

The boy held out his hand, a pleading gesture, begging Tom to stay. "My name's Caul."

Tom's mouth felt dry. Bits of Pennyroyal's stupid story clanged inside his head like an alarm bell: *Murdering the menfolk . . . the city an empty shell, a husk, its people dead. . . .*

"Don't worry," said Caul, grinning suddenly, as if he understood. "We're only burglars, and now we're going home. But you have to come with us. Uncle says."

Several things happened all at once. Tom turned to run and a net of thin metal mesh, flung from some gantry overhead, dropped over him and brought him crashing down. At the same instant as he heard Caul shout, "Skew! No!" another voice yelled, "Axel?" and he looked up to see Scabious standing at the far end of the gallery, transfixed by the sight of the frail-looking fair-haired boy whom he took to be his son's ghost. Then, in the shadows overhead, a gun went off with a cough and a sudden stab of blue flame, some kind of gas pistol, ricochet yowling like a hurt dog. Scabious cursed and flung himself sideways into cover as a second boy leaped down onto the stern gallery, bigger than Caul and with long dark hair whipping about his face. Together, he and Caul lifted Tom, who was still struggling to free himself from the net. They began to run, jostling their captive into the mouth of an underlit access alley.

It was very dark, and the floors throbbed and jarred with a steady rhythm. Thick ducts sprouted from the deck plates and rose into the shadows overhead like trees in a metal forest. Somewhere behind there was a dim glow of moonlight and the angry, hurt voice of Mr. Scabious shouting, "You young—! Come back here! Stop!"

"Mr. Scabious!" Tom shouted, pushing his face into the cold crosshatch of the net. "They're parasites! Thieves! They're—"

His captors dropped him unceremoniously on the deck. He rolled over and saw them crouching in a gap between two ducts. Caul's long hands had gripped a section of the deck plate and he was lifting it, *opening* it: a camouflaged manhole.

"Stop!" shouted Scabious, close now, his shadow flashing between the ducts astern. Caul's friend swung his gas pistol up and squeezed off another round, holing a duct that began to gush a great white geyser of steam.

"Tom!" yelled Scabious. "I'll fetch help!"

"Mr. Scabious!" Tom cried, but Scabious was gone; Tom could hear his voice shouting for aid in some neighboring tubeway. The lid of the manhole was open, blue light shafting up through steam. Caul and the other stranger picked him up and swung him toward it. He had a glimpse of a short companionway leading down into a dim, blue-lit chamber, and then he was falling, like a sack of coal dropped into a cellar, landing hard on a hard floor. His captors came clattering down the ladder, and the hatch above him slammed shut.

The
Screw Worm

ROUND-ROOFED HOLD, STUFFED with plunder like a well-filled belly. Blue bulbs in wire cages. A smell of damp and mildew and unwashed boys.

Tom struggled to sit up. In the fall down the companionway one of his hands had come free of the net, but just as he realized this, and before he could free himself entirely, Caul grabbed his arms from behind and Caul's friend, the boy called Skewer, squatted in front of him. Skewer had holstered his gas pistol, but there was a knife in his hand: a short blade of pale metal with a serrated edge. It flashed blue in the blue light as he pressed it against Tom's throat.

"No, please!" squeaked Tom. He didn't really think the strangers had gone to all the trouble of kidnapping him just to murder him, but the blade was cold, and the look in Skewer's pewter-colored eyes was wild.

"Don't, Skewer," said Caul.

"Just so he knows," Skewer explained, drawing the knife away slowly. "Just so he's clear what'll happen if he tries anything fancy."

"He's right, Tom," said Caul, helping Tom to stand. "You can't escape, so you'd better not try. You won't be very comfy if we have to lock you in a cargo container. . . ." He pulled a cord from his pockets and bound Tom's wrists together. "This is just till we're away from Anchorage. We'll untie you after, if you behave."

"Away from Anchorage?" asked Tom, watching Caul's fingers tie the complex knots. "Where are you going?"

"Home," said Caul. "Uncle wants to see you."

"Whose uncle?"

A circular door in the bulkhead behind Caul whirled open suddenly, like the iris of a camera. There were banks of dodgy-looking equipment cluttering the room beyond, and a third boy, startlingly young, who shouted, "Skewer, we've got to GO!"

Caul grinned quickly at Tom, said, "Welcome aboard the *Screw Worm*!" and ran through the door into the new room. Tom followed, shunted forward by Skewer's firm hand. This strange, blue-lit kennel was not some undercroft of Anchorage, as he'd thought at first, but it clearly wasn't one of Professor Pennyroyal's parasite towns either. It was a vehicle, and this was its control room; a crescent-shaped cabin with banks of dials and levers all around and bulbous windows looking out into a rushing darkness. On six oval screens above the controls, grainy blue views of Anchorage flickered: the Scabious Spheres, the stern gallery, Rasmussen Prospekt, a corridor in the Winter Palace. On the fifth screen, Freya Rasmussen was sleeping peacefully. On the sixth, Scabious led a gang of engine workers toward the secret manhole.

"They're onto us!" said the youngest of the burglars, sounding very scared.

"All right, Gargle. Time to go." Caul reached for a bank of levers. They had a homemade look, like everything else aboard this craft, and they grated and creaked as he pulled them, but they seemed to work. One by one the pictures on the screen folded up and dwindled to white dots. The cabin filled with a metallic hiss as the camera cables that had infested Anchorage's air ducts and plumbing like the tendrils of an invasive weed were reeled quickly in. Tom imagined people all over the city looking up in surprise at the sudden rush and rattle in their heating ducts. In the cabin the noise of the reels rose to a deafening shriek and then ended in a series of dull clangs as the crabs were jerked home into ports on the hull above his head and armored lids closed over them. As the echoes of the last one faded, he heard another, fainter clanging: Scabious and his engine-district workers hacking at the camouflaged hatch with picks and hammers.

Caul and Skewer stood side by side at the controls, their hands moving quickly and confidently over the crowded panels. Tom, who had always taken great care of the *Jenny Haniver*'s instruments, was shocked by the state of these: rusty, scuffed, and dirty, levers grating in their slots, dials cracked, sparks flashing blue each time a switch was tripped. But the cabin began to shake and hum and the needles in the crazed gauges flickered, and Tom saw that this stuff worked. This machine, whatever it was, might be about to snatch him away from Anchorage before Scabious and the others could do anything to save him.

"Going down!" whooped Skewer.

There was a new sound, not unlike the one made by the *Jenny Haniver*'s mooring clamps when they disengaged from a docking pan. Then an awful sensation of falling as the *Screw Worm* dropped free from its hiding place on Anchorage's underbelly. Tom's stomach turned over. He grabbed a handle on the bulkhead behind him for support. Was this an airship? But it was not flying, just falling, and now came a great juddering shock as it landed on the ice beneath the city. The huge shapes of gantries and skid supports rushed past beyond the windows, half hidden by a spray of grayish slush, and then suddenly the city was gone and he was looking out across open, moonlit snowfields.

Gargle checked his instruments. "Thin ice bearing east by northeast one half east, about six miles," he squeaked.

Tom still had little idea of the size or shape of the *Screw Worm*, but watchers on the upper tier saw it clearly in the moonlight now as it shot out from beneath the city, narrowly avoiding the drive wheel. It was a house-high metal spider, its fat hull supported by eight hydraulic legs, each ending in a broad, clawed disk of a foot. Black smoke spurted from exhaust ports on its flanks as it ran eastward, back along the track made by Anchorage's runners.

"A parasite!" growled Scabious, dashing out onto a maintenance platform above the drive wheel to watch it go. Anger bubbled up inside him, forcing apart the locks and bolts with which he had fastened down his feelings since his son had died. Some filthy parasite clinging to his city like a tick! Some thieving parasite boy tricking him into believing that his Axel had returned!

"We'll stop them!" he shouted to his people. "We'll teach them to steal from Anchorage! Tell the Wheelhouse ready about! Umiak, Kinvig, Kneaves, with me!"

Anchorage dug in its starboard ice rudders and came about. For a while nobody aboard could see anything for the glittering curtains of snow the runners had flung into the air. Then the parasite appeared again, a mile ahead, veering northeast. The city put on speed to give chase, while Scabious's people heaved the jaws open and gnashed them to clear the ice that had formed on the banks of steel teeth. Searchlights fumbled across the snow, stretching the parasite's crooked running shadow ahead of it. Closer, closer, until the jaws were snapping so near to the thing's stern that a puff of smoke from its exhausts was trapped inside. "Once more!" bellowed Scabious, standing on the floor of his city's small gut. "This time he's ours!"

But Windolene Pye peered at her charts and saw that the city was speeding toward a place the survey teams had marked with red crosses: a place where open water had skimmed over with ice that would not bear a city's weight. She swung the engine-district telegraph to ALL STOP and Anchorage backed its engines, dug in all its anchors, and came shivering to a halt with a shock that scattered black flocks of tiles from the rooftops and brought down an empty terrace of rust-sick buildings on the upper tier.

The parasite machine ran on, stilting its way out onto the

treacherous ice. Scabious stared out through the open jaws and watched it slow and halt there. "Ha! We've driven him onto the thin stuff! He'll dare go no farther! He's ours now!" He ran through the gut to the garage where the survey teams kept their sleds, snatching a wolf rifle from one of his men as he went. Someone dragged a sled out for him and fired the engines up, and he leaped aboard it and went rushing down the exit chute, a steel door sliding open ahead of him. Out on the ice, he swung around the city's jaws and sped toward the cornered spider-thing, a dozen of his men on other sleds whooping and shouting behind him.

Tom squinted through the limpet's windows, trying to shield his eyes against the glare of Anchorage's searchlights. He could already hear the faint shouts of his rescuers, the crack of wolf rifles fired into the air, the throaty stutter of sled engines hammering toward him across the ice.

"If you just let me go, I'll put in a good word for you," he promised his captors. "Scabious isn't a bad sort. He'll treat you well if you just hand back the things you've stolen from his engine district. And I know Freya won't want you punished."

The little boy, Gargle, looked as if he might be convinced, glancing fearfully from Tom to the approaching sleds. But Skewer just said, "Quiet," and Caul's pale hands kept dancing across the consoles. The *Screw Worm* lurched into motion again, settling its fat body lower until the hull was resting on the ice. Whirling saw blades slid out of its belly, and jets of heated water sprayed against the ice, sending up fierce clouds of steam. With clumsy movements of its legs the *Screw Worm* turned, turned, cutting an escape hole for itself. When the circle was complete, the blades folded back into the hull and the machine pushed itself down, shoving the plug of ice aside and forcing its body through, into the water below.

A hundred yards away, Scabious saw what was happening. Steering the sled with his knees, he took his hands off the controls and raised his rifle, but the bullet banged off the armored hull and went whining away across the ice like a lost bee. The parasite's bulbous eyeball windows sank out of sight. Wavelets lapped across its back, sloshing over magnetic grapples and crab-camera ports. Its long legs folded themselves one by one into the hole, and it was gone.

Scabious brought his sled to a stop and hurled his rifle away. His prey had escaped him, taking Tom and the parasite boys with it, and he could imagine neither where it was bound nor any way that he could follow. *Poor Tom*, he thought, for in spite of his gruffness he had liked that young aviator. Poor Tom. And poor Axel, who was dead, dead, dead, his ghost not walking Anchorage's byways after all. *Nobody returns from the Sunless Country, Mr. Scabious.*

He was glad of his cold-mask. It stopped his men from seeing the tears that were coursing down his face as they parked their own sleds close to his and ran to peer into the hole the escaping parasite had cut.

Not that there was anything there to see. Only a broad circle of open water, and the waves slapping and clopping at its edges with a sound like sarcastic applause.

Freya had been woken by the lurching of the city, by the noise of bottles of shampoo and jars of bath salts crashing down from the bathroom shelves where she had abandoned them. She rang and rang for Smew, but he did not come, and in the end she had to venture out of the Winter Palace alone, perhaps the first margravine to do such a thing since Dolly Rasmussen's time.

At the Wheelhouse everybody was shouting about ghost crabs and parasite boys. Not until it was all over did Freya understand that Tom was gone.

She couldn't let Windolene Pye and her staff see that she was crying. She hurried off the bridge and down the stairs. Mr. Scabious was on his way up, dripping snow and meltwater as he tugged off his gauntlets and cold-mask. He looked flushed, and more alive than she had seen him since the plague, as if the discovery of the parasite had freed something in him. He almost smiled at her.

"An amazing machine, Your Radiance! Drilled straight through the ice sheet. You have to hand it to the devils! I've heard legends of parasites on the High Ice, but I confess, I always thought them just old icewives' tales. I wish I'd been more open-minded."

"They took Tom," said Freya in a small voice.

"Yes. I'm sorry. He was a brave lad. Tried to warn me of them, and they caught him and dragged him inside their machine."

"What will they do with him?" she whispered.

The enginemaster looked at her, then shook his head and pulled off his hat as a mark of respect. He wasn't sure what the crew of a vampire-parasite-spider ice machine might want with the young aviator, but he couldn't imagine it was anything nice.

"Can't we do something?" Freya asked plaintively. "Can't we dig, or drill, or something? What if this parasite thing resurfaces? We must wait here and watch. . . ."

Scabious shook his head. "It's long gone, Your Radiance. We can't hang about here."

Freya gasped as if he'd slapped her. She wasn't used to having her orders questioned. She said, "But Tom's our friend! I won't just abandon him!"

"He is just one boy, Your Radiance. You have a whole city to think of. For all we know, Wolverinehampton is still on our trail. We must move on immediately."

Freya shook her head, but she knew her enginemaster was right. She had not turned back for Hester when Tom had begged her to, and she could not turn back now for Tom, no matter how much she wanted to. But if only she had been nicer to him these past weeks! If only her last words to him hadn't been so snappish and cold!

"Come, Margravine," said Scabious gently, and held out his hand. Freya stared at it for a moment, surprised, then reached out and took it, and they climbed the stairs together. It was quiet on the bridge. People turned to look at Freya as she entered, and there was something in the silence that told her they had all been talking about her until a moment before.

She sniffed, and wiped her eyes on her cuff, and said, "Please get us under way, Miss Pye."

"What course, Your Radiance?" asked Miss Pye gently.

"West," said Freya. "America."

"Oh, Clio!" sniffled Pennyroyal, huddled almost unnoticed in a corner. "Oh, Poskitt!"

The engines were starting up; Freya could feel the vibrations thrumming through the girders of the Wheelhouse. She pushed past Scabious and went to the back of the bridge, looking out over her city's stern as it began to move, leaving behind it nothing but a scrawl of sled tracks and a perfectly circular hole already skimming over with fresh ice.

Hidden Depths

DAYS PASSED, THOUGH IT WAS hard to say how many. The dim blue light aboard the *Screw Worm* made it feel as though time had stopped at a quarter to four on a wet November afternoon.

Tom slept in a corner of the hold on a pile of quilts and tapestries looted from the villas of Anchorage. Sometimes he dreamed that he was walking hand in hand with someone down the dusty corridors of the Winter Palace, and awoke not knowing if it had been Hester or Freya. Was it really possible that he would never see either of them again?

He imagined himself escaping, reaching the surface and going in search of Hester, but the *Screw Worm* was swimming through the luminous canyons beneath the ice, and there was no escape. He imagined fighting his way into the control cabin and sending signals to Anchorage, warning Freya of

Pennyroyal's lies, but even if he worked out which of those rusty machines was the radio, the boys who had kidnapped him would never let him near it.

They were all very wary of him. Skewer was distant and hostile, and when Tom was about, he scowled and swaggered a lot and talked very little. He reminded Tom of Melliphant, the bully who had menaced him during his apprenticeship. As for Gargle, who could not be more than ten or eleven years old, he just stared at Tom with wide round eyes when he thought Tom wasn't looking. Only Caul was prepared to talk, odd, half-friendly Caul, and even he seemed cautious and was unwilling to answer Tom's questions.

"You'll understand when we get there" was all he would say.

"Where?"

"Home. Our base. Where Uncle lives."

"But who *is* your uncle?"

"He's not my uncle; just Uncle. He's the leader of the Lost Boys. Nobody knows his real name, or where he came from. I heard a story that he'd been a great man once, aboard Breidhavik or Arkangel or one of those cities, and he got thrown out for some reason, and that's when he turned to thieving. He's a genius. He invented the limpets and the crab-cams, and found us, and built the Burglarium to train us in."

"Found you? Where?"

"I don't know," admitted Caul. "All over the place. On different cities. The limpets steal children to train up as Lost Boys, just like they steal everything else Uncle needs. I was so little when I was taken that I don't remember anything before. None of us do."

"But that's horrible!"

"No, it's not!" Caul laughed. He always ended up laughing. It was funny and frustrating, trying to explain the life he had always taken for granted to an outsider. How could he make Tom see that being taken to the Burglarium had been an honor, and that he would much rather be a Lost Boy than a boring Dry? "You'll understand when we get there," he promised. And then (because it made him uneasy, the thought of going home to explain himself to Uncle) he would change the subject and ask, "What's Freya really like?" or "Do you think it's true that Pennyroyal doesn't know the way to America?"

"He knows the way," said Tom bleakly. "Anybody with half a brain can work out a route to America from the old charts. The trouble is, I think he lied about what's at the end of it. I don't think the green places exist, except in Professor Pennyroyal's imagination." He hung his head, wishing he had managed to warn Freya of his fears before the Lost Boys had taken him. By now Anchorage would be so far on its way that it wouldn't have enough fuel to turn back.

"You never know," said Caul, reaching out to touch Tom's arm and then snatching his hand away quickly, as if the touch of a Dry burned. "He turned out to be right about the parasites, sort of."

There came a day (or maybe a night) when Tom was roused from his troubled dreams by Caul shouting, "Tom! We're home!" He scrambled out of his nest of stolen textiles and hurried to look, but when he reached the control cabin, he found that the *Screw Worm* was still deep under water. A repetitive, echoey ping came from one of the machines. Skewer, busy with his instruments, glanced up just long enough to say, "It's Uncle's beacon!"

There was a yawing, twisting sensation as the limpet adjusted its course. The darkness outside the windows was fading, turning to a twilight blue, and Tom realized that he was no longer beneath the ice sheet but out in open sea, and that sunlight was dazzling through a choppy surface several hundred feet above his head. The bottoms of gigantic icebergs slid past, like upside-down mountains. Then, in the dimness ahead, other shapes began to form: weed-furred gantries and girders; the barnacle-encrusted blade of a gigantic propeller; a tilted, silted plane where rows of rusty blocks shoved up out of the mud and litter. Like an airship flying above a landscape of mesas and canyons, the *Screw Worm* was cruising over the streets of an enormous sunken raft city.

"Welcome to Grimsby," said Skewer, steering toward the upper tier.

Tom had heard of Grimsby. Everybody had heard of Grimsby. Biggest and fiercest of the North Atlantic predator rafts, it had been sunk by pack ice during the Iron Winter of ninety years ago. Awed, Tom gazed out through the limpet's windows at the passing view: the swirls of fish glittering between the dead houses, the temples and great office buildings festooned with weed. And then, amid the grays and blues and blacks, something showed warm and golden. Gargle gave a cheer and Skewer grinned, easing the *Worm*'s steering levers forward and lifting it up over the brink of the city's topmost tier.

Tom gasped. Ahead, lights shone in the windows of the

Town Hall, and people were moving about inside, making this drowned building look warm and homely, like a house well lit on a winter night.

"What is it?" Tom wondered. "I mean, how—?"

"It's our home," said Caul. He had been quiet until now, worrying about what sort of welcome awaited him, but he felt proud that Grimsby had impressed Tom, who had seen so many strange cities.

"Uncle built it!" said Gargle.

The *Screw Worm* slid into the water-filled lower story of the Town Hall, then wound its way along tubular tunnels where it had to keep waiting for automatic doors to open ahead of it and close behind. This system of water-doors and air locks served to keep the rest of the building dry, but Tom did not understand that, and it came as a surprise and a huge relief when the limpet broke the surface and came to rest in a pool beneath a high domed roof.

The noise of the engines ceased, but from outside came clangs and thuds as docking arms engaged, hoisting the *Screw Worm* clear of the water. A hatch in the cabin roof sprang open with a sigh. Caul fetched a ladder and hooked it to the opening. "You go first," he told Tom, and Tom climbed out onto the limpet's broad back and stood there breathing cold, ammonia-smelling air and looking around.

The limpet had surfaced through a circular hole in the floor of a huge, echoing room that might once have been Grimsby's main council chamber (on the ceiling the spirit of Municipal Darwinism—a rather beefy young woman with wings—pointed the city fathers toward a prosperous future). Dozens of similar entrances dotted the broad floor, each overhung by a complicated docking crane. From several of them hung limpets, and Tom was startled to see how ramshackle the vessels looked, as if cobbled together from bits of anything that came to hand. Some were obviously undergoing repairs, but the people who had been working on them (all young men or boys, few much older than Caul or Skewer) had left their posts and were converging on the *Screw Worm*. They were all staring at Tom.

Tom stared back, feeling glad of Caul, who had climbed up to stand beside him. Even on the roughest of the cities the *Jenny Haniver* had visited, he had seldom seen a bunch as hostile-looking as this. Lads his own age, wiry, hard-looking young men, little boys smaller than Gargle, all glared at him with something that was half hate, half fear. They were shaggy-headed, and the few who were old enough to shave hadn't bothered. Their clothes were a mismatched assortment of too big and too small: bits of uniforms, ladies' shawls and bonnets, diving suits and aviators' helmets, tea cozies and colanders pressed into service as hats. They looked as if they'd been showered with debris by an exploding flea market.

A crackle came from overhead, then a high warbling shriek of feedback. All faces turned upward. Fluted speakers bolted to the docking cranes belched static, and a voice that seemed to come from everywhere at once. "Bring the Dry to my quarters, my boys," it said. "I will speak with him right away."

Uncle

GRIMSBY WAS NOT QUITE WHAT Tom would have expected of a master criminal's underwater lair. It was too chilly, and smelled too much of mold and boiled cabbage. The reclaimed building that had looked so magical from outside was poky and cluttered, packed like a junk shop with the spoils from years of burglary. Swags of stolen tapestry decked the corridors, the rich designs embroidered over with new patterns of mildew. On shelves, in cubbyholes, half glimpsed through the open doors of the rooms and workshops that he passed, Tom saw heaps of clothes; moldering moraines of books and documents, ornaments and jewelry, weapons and tools; snooty-looking mannequins from high-class shops; Goggle Screens and flywheels; batteries and bulbs; big, greasy machine parts torn from the bellies of towns.

And everywhere there were the crab-cameras. The ceilings

crawled with the little machines; dark corners glittered with their stilting legs. With no need to hide, they crouched on stacks of crockery or crept down the fronts of bookcases, scuttled over the wall hangings, and swung from the heavy, dangerous-looking electrical cables that festooned the walls. Their cyclops eyes glinted and whirred, tracking Tom as Caul and Skewer led him up the long flights of stairs toward Uncle's quarters. To live in Grimsby was to live forever in the gaze of Uncle.

And Uncle was expecting them, of course. He stood up from his chair as they entered his chamber, coming to meet them through the light of a thousand surveillance screens. He was a little man, both short and thin, pallid from living so long out of the sun's sight. Half-moon spectacles perched on his narrow nose. He wore fingerless mittens, a five-cornered hat, a braided tunic that might have belonged once to a general or an elevator attendant, a silk dressing gown whose hem drew patterns on the dusty floor, nankeen trousers, and bunny slippers. Strands of sparse white hair trailed over his shoulders. Books that his boys had snatched for him at random from the shelves of a dozen libraries poked from his pockets. Crumbs clung to the gray stubble on his chin.

"Caul, my dear boy!" he murmured. "Thank you for obeying your poor old Uncle so prompt, and bringing the Dry home so handy. He ain't been damaged, I take it? No harm done?"

Caul, remembering how he had behaved in Anchorage and the reports Skewer would have sent home about him, was too scared to answer. Skewer said gruffly, "Alive and well, Uncle, just like your orders."

"Excellent, excellent," Uncle purred. "And Skewer. Little Skewer. You've been busy too, I gather."

Skewer nodded, but before he could speak, Uncle lashed out at him, striking so hard that Skewer stumbled backward and fell over with a childish wail of pain and surprise. Uncle kicked him a few times for good measure. Beneath their cheerful bunny faces, his slippers had steel toe caps. "Who do you think you are," he shouted, "setting up as captain without my say-so? You know what happens to boys who disobey me, don't you? You remember what I did to young Sonar off the *Remora* when he pulled a trick like yours?"

"Yes, Uncle," sniveled Skewer. "But it wasn't my fault, Uncle. Caul talked to a Dry! I thought the rules—"

"So Caul bent the rules a little," said Uncle kindly, and kicked Skewer again. "I'm a reasonable man. I don't mind if my boys use their initiative. I mean, it wasn't just any old Dry young Caul revealed himself to, was it now? It was our friend Tom."

He had been circling closer to Tom all the while, and now he reached out a clammy hand and gripped Tom's chin, twisting his face up into the light.

"I won't help you," said Tom. "If you're planning to attack Anchorage or something, I won't help you."

Uncle's laugh was a thin little sound. "Attack Anchorage? That's no plan of mine, Tom. My boys are burglars, not warriors. Burglars and observers. They watch. Listen. Send me reports about what's going on aboard the cities, what's being said. Yes. That's how I keep my boys in plunder and prey. That's why I've never been found out. I get lots of reports and I put them together, compare and contrast, note things down, add two and two. I look out for names that crop up in odd places. Like Hester Shaw. Like Thomas Natsworthy."

"Hester?" said Tom, starting forward, restrained by Caul. "What have you heard about Hester?"

In the shadows behind Uncle's chair two guards, surprised at Tom's sudden movement, drew their swords. Uncle waved them back. "Caul's reports were right, then?" he asked. "You're Hester Shaw's sweetheart? Her lover?" There was a nasty, wheedling edge to his voice now, and Tom felt himself blush as he nodded. Uncle watched him for a moment, then chuckled, "It was the airship that first made me sit up and take notice. *Jenny Haniver*. That's a name I recognize, oh, yes. That's that witch Anna Fang's ship, ain't it?"

"Anna was a friend of ours," said Tom.

"A friend, eh?"

"She died."

"I know."

"We sort of inherited the *Jenny*."

"Inherited her, did you?" Uncle let out a long, sniggering laugh. "Oh, I like that, Tom! Inherited! As you can see, I've got a lot of stuff down here that me and my boys have *inherited*. I wish we'd taken you ten years ago, Tom; we could have made a Lost Boy of you." He laughed again, and went back to settle in his chair.

Tom looked at Caul, then at Skewer, who was on his feet again, his face still branded with the red imprint of Uncle's hand. *Why do they put up with him?* Tom wondered. *They're all younger and stronger than he is; why do they do his bidding?* But the answer flickered on the walls all around him, on looted Goggle Screens of every shape and size, where blue images of life in Grimsby moved and faint overheard conversations drizzled from the speakers. Who could challenge Uncle's power, when Uncle knew everything that they said and did?

"You mentioned something about Hester," he reminded the old man, straining to be polite.

"Information, Tom," said Uncle, ignoring him. Surveillance pictures danced in the lenses of his spectacles. "Information. That's the key to it all. The reports my burglars send back to me all fit together like the bits of a jigsaw. I probably know more than any man alive about what goes on in the north. And I pay attention to odd little details. To changes. Changes can be dangerous things."

"And Hester?" asked Tom again. "You know about Hester?"

"For example," Uncle said, "there's an island, Rogues' Roost, not far from here. Used to be lair to Red Loki and his air pirates. Not a bad sort, Red Loki. Never troubled us. Occupied different niches in the food chain, him and me. But now he's gone. Kicked out. Murdered. It's home to a bunch of Anti-Tractionists now. The Green Storm, they call themselves. A hard-line faction. Terrorists. Troublemakers. Have you ever heard of the Green Storm, Tom Natsworthy?"

Tom, still thinking about Hester, scrabbled for an answer. He remembered Pennyroyal shouting something about the Green Storm during that chase above the Tannhäusers, but so much had happened since that he could barely recall a word of it. "Not really," he said.

"Well, they've heard of you," said Uncle, leaning forward in his chair. "Why else would they have hired a spy to keep watch for your airship? And why else would your girlie be their houseguest?"

"Hester is with them?" gasped Tom. "You're sure?"

"That's what I said, ain't it?" Uncle sprang up again, rubbing his hands together, cracking the joints of his fingers as he circled Tom. "Though 'houseguest' isn't quite the word I'm looking for, perhaps. She ain't comfortable, exactly. Ain't happy, exactly. Stuck in a cell, all alone. Taken out now and then for who knows what—questionings, torturings . . ."

"But how did she come there? Why? What do they want with her?" Tom was flustered, not sure if Uncle was telling the truth or having some sort of joke at his expense. All he could think of was Hester, imprisoned, suffering. "I can't stay here!" he said. "I must get to this Roost place, try and help her. . . ."

Uncle's smile came back. "Of course you must, dear boy. That's why I brought you down here, isn't it? We got common interests, you and me. You're going to go and save your poor girlie from the Roost. And me and my boys are going to help you."

"Why?" asked Tom. He had a trusting nature—too trusting by half, Hester always used to say—but he was not so naive that he trusted Uncle. "Why would you want to help me and Hester? What's in it for you?"

"Ooh, good question!" Uncle chuckled, rubbing his hands together, knuckles cracking like a string of squibs. "Come, let's eat. Dinner is served in the Map Room. Caul, my boy, you come with us. Skewer, lose yourself."

Skewer slunk out like a naughty dog, and Uncle ushered the others out of the chamber of screens by a back way, up twining staircases to a room lined from floor to rafters with wooden shelves. Rolled and folded maps had been crammed tightly into every chink of space, and sad, pasty-looking boys—failed burglars, barred from limpet work—clambered from shelf to shelf, locating the charts and street plans that Uncle needed to prepare fresh burglaries, replacing those he'd finished with. *This is where poor little Gargle will end up*, thought Caul, for he knew that after the reports he'd had from Anchorage, Uncle would never send the boy out bur- gling again. It made him sad for a moment, imagining how the rest of Gargle's life would be spent bird's-nesting among these cliffs of parchment or tinkering with Uncle's spy cameras.

Uncle settled himself at the head of the table, switching on a little portable Goggle Screen beside his plate so that he could keep watch on his boys even while he ate. "Sit down!" he cried, gesturing generously at the food laid out on the table, the waiting chairs. "Eat! Eat!"

There was nothing to eat in Grimsby except what the Lost Boys stole, and the Lost Boys stole only what boys who have no one to nag them about balanced diets and no snacks between meals eat. Sugary cookies, cheap, soapy chocolate, bacon sandwiches oozing grease, thin rounds of algae bread smeared thick with garish spreads, glasses of ill-chosen wine that kicked like airship fuel. The only concession to healthy eating was a tureen of boiled spinach in the center of the table. "I always make sure the boys bring back a bit of green- stuff," explained Uncle, dishing up. "Helps keep the scurvy at bay." It spattered onto Tom's plate like something dredged from a blocked sump.

"So why am I helping you, you ask," said Uncle, eating quickly and talking with his mouth full, his eyes darting con- stantly to his Goggle Screen. "Well, Tom, the fact is this. It ain't so easy to spy on a place like Rogues' Roost as it is aboard a city. We've had a listening post set up there for months, and we still don't know what the Green Storm are up to. They're serious bunnies. We can barely get any crab-cams inside, and I daren't send one of my boys in; nine chances out of ten he'd be picked up by the sentries. So I thought I'd send you instead. You get a chance to rescue Hester, and I get to learn a bit about the Roost."

Tom stared at him. "But your boys are trained burglars! If they can't go in without getting caught, what makes you think I can?"

Uncle laughed. "If you got caught, it wouldn't matter. Not to me. I'd still learn a lot about their security from watching how you got on, and if they questioned you, you couldn't give away any of my secrets. You don't know where Grimsby lies. You don't know how many limpets I've got. And they probably wouldn't believe you anyway. It'll just look as if you were acting alone, out of love for your girlie. How sweet!"

"It sounds as if you're expecting them to catch me," said Tom.

"Not expecting, exactly," Uncle protested. "But we have to be prepared for all eventualities, Tom. With a bit of luck, and some help from my boys, you'll get in, get the girl, get out; and we'll all be sitting around this table again in a few days' time, listening to Hester tell us why the Green Storm are getting all secret and military on my territory."

He stuffed a handful of popcorn into his mouth and turned back to his screen, flicking idly from channel to channel. Caul stared unhappily at his plate, shocked at what

Uncle was suggesting. It sounded as if he just meant to use Tom as a sort of expendable two-legged crab-cam. . . .

"I won't go!" said Tom.

"But Tom!" cried Uncle, looking up.

"How can I? I want to help Hester, but it would be madness! This Rogues' Roost place sounds like a fortress! I'm a historian, not a commando!"

"But you've got to go," said Uncle. "Because it's Hester in there. I've read Caul and Skewer's sad little reports about you. The way you love her. The way you've tortured yourself since you drove her away. Think how much worse it'll be if you don't try to save her now you've got the chance. *She*'s probably being tortured for real. I don't like to imagine the things those Green Storm are doing to her. They blame her for murdering old Anna Fang, you know."

"But that's not fair! It's ridiculous!"

"Maybe that's so. Maybe that's what poor Hester's telling the Green Storm interrogators right now. But I don't suppose they believe her. And even if they do eventually decide she's innocent, they're hardly going to send her on her way with an apology, are they? It'll be a bullet in the head and over the cliffs with her. Can you picture that, Tom? Good. Get used to it. If you don't try and help her, you'll be seeing it every time you close your eyes for the rest of your life."

Tom pushed back his chair and strode away from the table. He wanted to find a window, to look at something other than Uncle's leering, knowing face, but there were no windows in the Map Room and nothing to look out at anyway except cold water and the roofs of a drowned city.

On a board near the door a huge chart had been pinned

up, showing Rogues' Roost and the trenches and ridges of the seafloor around it. Tom stared at it, wondering where Hester was, what was happening to her among those little squares of buildings marked in blue on the island's summit. He shut his eyes, but she was waiting for him in the dark behind his eyelids just as Uncle had promised.

It was all his fault. If he hadn't kissed Freya, Het would never have flown off like that, never been captured by the agents of the Green Storm. Freya was in danger too, but she was far away and there was nothing he could do to help her or her city. He could help Hester, though. He had one chance in ten of helping Hester.

He calmed himself as best he could, trying to make his voice sound steady and unafraid as he turned back to face Uncle. "All right," he said. "I'll go."

"Capital!" Uncle chuckled, clapping his mittened hands. "I knew you would! Caul will take you to the Roost aboard his *Screw Worm* first thing tomorrow."

And Caul, looking on, felt himself dragged in two directions at once by riptides of emotion such as he'd never felt: fear for Tom, of course, but elation too, because he'd been so afraid that Uncle would punish him for what he'd done in Freya's city, but here he was, commander of the *Screw Worm* still. He stood up and went to Tom, who was leaning on the back of his chair, staring at his hands, looking trembly and sick. "It's all right," he promised. "You won't be alone. You're with the Lost Boys now. We'll get you into that place and out again with Hester, and everything will be all right."

Uncle flicked quickly through the channels on his Goggle Screen, because there was no telling what devilry boys might get up to if they weren't watched all the time. Then, beaming at Tom and Caul, he topped up their glasses with more wine to wash down the pack of half-truths and outright lies he'd fed them.

The Cabinet
of Dr. Popjoy

TIME HAD PASSED SLOWLY FOR Hester. There was not much difference between day and night at Rogues' Roost, except that sometimes the little square of window high in the wall of her cell turned from black to gray. Once the moon peeked in at her, a little past full, and she realized that it must be more than a month since she'd left Tom.

She sat in a corner, ate when her guards shoved food in through the flap in the door, squatted over a tin bucket if nature called. She mapped the courses of Anchorage and Arkangel as best she could in the mold on the walls, trying to calculate where and when the great predator city would catch up with its prey. Mostly she just thought about being Valentine's daughter.

There were days when she wished she had killed him when she'd had the chance, and others when she wished that he were still alive, for there was a lot she would have liked to ask him. Had he loved her mother? Had he known who Hester was? Why had he cared so much about Katherine and not at all about his other child?

Sometimes the door would be kicked open and soldiers would come and take her to the Memory Chamber, where Sathya waited with Popjoy and the thing that had been Anna Fang. A huge, ugly photograph of Hester's face had been added to the other portraits on the walls of the Mnemonic Environment, but Sathya still seemed to feel that it would help to have Hester there in person while she patiently repeated stories of Anna Fang's life to the impassive Stalker. The anger she had felt toward Hester seemed to have faded, as if part of her understood that this scarred and undernourished girl was not really the ruthless London assassin she had imagined. And Hester, in turn, slowly began to understand a little more about Sathya, and why she was so determined to bring the dead aviatrix back.

Sathya had been born on the bare earth, in a squatter camp of curtain-doored caves dug into the wall of an old track mark down in the town-torn south of India. In the dry season her people had to uproot themselves every few months to escape being crushed under the tracks of some passing city: Chidanagaram, or Gutak, or Juggernautpur. When the rains came, the world melted into slurry beneath their shoeless feet. Everyone talked of the day when they would move to some settled static in the uplands, but as Sathya grew older, she began to understand that they would never really make the journey. Simply surviving took up all their time and energy.

And then the airship came. A red airship flown by a tall, kind, beautiful aviatrix, putting in to make repairs on her way north after a mission to the island of Palau Pinang. The children of the camp hung around her, fascinated, listening eagerly to the tales of her work for the Anti-Traction League. Anna Fang had sunk a whole raft city that threatened to attack the Hundred Islands. She had fought battles with the air scouts of Paris and Cittàmotore, and planted bombs in the engine rooms of other hungry cities.

Sathya, standing shyly at the back of the crowd, saw for the first time that she didn't have to live the rest of her life like a maggot. She could fight back.

A week later, halfway to the League's capital at Tienjing, Miss Fang heard noises in the *Jenny Haniver*'s hold and found Sathya crouched amid the cargo there. Taking pity on the girl, she paid to have her trained as a League aviator. Sathya worked hard, learned well, and was soon a wing commander in the Northern Air Fleet. Three quarters of her pay went south each month to help her family, but she seldom thought about them—the League was her family now, and Anna Fang was her mother and her sister and her wise, kind friend.

And how had she repaid all that kindness? By climbing with a squad of Green Storm activists to the ice-caves of Zhan Shan, where the League laid its greatest warriors to rest, and stealing the aviatrix's frozen corpse. By bringing her here to Rogues' Roost and letting Popjoy work his horrible alchemy on her. In spite of herself, Hester felt more and more sorry for the other girl as she watched her trying to cajole memories out of the Stalker. "I am not Anna Fang," the thing insisted again and again in its dune-grass voice. Sometimes it grew angry, and they had to leave. Once there were no sessions for several days, and later Hester learned that it had killed a guard and tried to break out of the Chamber.

On good days, when the creature seemed biddable, they all went together down an armored passageway that led from the Memory Chamber to the nearby cargo hangar where the *Jenny Haniver* was berthed. In the narrow confines of the gondola Hester was forced to re-enact everything she remembered of her two short voyages with the aviatrix, and Sathya told again the old story of how Anna had built this airship, stealing one part after another from the Arkangel salvage yard where she had been a slave, secretly piecing the *Jenny* together under the nose of her brutish master.

The Stalker watched her with its cold green eyes and whispered, "I am not Anna Fang. We are wasting time. You built me to lead the Green Storm, not languish here. I wish to destroy cities."

One night Sathya came alone to the cell. The trembly, staring, haunted expression in her face was more intense than ever, and there were purple shadows under her eyes. Her nails were gnawed down to the quick. A strange idea flicked into Hester's mind as she sat up to meet her visitor: *She is in a prison of her own.*

"Come" was all Sathya said.

She led Hester along deep midnight tunnels to a laboratory, where racks of test tubes welcomed them with cheerless grins. Dr. Popjoy was crouched at a workbench, his bald head gleaming in the light of an argon lamp as he tinkered with a delicate piece of machinery. Sathya had to call his name several times before he grunted, made a few last adjustments, and stepped away from his work.

"I want Hester to see everything, Doctor," Sathya said.

Popjoy's pink eyes blinked wetly, focusing on Hester. "Are you sure that's wise? I mean, if word got out . . . But I suppose Miss Shaw won't be leaving here alive, will she? At least, not in the conventional sense!" He made snuffling noises that might have been laughter and beckoned his visitors forward. As Hester followed Sathya between the benches, she saw that the thing he had been at work on was a Stalker's brain.

"Remarkable piece of machinery, eh, my dear?" said Popjoy proudly. "Of course, it needs a corpse to infest. Lying around out here, it's just a clever toy, but wait until I stick it into a stiff! A dash of chemicals, a soupçon of electricity, and bingo!"

He danced nimbly across the laboratory, past racks of glass retorts, past dead flesh in jars and half-built bits of Stalker. On a T-shaped stand a big dead bird perched, watching the visitors with glowing green eyes. When Popjoy reached out a hand to it, it stretched its ragged wings and opened its beak. "As you can see," the Engineer said, petting it, "I don't limit myself to resurrecting human beings. Prototype Stalker-birds already patrol the skies around the Facility, and I'm considering other ideas—a Stalker-cat, and maybe a Stalker-whale that could carry explosives under a raft city. In the meantime I've been making some great strides in the field of human resurrection. . . ."

Hester glanced at Sathya, but Sathya would not look at her; she just followed Popjoy toward a door in the far wall. It was fitted with a magnetic lock like the ones on the door of the Memory Chamber. The Engineer's long fingers went spidering over the ivory keys, punching in a code. The lock clunked and whirred, and the door swung open to reveal a cave of ice where strange statues waited under plastic covers.

"You see, those old Stalker builders lacked imaginative flair," explained Popjoy, his breath smoldering as he scurried around the big freezer cabinet, unveiling his creations. "Just because a Stalker needs a human brain and nervous system, that doesn't mean it has to be limited to a human shape. Why stick to two arms and two legs? Why only two eyes? Why bother with a mouth? These fellows don't eat, and we haven't built them for their sparkling conversation. . . ."

The frosty plastic sheets were dragged aside, exposing steel-plated centaurs with twenty arms and caterpillar tracks instead of legs, Stalker-spiders with clawed feet and machine-gun turrets in their bellies, Stalkers with spare eyes in the backs of their skulls. On a slab near the front of the cabinet lay something half finished, made from the corpse of poor Widgery Blinkoe.

Hester put a hand to her mouth, gulping and gasping. "That's the man who drugged me at Arkangel!"

"Oh, he was only a paid agent," said Sathya. "He knew too much. I had him liquidated the night he brought you in."

"And what if all his wives come searching for him?"

"Would you come searching for Blinkoe if you were his wife?" asked Sathya. She wasn't even looking at the dead spy; her gaze lingered on the other Stalkers, and on Popjoy.

"Anyway!" said Popjoy brightly, flicking the shrouds back into place. "Better step back outside, before these chaps overheat; there's a slight danger of decomposition before they're quickened."

Hester couldn't bring herself to move, but Sathya pulled her back into the laboratory, saying, "Thank you, Dr. Popjoy—this has been most interesting."

"A pleasure, dear lady," replied the Engineer, with a flirtatious little bow. "Always a pleasure. And soon, I'm certain, we shall find a way to restore your friend Anna's memory. . . . Good-bye! And good-bye, Miss Shaw! I shall look forward to working with you after your execution."

Out of the laboratory, down a short tunnel, through a door that opened onto a rusty walkway running across the cliff face. The wind boomed, roaring down over the ice from the top of the world. Hester gauged its direction before she leaned over the handrail to be sick.

"You asked me once why the Green Storm was backing my work here," said Sathya. "Now you know. They're not interested in Anna, not really. They want Popjoy to build them an army of Stalkers so that they can seize power inside the League and begin their war against the cities."

Hester wiped her mouth and stared down at the tumbled creamy tongues of foam licking through narrow passages in the rocks. "Why tell me?" she asked.

"Because I want you to know. Because when the bombs start falling and the Green Storm's Stalkers are unleashed, I want someone to know that it's not my fault. I did all this for Anna. Only for Anna."

"But Anna would have hated it. She wouldn't have wanted a war."

Sathya shook her head miserably. "She thought we

should attack cities only when they threatened our settlements. She never agreed that city people were all barbarians; she said they were just misguided. I thought that when Anna was herself again, she would show us all a new way: something stronger than the old League and less fierce than the Green Storm. But the Storm are becoming more and more powerful, their new Stalkers are almost ready, and Anna is still lost. . . ."

Hester felt her face twisting into a sarcastic smile and looked quickly away before Sathya noticed. It was hard to stomach all these ethical worries coming from a girl who had murdered old Blinkoe without a qualm, but she sensed an opportunity. Sathya's doubts were like a loose bar in a jail window, a weakness that she might be able to work at. She said, "You should warn the League. Send a messenger to the High Council and tell them what your friends are doing here."

"I can't," said Sathya. "If the Storm found out about it, I'd be killed."

Hester just kept looking at the sea, tasting the salt spray on her lips. "Then what if a prisoner escaped?" she asked. "They couldn't blame you for that, could they? If a prisoner who knew what was happening here escaped and stole an airship and flew away, that wouldn't be your fault."

Sathya looked up sharply. Hester felt herself trembling at the sudden prospect of escape. She could leave this place! There would still be time to save Tom! She felt proud of the way she was preying on Sathya's unhappiness; it seemed to her a clever, ruthless thing to do, and worthy of Valentine's daughter.

"Let me escape and take the *Jenny Haniver*," she said. "I'll fly to League territory. Find someone trustworthy, like Captain Khora. He'll bring warships north and retake this place. Throw Popjoy's new creatures into the sea before they can be used."

Sathya's eyes shone, as if she could already imagine the handsome African aviator leaping from the gondola of his Achebe 9000 to help her out of the trap she had made for herself. Then she shook her head.

"I can't," she said. "If Khora saw Anna in her present state, he might not understand. I can't let anything disrupt my work with her, Hester. We're so close now. Sometimes I can feel her, looking out at me from inside that mask. . . . And anyway, how can I let you go? You helped to kill her."

"You don't still believe that," said Hester. "Not anymore. Or you'd have killed me already."

Two tears went tracking down Sathya's face, silvery against the darkness of her skin. "I don't know," she said. "I have doubts. But I have doubts about so many things." Suddenly she hugged Hester, pulling her face against the starched, scratchy shoulder of her tunic. "It's good to have someone to talk to. I'm not going to kill you. When Anna is better, she will be able to tell me herself whether you were to blame for her death. You must stay here until Anna is better."

The Big Picture

I F YOU COULD LOOK DOWN on the world from somewhere high above—if you were a god, or a ghost haunting one of the old American weapons platforms that still hang in orbit high above the pole—the Ice Wastes would look at first as blank as the walls of Hester's cell: a whiteness spread over the crown of the poor old Earth like a cataract on a blue eye. But look a little closer and there are things moving in the blankness. See that tiny speck to the west of Greenland? That is Anchorage, a screen of survey sleds spreading ahead of it as it wriggles its way between glacier-slathered mountains and across uncharted stretches of sea ice. Wriggles carefully but not too slowly, because all aboard carry with them the memory of the parasite that stole poor Tom away, and the fear that more might erupt at any moment through the ice. Watches are set in the engine district now, and patrols inspect the hull each morning, searching for unwelcome visitors.

What no one aboard suspects, of course, is that the real danger comes not from below but from another speck (larger, darker) that is creeping toward them from the east, skids up, tracks down, hauling its great bulk across the hummocked spine of Greenland. It is Arkangel. In its gut Wolverinehampton and three small whaling towns are being torn apart, while deep in its Core, in the ivory-paneled office of the Direktor, Piotr Masgard is urging his father to increase the city's speed.

"But speed is expensive, my boy," the Direktor says, rubbing his beard. "We caught Wolverinehampton; I'm not sure it's worth crashing on westward after Anchorage. We may never find it. It may all be a trick. They tell me the girl who sold their course to you has vanished."

Piotr Masgard shrugs. "My songbirds often fly away before the catch. But in this case I have a feeling we'll see her again. She'll be back to claim her predator's gold." He brings his fists down hard on his father's desk. "We have to get them, Father! This isn't some scruggy whale town we're talking about! This is Anchorage! The riches of the Rasmussens' Winter Palace! And those engines of theirs. I checked the records. They're supposed to be twenty times more efficient than anything else on the ice."

"True," admits his father. "The Scabious family has always guarded the secret of their construction. Scared a predator might get hold of it, I suppose."

"Well, now one *will*," says Masgard triumphantly. "*Us!* Imagine, Søren Scabious could soon be working for *us!* He could redesign our engines so that we need half as much fuel and catch twice as much prey!"

"Very well." His father sighs.

"You won't regret it, Papa. Another week on this course. Then I'll take my Huntsmen out and find the place."

And if you were a ghost, up there among the endlessly tumbling papers and pens and plastic cups and frozen astronauts, you might use the instruments of that old space station to peer down through the waters into the secret halls of Grimsby, where Uncle sits watching on the largest of his screens as the *Screw Worm* pulls out of the limpet pens, Caul at the controls, Skewer for crew, carrying Tom Natsworthy away to Rogues' Roost.

"Zoom in, boy! Zoom!" snaps Uncle, savoring the glow of the limpet's running lights as it fades into the underwater dark. Gargle, seated beside him at the camera controls, obediently zooms. Uncle pats the boy's tousled head. He's a good boy and will be useful up here, helping him with his archives and his screens. Sometimes he thinks he likes them best, the little, helpless, gormless ones like Gargle. At least they're no trouble. That's more than can be said for soft, strange boys like Caul, who has been showing the nasty symptoms of a conscience lately, or for rough, ambitious ones like Skewer, who have to be watched and watched in case one day they turn the skills and cunning Uncle has given them against him.

"It's gone, Uncle," Gargle says. "Do you think it'll work? Do you think the Dry will make it?"

"Who cares?" Uncle replies, and chuckles. "We win either way, boy. It's true I don't know as much as I'd like to about what's going on in the Roost, but there have been some clues in Wrasse's reports. Little things, but to a man of my genius they all add up. A London Engineer . . . That coffin arriving from Shan Guo, packed in ice . . . The girl Sathya mithering on about her poor dead friend . . . Elementary, my dear Gargle."

Gargle stares at him with wide, round eyes, not understanding. "So . . . Tom?"

"Don't worry, boy," says Uncle, ruffling his hair again. "Putting that Dry inside is just a way of distracting the Green Storm's attention."

"Distracting it from what, Uncle?"

"Oh, you'll see, boy, you'll see."

The Stairs

T HE LOST BOYS HAD ESTABLISHED their listening post just off the eastern side of Rogues' Roost, where black cliffs dropped sheer into forty-fathom water. One of Red Loki's burned-out airships had foundered there during his battle with the Green Storm, and in the creel of its barnacled ribs three limpets had docked together to form a makeshift base, locking their long legs across each other's bodies like crabs in a lobster pot. The *Screw Worm* eased itself into the tangle, and an air lock on its belly linked to the hatch on the roof of the central limpet, *Ghost of a Flea*.

"So this is Uncle's new recruit?" asked a tall youth waiting inside the hatchway as Caul, Skewer, and Tom climbed through into the stale, cheesy air. He was the oldest member of Uncle's gang Tom had yet seen, and he was looking Tom up and down with a strange, condescending smile, as if he knew a joke that Tom wouldn't understand.

"Tom's girlfriend is Hester Shaw, the prisoner in Rogues' Roost," Caul started to explain.

"Yeah, yeah. Uncle's message-fish got here way ahead of you. I've heard all about these lovebirds. Mission of mercy, eh?"

He turned away, moving along a narrow passage. "His name's Wrasse," whispered Caul, following with Tom and Skewer. "He's one of the first ones."

"First at what?" Tom asked.

"One of the first Uncle brought down to Grimsby. One of the leaders. Uncle lets him keep half of everything he brings home. He's Uncle's right hand."

Uncle's right hand led them into a hold that had been cleared of cargo and fitted out as a surveillance station. Other boys, each younger than Wrasse but older than Skewer or Caul, lounged about looking bored or sat hunched over control panels in the blue half-light, watching a bank of circular screens that filled an entire wall. This place was crowded. Caul had never heard of so many boys being assigned to a single job. Why would Uncle send so many, just to spy? And why were so many of the screens dead?

"You've only got three crabs working!" he said. "We were running thirty aboard Anchorage!"

"Well, this isn't like burgling city folk, limpet boy," snapped Wrasse. "The Green Storm are hard-core. Guards and guns everywhere, all the time. The only way in for a crab-cam is up a sewage pipe that leads to an abandoned toilet block on the western side. We managed to get three cameras up that and into the heating ducts, but the Drys heard noises and started getting inquisitive, so we can't move 'em about much, and we haven't tried putting any more in. We wouldn't even have those three if Uncle hadn't sent us his latest models, remote-control jobs with no cables to trail around. Couple of other special features too."

That smile again. Caul glanced at the long control desks. Piles of notes lay among the abandoned coffee cups, listing timetables, shift patterns, the habits of the Green Storm sentries. A cluster of fat red buttons, each protected by its own glastic hood, caught his eye. "What do those do?" he asked.

"Never you mind," said Wrasse.

"So what do you reckon's going on up there?" asked Skewer.

Wrasse shrugged, flicking from channel to channel. "Dunno. The places that Uncle's most interested in—the laboratory and the Memory Chamber—we haven't been able to get into at all. We can eavesdrop in the main hangar, but we can't always understand what's going on. They don't talk Anglish or Nord like real people. Jibber and jabber away in Airsperanto and a lot of funny eastern languages. This girlie's their leader." (A dark head filled the screen, glimpsed from an odd angle, through the blurred grille of a ventilator in her office ceiling. She reminded Tom a bit of that girl who'd been so rude to him in Batmunkh Gompa.) "She's crazy. Keeps ranting about some dead friend of hers as if she's still alive. Uncle was very interested in her. Then there's this charming character. . . ."

Tom gasped. On the screen Wrasse was pointing to, someone sat hunched at the bottom of a deep, well-like room. The picture was so blurred and underlit that if you stared too long, it stopped looking like a person at all and dissolved into a soup of abstract shapes, but Tom didn't need to look for long.

"That's Hester!" he shouted.

The Lost Boys grinned and chuckled and nudged each other. They'd seen Hester's face on their screens, and they thought it a great joke that anyone should care about her.

"I've got to get to her," Tom said, leaning closer, wishing he could reach through the glass of the Goggle Screen and touch her, just to let her know that he was there.

"Oh, you will," Wrasse said. He took Tom by the arm and pulled him through a bulkhead door into a small compartment, the walls lined with racks of guns, swords, pikes. "We're all ready. Got our instructions from Uncle. Got our plans laid." He chose a small gas pistol and handed it to Tom, then a curious little metal device. "Lockpick," he said.

Behind him in the operations room Tom could hear a rising buzz of activity. Nobody was looking bored now; through the half-open door he could see boys hurrying to and fro with papers and clipboards, flicking switches on the long banks of camera controls, trying on headphones. "You're not sending me inside now?" he asked. "Not right now?" He'd expected time to prepare himself, maybe some sort of briefing about whatever the Lost Boys had learned of the layout inside Rogues' Roost. He hadn't imagined being pushed into action as soon as he arrived.

But Wrasse had him by the arm again and was propelling him back through the operations room, back along the tangle of passageways. "No time like the present," he said.

❀ ❀ ❀

An old metal stairway zigzagged down the cliffs on the western side of Rogues' Roost, and at its foot an iron jetty jutted into the surf, sheltered by long spurs of rock. It had sometimes been used for supply boats to tie up at, back in the pirate days, but no boat had come since the Green Storm took over, and already the jetty was looking tatty and unloved, eroded by rust and the unresting sea.

The *Screw Worm* surfaced in its shadow just as the sun sank into a thick bank of fog on the horizon. The wind had died to almost nothing, but there was still a heavy swell running, and surf crashed over the limpet's carapace as its magnetic grapples made contact with the jetty.

Tom looked up through the wet windows at lights coming on in the buildings high above him, and felt as if he were about to be sick. All the way from Grimsby he had been telling himself it would be all right, but here in the swell beneath the jetty he could not believe that he would ever get inside this Green Storm stronghold, let alone escape again with Hester.

He wished that Caul were here, but Wrasse had piloted the *Screw Worm* himself, making Caul stay back aboard the *Ghost of a Flea*. "Good luck!" the boy had said, hugging him in the airlock, and Tom was beginning to realize just how much good luck he would need.

"The stairs lead to a door about a hundred feet up," Wrasse said. "It's not guarded: They don't expect an attack from the sea. It'll be locked, but nothing our tools can't handle. Got the lockpick?"

Tom patted the pocket of his coat. Another roller lifted and twisted the *Screw Worm*. "Well, then," he said nervously, wondering if it was too late to turn back.

"I'll be waiting right here," promised Wrasse, with that faint, suspicious smile. Tom wished he could trust him.

He climbed quickly up the ladder, trying to think only of Hester, because he knew that if he thought for one moment about all the soldiers and guns in that fortress above him, he would lose his nerve. A wave sloshed over the *Screw Worm* as he sprang the hatch, drenching him in ice-cold water; then he was out on the hull, in the dark and the cold fresh air, the noise of the sea loud around him. He squeezed himself between the struts under the jetty as another wave heaved past, then groped his way up onto the top. He was soaked through and already beginning to shiver. As he ran toward the stairs, the jetty bucked beneath him like an animal, straining at its tethers, trying to shrug him off.

He climbed fast, glad of a chance to get warm. Birds whirled above him in the twilight, the movement startling him. *Just think of Hester,* he kept reminding himself, but even remembering the best of his times with her could not quite blot out his growing fear. He tried to stop thinking altogether, told himself he had a job to do, but the thoughts kept slipping into his brain. This was a suicide mission. Uncle was just using him. That story about needing a spy inside the Roost hadn't been the whole truth—he was sure of that now. And the listening post, with all its guns—he'd seen how shocked Caul looked when he caught a glimpse of those. He'd been set up. He was a pawn in a game whose rules he couldn't fathom. Maybe he should just surrender himself to the Green Storm, shout for the sentries and give himself up. They might not be as bad as everyone said, and at least he'd have a chance of seeing Hester. . . .

A black shape dropped out of the twilight. He flung his arms up and turned his face away, squeezing his eyes shut. There was a hoarse cry, and he felt a beak strike his head: a sharp, painful blow like a tap from a small hammer. Then a flapping and fluttering of wings, and nothing. He looked up and around. He'd heard about this, about seabirds that attacked anyone who came near their nesting grounds. High above him thousands wheeled against the gathering dark. He started to hurry up the stairs, hoping that they didn't all get the same idea.

He had made it up another flight before the bird came at him again, sweeping in from the side with a long, guttural squawk. He had a better look at it this time: wide, grubby wings like a raggedy cloak, and the eyes glinting green above the open beak. He struck at it with his fist and his forearm and flung it away. As he hurried on up, he felt pain and looked down to see blood welling out of three long cuts on the side of his hand. What sort of bird was this? Its talons had gone straight through his best leather mittens!

Another shriek, shrill and close enough to be heard through the racket of the birds overhead. Wings flapped around his head, a confusion of feathers, batting at his face and his hair. He could smell a chemical smell, and this time he saw that the green glare in the bird's eyes was not the reflection of the lights above. He pulled out the gun Wrasse had given him and struck at the thing. It whirled away to windward, but an instant later more claws raked his scalp; he was being attacked by two of the creatures.

He started to run, up and up, with the birds—if they *were* birds—squabbling and screeching around him, sometimes lunging in to strike at his head or his neck. There were only two of them—the other birds were minding their own business, circling the island's summit. Only two, but two were more than enough. Little flashes of light rebounded from razor-blade claws and clacking metal beaks; wings stuttered and snapped like flags in a gale. "Help!" he shouted pointlessly, and "Get off! Get off!" He thought of running back down to the safety of the waiting limpet, but the birds flung themselves at his face when he turned, and the door was close now, only one more flight of stairs to go.

He scrambled up, slithering on the icy steps, holding up his hands in his slashed mittens to try and protect his head. He could feel hot trickles of blood running down his face. In the last light of the dying day he saw the door ahead and flung himself at it, but he was too busy fending off the darting beaks and slicing claws to fumble with the lockpick. In desperation he raised the gun and aimed it upward. A flat crack echoed from the cliffs and one of the green-eyed birds dropped away, trailing a long plume of smoke behind it as it plunged toward the surf. The other drew back, then swept down again. Tom hid his face, and the gun slipped from his bloody hands and bounced off the handrails and fell away from him into the dark.

The white blade of a searchlight beam slashed across the cliff face, stabbing at him through the whirlwind of wings and flapping shadow. He cowered against the door. A siren started to howl, then another and another, long echoes bounding from the cliffs. "Wrasse!" he shouted. "Caul! Help!"

It seemed impossible that everything had gone so wrong so quickly.

✿ ✿ ✿

A voice crackled over the *Screw Worm*'s radio. "They've got him."

Wrasse nodded calmly. Uncle had told him that it would probably go this way. "Get those crabs moving," he told the radio. "We've only got a few minutes before they realize he's all by himself."

He began pressing buttons, throwing switches. A hatch on the hull opened to release a battered old cargo balloon. As the balloon drifted up into the storm of birds and searchlight beams around the island's summit, the *Screw Worm*'s magnets came free of the jetty one by one, and it folded its legs and sank into the surf like a stone.

The metal door opened, splashing Tom with yellow light. He was so glad to get away from the birds that it seemed a relief when the guards grabbed him. They pinned his arms behind his back and held his flailing legs, and someone jammed the muzzle of a Weltschmerz automatic under his chin. "Thank you," he kept blurting out, and "Sorry," as they manhandled him inside and slammed the door and flung him down on the cold floor. He was picked up and carried and set down while voices dinned from the low roof. Rocket projectors were firing outside. The voices spoke Airsperanto, with eastern accents and a lot of dialect words he couldn't grasp.

"Is he alone?" A woman's voice, oddly familiar.

"We think so, Commander; the (something) found him on the stair."

The woman spoke again. Tom didn't catch what she said, but she must have been asking how he had come here, because one of the other voices answered, "Balloon. A two-man balloon. Our batteries shot it down."

Something that sounded like swearing. "Why didn't the watchtowers see it coming?"

"The sentry said it just appeared."

"There wasn't a balloon," Tom whispered, confused.

"The prisoner, Commander . . ."

"Let's have a look at him. . . ."

"Sorry," Tom mumbled, tasting blood. Somebody shone a flashlight in his face, and when he could see again, he saw that the girl who looked like that girl Sathya was stooping over him, only she didn't just look like Sathya, she *was* Sathya. "Hello. Thank you. Sorry," he whispered. She peered through the blood and the straggles of wet hair, and her eyes went wide and then fierce and narrow as she recognized him.

After months of having not enough to watch, the Lost Boys suddenly had too much. They jostled one another in front of the screens, struggling to make out what was going on among the Drys. Caul, pushing his way to the front, glimpsed Tom being hurried along in a scrum of white-uniformed guards. On another screen the commander's office lay empty, her evening meal half eaten on her desk. A third showed aviators gathering by their airships in the big hangar, as if the Green Storm imagined Tom's arrival might be the beginning of an attack. The rest of the screens were filled with scurrying darkness. Dozens of remote crabs had been waiting outside the Roost's sewage outlet, and now the Lost Boys were taking advantage of the uproar to send them scuttling up into the base. Swarming out of a broken toilet, the little machines darted through an air vent and scattered into the ducts and flues of the Facility, cutting their way through security grilles and disabling sensors, their noise drowned out by the honking sirens.

In the midst of it all Caul felt the post shudder as the *Screw Worm* docked. A moment later Wrasse came pushing in through the air lock, looking tense and excited, snapping out questions about the Green Storm's response time.

"They're quick," one of his boys replied.

"I'm glad Uncle didn't send me to check them out!"

"Some kind of trained birds guarding the stairway, they're what first raised the alarm."

"We'll be ready for them."

Caul tugged and tugged at the sleeve of Wrasse's jacket until the older boy looked around, annoyed. "You're supposed to be waiting for Tom!" Caul shouted. "What if he escapes? How will he get clear without the *Screw Worm*?"

"Your boyfriend's had it, Dry-lover," said Wrasse, shoving him away. "Don't worry. It's all going as Uncle planned."

Keys in the lock, the jolt of the door kicked open. The noises jerked Hester awake. She scrambled up, and Sathya strode into the cell and knocked her down again. Soldiers were crowding in, dragging a sodden, dripping figure between them. Hester didn't know who it was, not even when Sathya lifted the wet head and showed her that bruised, blood-drizzled face, but she saw the long leather aviator's coat and thought, *Tom has a coat like that*, and that made her look again, even though it couldn't possibly be him.

"Tom?" she whispered.

"Don't pretend to be surprised!" screamed Sathya. "Do you ask me to believe you weren't expecting him? How did he know you were here? What had you planned? Who are you working for?"

"Nobody!" said Hester. "Nobody!" She started to cry as the guards forced Tom down on his knees beside her. He had come to rescue her, and he looked so frightened and so hurt, and the worst of it was that he didn't know what she'd done: He'd come all this way to try and save her, and she didn't deserve to be saved. "Tom," she sobbed.

"I trusted you!" Sathya shouted. "You ensnared me just as you did poor Anna, playing the innocent, making me doubt myself, and all the time your barbarian accomplice was on his way here! What was your plan? Is there a ship waiting? Was Blinkoe in league with you? I suppose you meant to kidnap Popjoy and take him to one of your filthy cities so that *they* could have his Stalkers?"

"No, no, no, you've got it all twisted around," Hester wept, but she could see that nothing she could say would convince the girl that Tom's sudden appearance was not part of some Tractionist plot.

As for Tom, he was too cold and shocked to take in much of what was happening, but he heard Hester's voice and looked up and saw her crouching beside him. He had forgotten how ugly she was.

Then Sathya grabbed him by his hair and forced his head down again, baring his neck. He heard her sword come out of its scabbard with a slithery hiss, heard a rattle and scrabble in the ducts on the ceiling, heard Hester saying, "Tom!" He shut his eyes.

✿ ✿ ✿

On the Lost Boys' screens the drawn sword was a flare of white. Sathya's voice came tinnily over the crabs' radios, shouting insane things about plots and betrayal.

"Do something!" Caul yelled.

"He's only a Dry, Caul," warned Skewer, not unkindly. "Leave it!"

"We've got to help him! He'll die!"

Wrasse threw Caul aside. "He was always going to die, you fool!" he shouted. "Do you think Uncle really planned to let him go, with what he's seen? Even if he got the girl out, my orders were Question 'em and kill 'em. Tom's just supposed to create a diversion."

"Why?" wailed Caul. "Just so you can move a few more cameras inside? Just so Uncle can see what's in the Memory Chamber?"

Wrasse punched him, flinging him against the control panels. "Uncle worked out what's in the Memory Chamber months ago. Those aren't just cameras. They're bombs. We're going to move them into position, give the Drys a few hours to settle down again, then blow the lot and go in and do some real burgling."

Caul looked at the screens, tasting the blood that was spilling from his nose. The other boys had drawn back from him, as if caring too much about Drys were something they could catch, like the flu. He started to raise himself and saw the pad of hooded red buttons near his hand. He stared at them a moment. He'd never seen controls like those before, but he could guess what they must do.

"No!" someone shouted. "Not yet!"

In the instant before they reached him, he flipped up the hoods of as many buttons as he could and brought both his fists down on them, hard.

The screens went dead.

Untie
the Wind

SOMETHING HIT HIM IN THE back and he went forward, face on the cold floor, thinking, *This is it, I'm dead*, but he wasn't dead, he could feel the dampness of the stone against his cheek, and when he rolled over, he saw that an explosion had brought the ceiling down: a big explosion, judging by all the rubble and the dust, and he would have expected it to make a noise, but he hadn't heard anything, and he still couldn't hear anything, even though quite large chunks of the roof were coming down and people were flailing about waving flashlights and shouting with their mouths wide open, no, there was just a whine and a whistle and a buzz going on somewhere inside his skull, and when he sneezed it made no sound, but small, hot fingers closed around his hand and tugged at him, and he looked up and saw Hester, white in the sweep and flare of a flashlight beam like a floodlit statue of herself, except that she was mouthing something at him, tugging and tugging him and pointing toward the doorway, and he scrambled out from under the thing that had fallen on him, which turned out to be Sathya, and he wondered if she was badly hurt and if he should try to help her, but Hester was pulling him toward the door, stumbling over the bodies of men who were quite definitely dead, stooping under the remains of a heating duct that was all twisted open and smoking as if it had exploded from inside, and as he looked back, somebody fired a gun at him and he saw the flash and felt the bullet flick past his ear, but he couldn't hear that either.

And then they were hurtling down a stairway. Through other doors. Slamming them silently shut behind them. They paused for breath, bent double, coughing, and he tried to make sense of what had happened. The explosion—-the heating duct . . .

"Tom!" Hester was leaning close to him, but her voice sounded far away, blurring and wobbling as if she were shouting underwater.

"What?"

"Ship!" she shouted. "Where's your ship? How did you get here?"

"Submarine," he said, "but I expect it's gone."

"What?" She was as deaf as him.

"Gone!"

"What?" Flashlights flashed through the dust and smoke at the far end of the corridor. "We'll take the *Jenny*!" she yelled, and began pushing Tom toward yet another stairway. It was dark, like the corridor, and full of smoke, and he began to realize that there had been other explosions, not just the one in the cell. In some corridors lights still flickered, but in most the power was down. Groups of frightened and bewildered soldiers hurried about with flashlights. It was easy enough for Tom and Hester to see them coming and hide, squeezing into deep doorways or ducking down rubble-strewn side passages. Slowly, Tom's hearing came back, and the whistling in his ears gave way to the steady, anxious honking of alarms. Hester shoved him into the mouth of a stairway as more people scurried past—aviators this time. "I don't even know where we are," she grumbled, when they were gone. "It all looks different in the dark." She looked at Tom, her face piebald with dust. Grinned. "How did you manage that explosion?"

It had been the toughest decision of Wrasse's life. For a moment he nearly lost it, down there in the *Ghost of a Flea*, staring in panic at the blank screens. All Uncle's plans in ruins! Everything they'd worked for wrecked! The crabs blown before most of them were even in position!

"What do we do, Wrasse?" one of his boys asked.

Only two things they could do. Go home, and let Uncle skin them alive for coming back empty-handed. Or go for it.

"We'll go for it," he decided, and felt his strength return as the others started running for guns and nets and gadgets, strapping flashlights to their heads, dragging Caul away. "Skewer, Baitball, you lot on the cameras, you stay here; the rest of you come with me!"

And so, as the Green Storm panicked and argued and tried to fight the fires the crabs had started, as searchlights prodded the sky and rocket batteries fired salvo after salvo at imaginary attackers, a sleek, customized limpet detached itself from the listening post and swam up to the jetty. The Lost Boys bundled out, running quickly and silently up the same stairs Tom had climbed an hour before.

Near the top a Stalker-bird found them, and one boy went over the handrail and screaming down into the surf. Another was winged by gunfire from an emplacement on the cliffs and Wrasse had to finish him off, because Uncle's orders were to leave no one behind for the Drys to question. Then they were at the door, and through it, following their sketchy floor plans toward the Memory Chamber, leaving boys behind at this junction and that to guard the escape route. Panicking Green Storm soldiers blundered through the smoke and the Lost Boys killed them, because that was in Uncle's orders too: Leave no witnesses.

The Memory Chamber's guards had fled. The massive locks dismayed Wrasse for only a moment; the power was out, and when he heaved at the door, it swung sweetly open. The Lost Boys' flashlights lit up a bridge stretching to a central platform where someone paced like a caged wild thing. A gleaming bronze mask swung suddenly toward the light.

They flinched back, all of them. Only Wrasse had been given any idea what it was they were being sent to steal, and even he had never actually seen it. Uncle had warned him not to confront the thing face on: *Take it by surprise*, his orders said, *from above or behind; get the nets over it and the grapples on before it knows what's happening.* But there was no time for that now, and even if there had been, Wrasse wasn't sure it would have worked. It looked so *strong*! For the first time in his life he began to wonder if Uncle really did Know Best.

He hid his fear as best he could. "That's it," he said. "That's what Uncle wants. Let's nick it."

The Lost Boys raised their guns, their blades, the ropes and chains and magnetic grapples and heavy throwing nets that Uncle had equipped them with and began to edge across the bridge.

And the Stalker flexed its hands and came to meet them.

Gunfire popped and bickered, though it was hard to tell where with the echoes all mixed up, rebounding along the low corridors. Tom and Hester ran on, following Hester's vague mental map of the air base. They began to pass bodies: three Green Storm troopers in a heap, then a young man in mismatched dark clothes, a furze of fair hair under his black wool cap. For a jolting instant Tom thought it was Caul, but this boy was older and bigger: one of Wrasse's crew. "The Lost Boys are here!" he said.

"Who are they?" asked Hester. Tom didn't answer, too busy trying to grasp what was going on and what part he had played in it all. Before she could ask again, a storm of noise interrupted, booming somewhere nearby: gunfire, massed at first but thinning, growing patchy and frantic and spiked with shrieks; then one last, bubbling scream and silence.

Even the sirens had stopped.

"What was *that*?" asked Tom.

"How should I know?" Hester took the dead Lost Boy's flashlight and ducked down another stairwell, dragging Tom after her. "Let's get out of here. . . ."

Tom followed gladly. He loved the feeling of her hand holding his, guiding him. He wondered if he should tell her so, and whether this was the moment to apologize for what had happened back in Anchorage, but before he could say anything, they reached the bottom of the stairs and Hester stopped, breathing hard, motioning for him to stay still and quiet.

They were in a sort of antechamber, where a circular metal door stood wide open.

"Oh, Gods and Goddesses!" said Hester softly.

"What?"

"The power! The locks failed! The electric barrier! It's escaped!"

"But *what?*"

She took a deep breath and crept toward the door. "Come on!" she told Tom. "There's a way through to the hangar. . . ."

They stepped together through the door. Just above their heads hung a thick haze of gun smoke, filling and billowing like a white awning. The shadows were full of the drip of falling liquid. Hester shone her flashlight along the bridge, sweeping the beam over puddles and scrawls of blood, over patterns of bloody footprints like the diagram of some violent dance, past drips of blood falling from the curved roof high above. Things lay on the bridge. At first they looked like bundles of old clothes, until you looked closer and began to make out hands, faces. Tom recognized some of those faces from the listening post. But what had they come here for? What had happened to them? He began to shake uncontrollably.

"It's all right," said Hester, flicking her flashlight toward the central platform. Empty, except for a blood-sodden gray robe abandoned like a cast-off chrysalis in the very center. The Stalker had left, doubtless hunting for fresh victims in the maze of rooms and corridors above them. Hester took Tom's hand again, leading him quickly around the outer edge of the chamber to the door that she had gone through so often with Sathya and the others, on the Stalker's good days. In the stairway beyond, the air moaned softly, like the voices of ghosts. "This leads to the hangar where the *Jenny*'s kept," she explained, hurrying down and down with Tom behind her.

The stairs ended; the passage made a tight dogleg and widened suddenly into the hangar. In the jitter of Hester's flashlight beam Tom glimpsed the *Jenny Haniver*'s patched red envelope hanging above him. Hester found a panel of controls on the wall and pulled on one of the levers. Pulleys grumbled into life somewhere up on the dark roof, and flakes of rust came showering down as wheels turned and hawsers tightened, heaving open the huge storm doors at the hangar's mouth. The widening gap revealed a narrow landing apron jutting from the cliff outside, and fog, fog all around the Roost, a dense white dreamscape of hills and folds and billows veiling the sea. Above it the sky was clear, and the light of stars and dead satellites reached into the hangar, revealing the *Jenny Haniver* on her docking pan, revealing the line of bloody footprints on the concrete floor.

From the shadows under the *Jenny*'s steering vanes stepped a tall shape, blocking the way back to the door. Two green eyes hung in the dark like fireflies.

"Oh, Quirke!" Tom squeaked. "Is that—? That's not a—? Is it?"

"It's Miss Fang," said Hester. "But she's not herself."

The Stalker walked forward into the spill of light from the open storm doors. Faint reflections slithered over its long steel limbs, its armored torso, the bronze mask of its face, glinting on small dents and scars that the Lost Boys' useless bullets had made. Their blood still dripped from the Stalker's claws and covered its hands and its forearms like long red gloves.

The Stalker had enjoyed the massacre in the Memory Chamber, but when the last of the Lost Boys was dead, it had not known what to do next. The smell of gun smoke and the muffled sounds of battle echoing down the corridors aroused its Stalkerish instincts, but it regarded the open door cautiously, remembering the electric barriers that had sprung up the last time it had tried to leave. At last it chose the other door, drawn by feelings it did not understand, down to the hangar and the old red airship that waited there. It had been circling the *Jenny* in the darkness, running its metal fingers over the grain of her gondola planking, when Hester and Tom came bursting in. Its claws sprang out again, and the fierce yearning to kill crackled through its electric veins like a power surge.

Tom turned, thinking to run out onto the apron, but crashed against Hester, who slipped on the bloody floor and went down hard. He bent down to help her, and suddenly the Stalker was standing over them.

"Miss Fang?" Tom whispered, looking up into that strange, familiar face.

The Stalker watched him crouching over the girl on the

blood-speckled concrete, and a little meaningless flake of memory fluttered suddenly into the machinery of its brain, itchy and confusing. It hesitated, claws twitching. Where had it seen this boy before? He had not been among the portraits on the walls of its chamber, but it knew him. It remembered lying in snow with his face staring down. Behind the mask, its dead lips shaped a name.

"Tom Nitsworthy?"

"Natsworthy," said Tom.

That alien memory stirred again inside the Stalker's skull. It did not know why this boy seemed so familiar, only that it did not want him to die. It took a step backward, then another. Its claws slipped back into their sheaths.

"Anna!"

The voice, a brittle scream, echoed loudly in the cavernous hangar, making all three of them look toward the door. Sathya stood there, a lantern in one hand and her sword in the other, her face and hair still white with plaster dust, blood dribbling from the wound on her head where shrapnel from the exploding duct had caught her. She set the lantern down and walked quickly toward her beloved Stalker. "Oh, Anna! I've been looking everywhere for you! I should have known you'd be here, with the *Jenny*. . . ."

The Stalker did not move, just swung its metal face to stare down at Tom again. Sathya stopped short, noticing for the first time the figures huddled at its feet. "You've caught them, Anna! Well done! They are enemies, in league with the intruders! They were your murderers! Kill them!"

"All enemies of the Green Storm must die," agreed the Stalker.

"That's right, Anna!" Sathya urged. "Kill them now! Kill them, like you killed those others!"

The Stalker put its head on one side. The green light from its eyes washed Tom's face.

"Then I'll do it!" Sathya shouted, striding forward, lifting her sword. The Stalker made a quick movement. Tom squealed in terror and felt Hester scrunch closer to him. Steel claws blazed in the lantern light, and Sathya's sword clattered on the floor, her hand still wrapped around the hilt.

"No," said the Stalker.

For a brief time there was silence while Sathya stared at the blood that came in unbelievable jets from the stump of her arm. "Anna!" she whispered, falling to her knees, crumpling forward onto her face.

Tom and Hester watched, not speaking, not breathing, crouched as still and small as they could, as if in their stillness the Stalker might forget them. But it turned, gliding back toward them, and raised its dripping claws again. "Go," it whispered, pointing toward the *Jenny Haniver.* "Go, and do not cross the path of the Green Storm again."

Tom just stared, crouched against Hester, too scared to move, but Hester took the Stalker at its word and eased herself up and backward, dragging him with her, urging him toward the airship. "Come on, for the gods' sake! You heard what it said!"

"Thank you," Tom managed to whisper, remembering his manners as they edged past the Stalker and up the *Jenny's* gangplank. The inside of the gondola smelled cold and strange after her long grounding, but when Hester switched on the engines, they came sputtering to life with their old,

familiar shudder, their roar filling the hangar. Tom eased himself into the pilot's seat, trying not to look out at the thing
that stood watching him, its armor gaudy with the green and
red reflections of the running lights.

"Is she really going to let us go?" he asked. His teeth were
chattering, and he was trembling so violently that he could
barely grip the controls. "Why? Why doesn't she kill us like
the others?"

Hester shook her head, switching on instruments,
heaters. She was remembering Grike, and the strange emo-
tions that had prompted him to collect broken automata or
rescue a disfigured, dying child. But all she said was "It's an
it, not a *she*, and we can't know what it's thinking. Just go,
before it changes its mind."

The clamps released, the pods swung into takeoff position, and the *Jenny* lifted uncertainly from its pan and edged
out into the night, grazing a vane on the hangar wall as it
went. The Stalker walked out onto the landing apron and
watched as the old airship pulled clear of Rogues' Roost,
dropping into the fog before the Green Storm's rocket batteries could decide whether she was friend or foe. And again that
strange half-memory brushed mothlike against the Stalker's
mind: the Once-Born called Tom kneeling over it in snow and
saying, "It's not fair! He waited till you were dazzled!"

For a moment it felt an odd satisfaction, as though it had
returned a favor.

"Which way?" asked Tom, when Rogues' Roost was a mile
behind him in the fog and he felt calm enough to speak again.

"Northwest," Hester replied. "Anchorage. I've got to go
back there. A terrible thing's happened."

"Pennyroyal!" guessed Tom. "I know. I worked it out just before I left. There wasn't time to tell anyone. You were right about him. I should have listened to you."

"Pennyroyal?" Hester was staring at him as if he'd spoken in a language she didn't understand. She shook her head. "Arkangel is on their tail."

"Oh, Great Quirke!" whispered Tom. "Are you sure? But how could Arkangel have learned Anchorage's course?"

Hester just took the controls and locked in a course, north by northwest. Then she turned, her hands behind her, clutching the edge of the control panel so hard it hurt. She said, "I saw you kissing Freya—and I—I—" Patches of silence formed between her words like ice. She wanted to tell him the truth, she really did, but as she looked at his poor, scratched, frightened face, she found she couldn't bear to.

"Het, I'm sorry," he said suddenly.

"It doesn't matter," she said. "I mean, me too."

"What are we going to do?"

"About Anchorage?"

"They can't go on if there's only a Dead Continent ahead of them, and they can't turn back if Arkangel's behind."

"I don't know," said Hester. "Let's just get there first. Then we'll think of something."

"But what?" Tom started to ask, but he didn't finish, because Hester had taken his face between her hands and was busy kissing him.

The sound of the *Jenny Haniver*'s engines grew fainter and fainter until at last not even the Stalker's ears could hear it. The memory that had prompted it to spare Tom and Hester was fading too, vanishing like a dream. It switched its eyes to night vision and went back into the hangar. Sathya's severed hand was cooling fast, but her body still showed a fuzzy blur of warmth. The Stalker padded to where she lay, lifted her up by her hair, and shook her till she woke and started whimpering.

"You will prepare airships, and weapons. We are leaving the Facility."

Sathya gurgled at her, her eyes bulging with pain and fear. Had the Stalker been waiting for this all along while she kept it locked in the Memory Chamber, showing it photographs and playing it poor Anna's favorite music? But of course, this was what it had been built for! Had she not told Popjoy to bring Anna back ready to command the League? "Yes, Anna," she sobbed. "Of course, Anna!"

"I am not Anna," said the Stalker. "I am the Stalker Fang, and I am tired of hiding here."

Other Once-Borns were edging into the hangar now: soldiers and scientists and aviators shocked and leaderless in the smoky aftermath of their battle with the mysterious intruders. Dr. Popjoy was with them, and as the Stalker turned to face them, they pushed him quickly to the front. With Sathya trailing like a broken doll, the Stalker went close to him, close enough to smell the salt sweat oozing out of his pores and hear the sharp staccato of his frightened breath. "You will obey me," it said. "Your prototypes must be quickened at once, Doctor. We will return to Shan Guo, gathering our forces from the other Green Storm bases as we go. Elements of the Anti-Traction League who resist us will be liquidated. We will take control of shipyards, training camps, weapons factories. And then we will unleash a storm that will scour the Earth clean of Traction Cities forever."

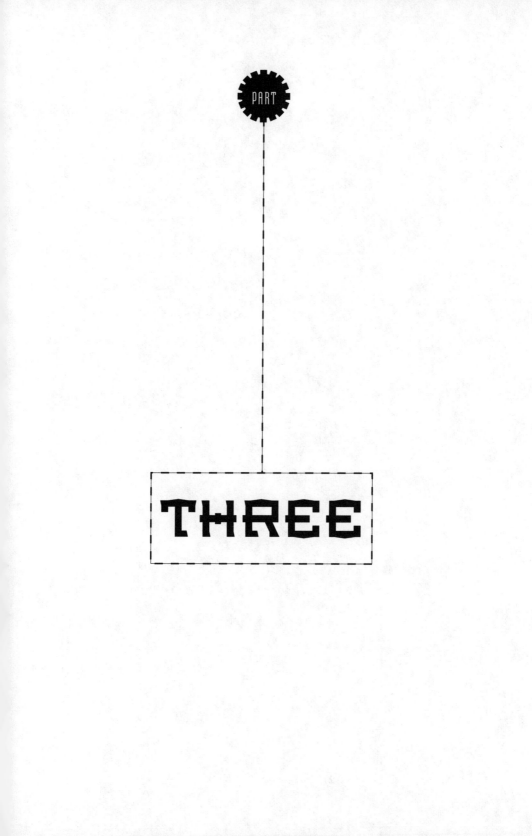

PART

THREE

The Crane

I WANT TO TELL YOU A LITTLE story," said the voice. "Are you hanging comfortably? Then I'll begin."

Caul opened his eyes. Rather, he opened one eye, for the other was swollen shut with bruises. What a beating the survivors of poor Wrasse's crew had given him as the *Screw Worm* carried him home in disgrace from Rogues' Roost! When unconsciousness had finally claimed him, he had mistaken it for death and welcomed it, and his last thought was that he was proud he'd helped Tom and Hester get away. Then he woke up back in Grimsby, and the beatings started again, and pretty soon he didn't feel proud anymore. He couldn't believe how stupid he'd been, throwing his life away to save a pair of Drys.

Uncle reserved a special punishment for boys who really disappointed him. They dragged Caul to the limpet pens and put a rope around his neck and attached the other end to the *Screw Worm*'s docking crane and hoisted him up to slowly strangle. All through the day shift, while he swung there gasping for breath, the Lost Boys stood around jeering and shouting and pelting him with scraps of food and litter. And when the night shift started and everyone returned to the sleeping quarters, the voice began. It was so faint and whispery that Caul thought at first he was imagining it, but it was real enough. It was Uncle's voice, coming softly from the big speaker near his head.

"Still awake, Caul? Still alive? Young Sonar lasted nearly a week strung up like that. Remember?"

Caul sucked air in through his cut and swollen lips, through the spaces where his front teeth had been. Above him the rope creaked, slowly twisting so that the limpet pen seemed to spin endlessly around him, the shadowy pools and the silent limpets, the painted figures looking down from the ceiling. He could hear Uncle's wet, steady breathing coming from the speaker.

"When I was a young man," Uncle said, "and I was a young man once, as young as you—although, unlike you, I got older—I lived aboard Arkangel. Stilton Kael, that was my name. The Kaels were a good family. Ran stores, hotels, salvage, the track-plate franchise. By the time I was eighteen, I was in charge of the family salvage yard. Not that I saw salvage as my destiny, you understand. What I longed for was to be a poet, a writer of great epics, someone whose name would live forever, like old whatsisname, you know, Thingy— the Greek bloke, blind. . . . Funny how youthful dreams come to nothing. But you'd know all about that, young Caul."

Caul swung and gasped, hands tied behind him, rope biting into his neck. Sometimes he blacked out, but when he came round the voice was still there, hissing its insistent story into his ears.

"Slaves were what kept the salvage racket running. I was in charge of whole gangs of 'em. Power of life or death, I had. And then one arrived, a girl, who turned my head. Beautiful, she was. A poet notices these things. Hair like a waterfall of India ink. Skin the color of lamplight. Eyes like the Arctic night: black, but full of lights and mysteries. Get the picture, Caul? Of course, I'm only telling you this because you'll be fish food soon. I wouldn't want my Lost Boys thinking I was ever soft enough to fall in love. Softness and love won't do in a Lost Boy, Caul."

Caul thought of Freya Rasmussen, and wondered where she was and how her journey to America was going. For a moment he saw her so close and clear that he could almost feel her warmth, but Uncle's voice went whispering on, shattering the dream.

"Anna, this slave's name was. Anna Fang. It had a certain ring to it, for a poet. I kept her away from the hard, dangerous work, and got her good food, good clothes. I loved her, and she told me she loved me. I planned to free her and marry her, and not care what my family said about it. But it turned out my Anna was playing me for a fool the whole time. While I was mooning over her, she was sneaking around my salvage yards, setting aside an old airship envelope here, a couple of engine pods there; getting my workers to fit them to a gondola on the pretext I'd ordered it; selling the presents I gave her to buy fuel and lifting gas. And one day, while I was still trying to find something that rhymed with 'Fang' and a word to describe the precise color of her ears, they came to tell me she was gone. Built herself an airship out of all the bits she stole, see. And that was the end of my life in Arkangel. My family disowned me; the Direktor had me arrested for aiding a slave escape, and I was banished onto the ice with nothing: nothing."

Caul took little sips of air, but never quite enough to fill his lungs.

"Oh, it was character-building stuff, Caul. I took up with a gang of Snowmad scavengers who were bringing up salvage from the wreck of Grimsby. Killed 'em one by one. Nicked their submarine. Came down here. Started doing a spot of burgling, snapping up a few unconsidered trifles to replace all the things I'd lost. Snapped up information too, because I'd sworn by then that nobody would ever keep a secret from me again. So in a way, you could say she made me the man I am today, that witch Anna Fang."

The name, repeated and repeated, found its way through the swirls of colored lights that were exploding in Caul's head. "Fang," he tried to say.

"Exactly," whispered Uncle. "I worked out what was going on at Rogues' Roost a while ago. All those pictures turning up, and the way they were so keen to find the *Jenny Haniver*. Either they're setting up an Anna Fang museum, I told myself, or they've brought her back."

Caul remembered the listening post and the violent, confusing aftermath of the raid. A few cameras had still been functioning, and as their operators sought desperately for some trace of the burgling party, they had caught glimpses of the Stalker Fang, and picked up the sound of its terrible dead voice whispering of war.

"That's why I put so much effort into the Rogues' Roost job," Uncle said. "Just think of it! Burgling back the very person who'd led to my downfall all those years ago. My career turning back to its start, like a snake eating its tail! Poetic justice! I was going to bring that Stalkerette down here and reprogram her and set her slaving for me again, on and on, never resting, till the sun goes out and the world freezes over!

"And I'd've done it too. If you hadn't blown them crab-bombs when you did, and made Wrasse take his lads in too soon, it would all have worked out. But you spoiled it, Caul. You went and ruined everything."

"Please . . ." Caul managed to say, gathering enough breath with a great effort and shaping it carefully into a word. "Please . . ."

"Please what?" sneered Uncle. "Let you live? Let you die? Not after what you did, Caul, my lad. The boys have got to have someone to blame for what happened to Wrasse, and I'm damned if it's going to be me. So you'll hang there till you croak, and then you'll hang there till the smell gets too bad for even the Lost Boys to stick, and then we'll flush you out the water-door. Just to remind everybody that Uncle Knows Best."

A long sigh, a fumble of fingers against the microphone, then that flicked-balloon sound of the speaker switching off, and even the background hiss of static died. The rope creaked, the room spun, the sea pressed against the walls and windowpanes of Grimsby, looking for ways in. Caul drifted through blackness, woke, drifted again.

In his high chamber, Uncle watched the dying boy's face turn on a half dozen screens: close-up, medium close-up, long shot. He stifled a yawn and turned away. Even all-seeing eyes have to sleep sometimes, although he didn't like any but the most faithful of his boys to know about it. "Keep a good watch on him, Gargle," he said to his young assistant, and climbed the stairs to his bedchamber. The bed was almost hidden now by heaps of papers, by folders and files and books and documents in tin containers. Uncle snuggled under the counterpane (gold-embroidered, stolen from the Margrave of Kodz) and went quickly to sleep.

In his dreams, which were always the same, he was young again: exiled and penniless and brokenhearted.

When Caul next came round it was still night, and the rope that was strangling him had started to jerk and twist. He fought for breath, making horrible wet rattling sounds, and someone just above him hissed, "Stay still!"

He opened his good eye and looked up. In the shadows above his head a knife shone, sawing through the thick, tarry strands of the rope.

"Hey!" he tried to say.

The last strand broke. He fell through darkness, landed hard on the hull of the *Screw Worm*, and lay there gasping for breath with great helpless whooping sounds. He felt someone cut the cords on his wrists. Hands found his shoulders and rolled him over. Gargle was looking down at him.

Caul tried to speak, but his body was too busy breathing to bother with words.

"Pull yourself together," Gargle said softly. "You've got to go."

"Go?" croaked Caul. "But Uncle will see!"

Gargle shook his head. "Uncle's asleep."

"Uncle never sleeps!"

"That's what you think. Anyway, all the crab-cams that were watching you have gone wrong. I arranged it."

"But when he finds out what you've done—"

"He won't." Gargle's grin flashed white. "I hid the bits of the crabs I busted in Skewer's bunk. Uncle'll think Skewer did it."

"Skewer hates me! Uncle knows that!"

"No, he doesn't. I've been telling Uncle how well the two of you got on aboard the *Screw Worm*. How Skew only took charge because he was worried about you. How he'd do *anything* for you. Uncle thinks you and Skew are thick as thieves."

"Gods!" Caul said hoarsely, surprised at the newbie's cunning and appalled at the thought of what was going to happen to Skewer.

"I couldn't let Uncle kill you," Gargle said. "You were good to me aboard Anchorage. And that's where you belong, Caul. Take the *Screw Worm* and get back to Anchorage."

Caul massaged his throat. All his years of training were screaming at him that stealing a limpet was the most terrible sin a Lost Boy could contemplate. On the other hand, it felt good to be alive, and every breath that he drew into his starved lungs made him more determined to stay that way.

"Why Anchorage?" he said. "You heard Tom and Pennyroyal talking. Anchorage is doomed. And I'd not be welcome there anyway. Not a burglar like me."

"They'll welcome you, all right. When they find out how much they need you, they'll soon forget you ever burgled them. You'll want this." Gargle shoved something into his hand: a long tube of thin metal. "No time to talk, Caul," he said. "You don't belong here. You never belonged here, really. Now get into that limpet and clear off."

"Aren't you coming too?"

"Me? Course not. I'm a Lost Boy. I'm going to stay here and make myself useful to Uncle. He's an old man, Caul. His eyesight and his ears are going. He's going to need someone he can trust to run his cameras and his archives. Give me a few years and I'll be his right hand. A few more, and who knows? Maybe I'll be running Grimsby myself."

"That'd be good, Gargle," said Caul, laughing painfully. "I'd like to see you in charge of Grimsby. Put a stop to all that bullying."

"Put a stop to it?" Gargle wore a grin Caul hadn't seen before, a cold, sharp grin he didn't like at all. "Not likely! I'm going to be the biggest bully of them all! That's what kept me going, Caul, all the time Skewer and the others were roughing me up in the Burglarium. Thinking about what I'd do to them when my turn came."

Caul stared at him a moment longer, half inclined to believe that this was all just another dream. "Go," Gargle said again, and opened the *Screw Worm*'s hatch. Dream or not, there was no arguing with him; there was such a sureness in his voice that Caul felt like a newbie again, being ordered about by some confident older boy. He almost dropped the thing Gargle had given him, but Gargle caught it and thrust it at him again. "Go, and stay gone, and good luck!"

Caul took it and pulled himself weakly to the hatch and then inside and down the ladder, wondering how this battered tube of japanned tin was supposed to help him.

Anchorage

FREYA AWOKE EARLY AND LAY for a while in the dark, feeling her city shudder beneath her as it went bucketing over pressure ridges. Anchorage was far to the west of Greenland now, heading south over unknown ice and the humped, rocky backs of frozen islands. Several times Mr. Scabious had had to hoist up the drive wheel and let the cats haul the city across solid, snow-covered rocks and riven glaciers. Now sea ice stretched ahead of them again, reaching unbroken toward the horizon. Miss Pye thought it was Hudson Bay, the great ice plain that Professor Pennyroyal claimed would carry them into the heart of the Dead Continent, almost to the borders of his green places. But would it be strong enough to bear Anchorage's weight?

If only Professor Pennyroyal could tell us for sure, thought Freya, kicking off her covers and padding to the window. But

Pennyroyal had come this way on foot, and the descriptions in his book were really surprisingly vague. Miss Pye and Mr. Scabious had tried to make him go into more detail, but he had just grown sulky and rude, and after a while he had stopped coming to Steering Committee meetings altogether. In fact, ever since Hester had flown off in the *Jenny Haniver*, the good professor had been acting very oddly indeed.

A breath of cold blew in Freya's face as she parted the curtains to look out at the ice. Strange to think that this was the far side of the world! Stranger still to remember that soon they would be in the new hunting ground, and the views from her windows would all be green: grass and bushes and trees. The idea still scared her a little. Would the Ice Gods rule in lands where snow lay for only a few months of each year? Or would Anchorage need new gods?

A wedge of light yellowed the snow outside the Wheelhouse as a door opened and someone slipped out. Freya wiped away the fog her breath had made and put her face close to the glass. There was no mistaking that silhouette: a portly figure in heated robes and an outsize fur turban, creeping guiltily along Rasmussen Prospekt.

Even by Professor Pennyroyal's recent standards this was strange behavior. Freya dressed quickly, pulling on the simple, fleece-lined working clothes that were her usual outfit these days and pocketing a flashlight. She crept out of the palace without bothering to wake Smew. Pennyroyal was nowhere to be seen, but his deep, wandering footprints gaped in the snow, showing her the way he had gone.

A few months ago Freya would not have dared to venture out of the palace precincts alone, but she had changed a lot during the long journey around the top of Greenland. At first the shock of losing Tom had almost plunged her back into her old ways: staying in her quarters, seeing nobody, issuing her orders through Scabious or Smew. But she had soon grown bored, cooped up in the Winter Palace. She itched to know what was happening outside. And so she ventured out, and threw herself into the life of her city in ways she never had before. She sat gossiping with off-duty workers who ate their lunches in the heated pavilions on the edge of the upper city, watching the ice go by. She learned from Windolene Pye how to turn on the shower and wash herself, and clean her teeth, and she had cut her hair short. She joined the patrols that Scabious sent down onto the skid supports each morning to check for parasites; she drove cargo machines in the engine district; she had even gone out onto the ice ahead of Anchorage with a startled and rather embarrassed survey team. She had thrown away all her family's traditions with a feeling of relief that was like getting rid of old, ill-fitting clothes.

And now she was sneaking through the shadows on the starboard side of Rasmussen Prospekt, spying on her own chief navigator!

Ahead of her, the professor's gaudy turban made a sudden blotch of color against the dingy, ice-caked buildings as he slipped between the gates of the air harbor.

Freya ran after him, dashing from one patch of shadow to the next until she threw herself down in the shelter of the customs booth just inside the harbor gates. Wreathed in the mist of her own hot breath, she looked around, thinking for a moment that she had lost her quarry among these snowy hangars and docking pans. No—there he was! The bright blob of his turban bobbed under a streetlamp on the far side of the harbor, then blinked out as he stepped into the shadows at the entrance to Aakiuq's warehouse.

Freya crossed the harbor, tracing the jittery path of the explorer's footsteps through the snow. The warehouse door stood open. She paused a moment, peering nervously into the darkness inside and remembering the parasite boys who had used the dark as a cloak to haunt and plunder her city. But there was no danger now; the flashlight that she could see moving about in the far reaches of the warehouse did not belong to some malevolent ice pirate, just to an odd explorer.

She could hear his voice muttering in the dusty silence. Who was he talking to? Himself? Windolene Pye had told her that he'd drained the chief navigator's wine cellar and now stole liquor from the empty restaurants in the Ultima Arcade. Maybe he was drunk, and raving. She moved closer, easing her way between mountains of old engine parts.

"Pennyroyal calling anyone!" said his voice, low but desperate-sounding. "Pennyroyal calling anyone! Come in, please! Please!"

He crouched in a pool of green light cast by the glowing dials of an ancient radio set that he must somehow have managed to get working. Headphones were clamped over his ears, and his hand trembled slightly as it clutched the microphone. "Is there anybody out there? Please! I'll pay you anything! Just get me off this city of fools!"

"Professor Pennyroyal?" said Freya loudly.

"Warrgh! Clio! Poskitt! Knickers!" yelped the professor. He leaped up, and there was a sliding clatter as the cord of his headphones tugged an avalanche of old wireless components down around his feet. The light from the dials went out, and a few valves burst with little showers of sparks, like disappointing fireworks. Freya pulled out her flashlight and switched it on. Caught in the dusty beam, Pennyroyal's face looked pallid and sweaty, fear changing to a simpering smile as he squinted past the light and made out Freya.

"Your Radiance?"

Almost nobody bothered calling her that these days. Even Miss Pye and Smew called her Freya. How out of touch the professor had become!

"I'm glad to see you're keeping busy, Professor," she said. "Does Mr. Aakiuq know you're snooping about in his warehouse?"

"Snooping, Your Radiance?" Pennyroyal looked shocked. "A Pennyroyal never snoops! No, no, no . . . I was merely—I didn't want to trouble Mr. Aakiuq. . . ."

Freya's flashlight flickered, and she remembered that there probably weren't that many batteries left aboard Anchorage. She found a switch and turned on one of the argon lamps that swung from the rusty rafters overhead. Pennyroyal blinked in the sudden brightness. He looked terrible: pasty-skinned, red-eyed, a fuzz of white stubble blurring the neat edges of his beard.

"Who were you talking to?" she asked.

"To anyone. No one."

"And why do you want them to get you off this city of fools? I thought you were coming with us. I thought you were keen to return to the green valleys of America and the beautiful Zip Code, the chief's daughter."

She would not have thought it possible for him to get any paler, but he did. "Ah!" he said. "Um."

Sometimes, during the past few weeks, a horrible thought had come to Freya. It came at odd moments—when she was in the shower, or lying awake at three in the morning, or eating dinner with Miss Pye and Mr. Scabious—and she had never spoken of it to anyone else, although she was sure that they must have thought it too. Usually, when she felt it slithering into her mind, she tried to think about something else, because—well, it was silly, wasn't it?

Only it wasn't silly. It was the truth.

"You don't know the way to America, do you?" she asked, trying to keep the trembly sound out of her voice.

"Um."

"We've come all this way, following your advice and your book, and you don't know how to find your green valleys again. Or maybe there aren't even any to find? Have you ever *been* to America, Professor?"

"How dare you!" Pennyroyal was about to say, and then, as if realizing that there was no more mileage in lies, sighed and shook his head. "No. No, I made it all up." He sank down on an upturned engine cowling, miserable and defeated. "I never went anywhere, Your Radiance. I just read other people's books, and looked at pictures, and made it all up. I wrote *America the Beautiful* whilst lounging by a hotel swimming pool on the top tier of Paris, in the company of a delectable young person named Peaches Zanzibar. Took care to set it all somewhere nice and remote, of course. I never dreamed that anyone would actually want to *go* there."

"So why didn't you just admit it was all a fib?" asked

Freya. "When I appointed you chief navigator, why didn't you tell me it was all lies?"

"And pass up the chance of all that money, and posh apartments, and the chief navigator's wine cellar? I'm only human, Freya. Besides, if word got back to the Hunting Ground, I'd have been a laughingstock! I just thought I'd leave with Tom and Hester."

"That's why you were so upset when Hester took the *Jenny Haniver*!"

"Exactly! She cut off my escape route! I had no way off this city, and I couldn't admit what I'd done because you'd have killed me."

"I would not!"

"Well, your people would. So I've been using these old radios to try and call for help; hoped there might be a lost air trader or an exploration vessel within range, someone who could take me off."

It was remarkable how sorry he could feel for himself while not worrying at all about the city he had led to its doom. Freya shivered with anger. "You— You— You are dismissed, Professor Pennyroyal! You are no longer my chief navigator! You will hand back your ceremonial compasses and the keys to the Wheelhouse immediately!"

It didn't make her feel any better. She collapsed on a heap of old gaskets that creaked and shifted under her weight. How was she going to break this news to Miss Pye and Mr. Scabious and everybody else? That they were stuck on the wrong side of the world, with nothing ahead of them but a Dead Continent and not enough fuel to ever get home again, and that it was *she* who had brought them here! She had told everyone this voyage west was what the Ice Gods wanted, when all along it was only what *she* had wanted. If only she had not been taken in by Pennyroyal and his stupid book!

"What am I going to do?" she asked. "What am I going to do?"

Someone shouted something, out in the streets behind the air harbor. Pennyroyal looked up. There was a whirring, purring noise coming from somewhere. It was very faint, a muttering that rose and fell, sounding for all the world like—

"Aero-engines!" Pennyroyal leaped up, knocking over more heaps of spares in his haste to reach the door. "Thank Clio! We're saved!"

Freya ran after him, wiping away tears, tugging up her cold-mask. Outside, the dark had faded to a steely twilight. Pennyroyal was pounding away from her across the harbor, stopping once to turn and point as something slid across the sky beyond the harbor office. Freya squinted into the wind and saw a cluster of lights, a creamy trail of exhaust smoke smeared on the darkness. "Airship!" Pennyroyal yelled, doing a mad little dance in the middle of a snowy docking pan. "Someone heard my message! We're saved! Saved!"

Freya ran past him, trying to keep the machine in sight. The Aakiuqs were standing outside the harbor office, looking up. "An airship, all the way out here?" she heard the harbormaster say. "Who can it be?"

"Did the Ice Gods tell you they were coming, Freya, dear?" asked Mrs. Aakiuq.

A man called Lemuel Quaanik ran up, snowshoes flapping from his big feet. He was one of the surveyors with whom Freya had worked, and so he did not feel too much in awe of her to speak. "Radiance? I seen that ship before. That's Piotr Masgard's rig, the *Clear Air Turbulence*!"

"The Huntsmen of Arkangel!" gasped Mrs. Aakiuq.

"Here?" cried Freya. "It can't be! Arkangel would never hunt west of Greenland. There's nothing here for it to eat."

"There's us," said Mr. Quaanik.

The *Clear Air Turbulence* circled Anchorage, then hung off the stern like a lone wolf shadowing its prey. Freya ran to the Wheelhouse and up to the bridge. Windolene Pye was already there, still in her nightgown, with her long, graying hair undone. "It's the Huntsmen, Freya!" she said. "How did they find us? How in all the gods' names did they know where we were?"

"Pennyroyal," Freya said. "Professor Pennyroyal and his stupid broadcasts . . ."

"They're signaling," called Mr. Umiak, leaning out of the radio room. "They're ordering us to cut our engines."

Freya glanced sternward. In this half-light the ice was pale and faintly luminous. She could see the scumbled track of her city's stern wheel stretching away toward the northeast, fading into mist. There was no sign of pursuit, just that black ship, shifting and trembling as it rode the city's slipstream.

"Shall I answer them, Freya?"

"No! Pretend we haven't heard."

That didn't stop Piotr Masgard for long. The *Clear Air Turbulence* slid closer until it was hanging abreast of the Wheelhouse, and Freya stared out at it through the glass wall and saw the aviators bent over their controls on the flight deck and a gunner grinning at her from a little armored blister slung under the engine pods. She saw a hatch open and Piotr Masgard himself lean out, shouting something through a bullhorn.

Miss Pye opened a ventilator, and the big voice came booming in at them.

"Congratulations, people of Anchorage! Your city has been chosen as prey by great Arkangel! The Scourge of the North is a day's journey from here, and gaining fast. Shut down your engines and save us a chase, and you will be treated well."

"They can't eat us!" said Miss Pye. "Not now! Oh, it really is too bad!"

Freya felt a spreading numbness, as if she'd fallen into icy water. Miss Pye was looking at her, as was everyone else on the bridge, all waiting for the Gods of the Ice to speak through her and tell them what to do. She wondered if she should tell them the truth. It might be better to be eaten by Arkangel than to run on endlessly over this uncharted ice toward a continent that really was dead after all. Then she thought of all that she had heard about Arkangel, and the way it treated the people it ate, and she thought, *No, no, anything is better than that. I don't care if we fall through the ice or starve in dead America, they shall not have us!*

"Shut down your engines!" bellowed Masgard.

Freya looked east. If Arkangel had cut across the spine of Greenland, it might be as close as Masgard claimed, but Anchorage could still outrun it. The predator city would not want to venture far onto this uncharted ice plain. That was why they had resorted to sending out their Huntsmen. . . .

She had no loud-hailer to reply with, so she took a china-graph pencil from the chart table and wrote, in big letters on the back of a map, *NO!* "Miss Pye," she said, "please tell Mr. Scabious, Full Speed Ahead!"

Miss Pye stepped to the speaking tubes. Freya pressed her message to the glass. She saw Masgard strain to read it, and the way his face changed when he understood. He went back inside his gondola and slammed the hatch shut, and the airship veered away.

"What can they do, after all?" said one of the navigators. "They won't attack us, for they'd risk damaging the very things they want to eat us for."

"I bet Arkangel is much more than a day away!" declared Miss Pye. "That great lumbering urbivore! They must be desperate, or they wouldn't have to send out spoiled toffs to play at air pirates. Well, Freya, you called their bluff, all right. We shall outrun them easily!"

The *Clear Air Turbulence* dropped down into the sleet of powdered ice behind the city and fired a flight of rockets into the larboard supports of the stern wheel. Smoke, sparks, flames spewed from Anchorage's stern; the axle gave way, and the wheel fell sideways and slewed across the ice, still attached by a tangle of drive chains and twisted stanchions at its starboard end, an anchor of wreckage that brought the city skidding and shuddering to a standstill.

"Quickly!" shouted Freya, feeling panic rise in her as the lights of the airship lifted out of the fading cloud of ice astern. "Get us moving again! Lower the cats. . . ."

Miss Pye was at the speaking tubes, listening to the garbled reports from below. "Oh, Freya, we can't; the wheel is too heavy to drag—it must be cut away, and Søren says that will take hours!"

"But we don't have hours!" screamed Freya, and then realized that they didn't have even minutes. She clung to Miss Pye, and together they stared toward the air harbor. The *Clear Air Turbulence* landed there just long enough to vomit out a score of dark, armored figures who went hurrying down the stairways to secure the engine district. Then she was aloft again, hanging in the sky above the Wheelhouse. The glass walls gave way under the boots of more men, swinging down on ropes from her gondola. They crashed onto the bridge in a spray of glittering fragments, a blur of screams, shouts, and swords bright in the lamplight. The chart table overturned. Freya had lost Miss Pye. She ran for the elevator, but someone was there ahead of her, fur and armor and a grinning face and big, gloved hands reaching out to catch her, and all she could think was *All this way! We've come all this way, only to be eaten!*

31

The
Knife
Drawer

A FEW HUNDRED FEET BELOW the *Jenny Haniver*'s gondola,
vast rough pans of sea ice were sliding by, crisscrossed with
dikes and jagged, shattered ridges. Tom and Hester, looking
down from the flight-deck windows at the never-ending
whiteness, felt as if they had been flying forever over this
armored ocean.

The day after their escape from Rogues' Roost, they had
set down at a tiny Snowmad whaling station and bought fuel
with the last of Pennyroyal's sovereigns. Since then they had
just been flying north and west in search of Anchorage. They
had not slept much, for fear of the fallen aviatrix who stalked
their dreams. They stayed on the flight deck, nibbling stale
cookies, drinking coffee, telling each other in awkward little
bursts of the things they had each seen since they parted.

They did not speak of Hester's flight from Anchorage, or

of what caused it. They had not mentioned it since that first night, when they lay all breathless and shivery and tangled together on the hard deck, and Hester in a small voice had said, "There's something I haven't explained. After I left you, I did something terrible. . . ."

"You got upset and flew off," Tom said, misunderstanding. He was so glad to have her back that he didn't want to risk an argument, so he tried to make it sound as if it had been a small thing, and easy to forgive.

Hester shook her head. "I don't mean—" But she could not explain.

So they had flown on, day after day, over rippled sea ice and deep-frozen land, until today, when Tom said suddenly, "I didn't mean what happened, with me and Freya. When we get to Anchorage, it won't be like last time, I promise. We'll just warn them about Arkangel coming, and then we'll take off again. Head for the Hundred Islands or somewhere, just the two of us, like it used to be."

Hester just shook her head. "It's too dangerous, Tom. There's a war coming. Maybe not this year or next, but soon, and bad, and it's too late to do anything about it. And the League still believes we burned its Northern Air Fleet, and the Green Storm will blame us for the attack on Rogues' Roost, and that Stalker won't always be around to protect us."

"Then where can we go that will be safe?"

"Anchorage," said Hester. "We'll find a way to keep Anchorage safe, and lie low there for a few years, and then, maybe . . ."

But even if there was some way to save the city, she knew that there was no place aboard it for her. She would leave Tom there, safe with Freya, and fly on alone. Anchorage was good and kind and peaceful: no place for Valentine's daughter.

That night, as the lights of the Aurora danced above him, Tom looked down through a gap in the clouds and saw a great scar drawn across the ice below, hundreds of deep, parallel grooves stretching eastward into clouded uplands and vanishing west into the empty night.

"City tracks!" he shouted, hurrying to wake Hester.

"Arkangel," said Hester. She felt sick and frightened. The wide wake of the predator city brought back to her just how immense it was. How could she hope to stop something like that?

They swung the *Jenny* onto Arkangel's course. An hour later, Tom picked up the harsh scream of the predator's homing beacon slicing through the static on the radio, and soon they saw its lights twinkling in the mist ahead of them.

The city was moving at quarter speed, with a screen of survey vehicles and stripped-down drone-suburbs spread out ahead of it to test the ice. Airships hung about it, mostly traders leaving the air harbor and turning east, reluctant to let Arkangel carry them so far off the edges of all maps. Tom wanted to talk to them, but Hester warned him off. "You can't trust the sort of ships that deal with Arkangel," she said. She was afraid one of the traders might recognize her and let Tom know what she had done. She said, "Let's stay well clear of the place and keep moving."

They stayed clear and kept moving, and the glow of Arkangel dwindled into the dark behind them as snow began blowing in from the north. But as the signal of its beacon began to fade, it was replaced by another, very faint at first but growing louder, coming from somewhere on the ice ahead. They stared into the dark while the wind boomed against the *Jenny*'s envelope and snowflakes padded at her windows. Faint and far away, a cluster of lights sparkled, and the long, somber note of the homing beacon curled up out of the static, lonely as the cry of wolves.

"It's Anchorage."

"It's not moving!"

"Something's wrong. . . ."

"We're too late!" cried Tom. "Don't you remember? Arkangel sends its Huntsmen to capture the towns it wants to eat. That brute we met at Airhaven! He turns them around and steers them into its jaws. . . . We'll have to turn back. If we land there, the Huntsmen will hold us until Arkangel arrives, and the *Jenny* will be eaten along with the city. . . ."

"No," said Hester. "We've got to land. We've got to do something." She looked at Tom, longing to tell him why this was so important to her. She knew now that if she were to redeem herself, she would have to fight the Huntsmen, and that she would very probably be killed. She wanted to explain to Tom about her deal with Masgard, and have him forgive her. But what if he couldn't forgive? What if he just pushed her away, horrified? The words crouched in her mouth, but she dared not let them out.

Tom cut the *Jenny*'s engines and let the wind carry her silently closer. He was touched by Hester's sudden, surprising concern for the ice city. He had not quite realized, until he saw it again, how much he'd missed it. His eyes filled with tears, making the lights of the Wheelhouse and the Winter

Palace flare into spidery patterns. "Everything's lit up like a Quirkemas tree. . . ."

"That's so Arkangel can see it," Hester said. "Masgard and his Huntsmen must've stopped the engines and switched on all the lights and the homing beacon. They're probably waiting in Freya's palace right now for their city to arrive."

"And what about Freya?" asked Tom. "What about all the people?"

Hester had no answer to that.

The air harbor looked unusually well lit and welcoming, but there was no question of landing there. Hester doused the *Jenny*'s running lights and left the flying to Tom, who had always been so much better at it than her. He took the *Jenny* so low that the keel of the gondola was almost scraping the ice before he jerked her suddenly upward again, slipping her through a narrow gap between two warehouses on the larboard edge of the lower tier. The clang of the docking clamps sounded horribly loud on the flight deck, but no one came running to see what had happened, and when they ventured outside, they found nothing moving in the silent, snow-deep streets.

They climbed quickly and quietly to the air harbor, not speaking, wrapped in their different memories of this city. The *Clear Air Turbulence* was docked on an open pan near the middle of the harbor, the wolf mark of Arkangel shining red on her envelope. A fur-clad guard stood watch beside her, and there was light and movement behind the windows of the gondola.

Tom looked at Hester. "What are we going to do?"

She shook her head, not yet sure. Tom followed her

through the spills of thick shadow behind the fuel tanks, and they let themselves in at the back door of the harbormaster's house. Here there was darkness, broken only by the glow of the harbor lights seeping in through frosty windows. A tornado seemed to have swept the once-tidy parlor and kitchen, smashing the collection of commemorative plates, shattering crockery, dashing the portraits of the Aakiuqs' children from the household shrine. The antique wolf rifle that used to hang on the parlor wall was gone, and the stove was cold. Hester crunched over the broken fragments of beaming Rasmussen faces to the cupboard and opened the knife drawer.

Behind her a loose stair creaked. Tom, who was closest to the staircase, whirled around in time to see the gray smudge of a face peering down at him between the banisters. It was gone almost at once as whoever was hiding there went scrambling up toward the second floor. Tom shouted in surprise and quickly clamped a hand over his mouth, remembering the man outside. Hester shoved roughly past him, Mrs. Aakiuq's sharpest kitchen knife a dull gleam in her hand. There was a confused tussle in the tigerish shadows behind the banisters, a voice gasping, "Mercy! Spare me!" and the slithering thuds of a heavy body dragged back down the stairs by the seat of its trousers. Hester stood back, panting, the knife still ready, and Tom looked down at her captive.

It was Pennyroyal. Filthy and straggle-haired, white bristles thick in the hollows of his face, the explorer seemed to have aged ten years while they'd been away, as though time had passed faster aboard Anchorage than in the outside world. He whimpered slightly, his bulging eyes darting between their faces. "Tom? Hester? Gods and Goddesses, I thought you were more of those damned Huntsmen. But how did you come here? Have you got the *Jenny* with you? Oh, thank heavens! We must leave at once!"

"What's been happening here, Professor?" asked Tom. "Where is everybody?"

Pennyroyal, still keeping a wary eye on Hester's knife hand, dragged himself into a more comfortable position, leaning back against the newel-post. "The Huntsmen of Arkangel, Tom. Aero-hooligans, led by that scoundrel Masgard. They arrived about ten hours ago, smashed the drive wheel, and took charge of the city."

"Anyone dead?" asked Hester.

Pennyroyal shook his head. "Don't think so. They wanted to keep everyone in good shape for their beastly slave holds, so they just rounded them all up and imprisoned them in the Winter Palace while they wait for their city to catch up. A few of Scabious's brave fellows tried to argue and got roughed up pretty badly, but otherwise I don't think anyone's been hurt."

"And you?" Hester leaned forward into the light and let him feel her Gorgon stare. "How come you're not locked up with the others?"

Pennyroyal flicked a narrow, watery smile at her. "Oh, you know the motto of the Pennyroyals, Miss Shaw: 'When the Going Gets Tough, the Sensible Conceal Themselves Beneath Large Items of Furniture.' I happened to be at the air harbor when they landed. With typical quick thinking, I nipped in here and hid under the bed. Didn't emerge until it was all over. I've thought of presenting myself to young Masgard, of course, and claiming the finder's fee, but frankly

I don't think he can be trusted, so I've been lying low ever since."

"What finder's fee?" asked Tom.

"Oh, ah . . ." Pennyroyal looked a little shamefaced and tried to hide it with his old, roguish smile. "Thing is, Tom, I think it was me who brought the Huntsmen here."

For no reason that Tom could understand, Hester started to laugh.

"I only sent a couple of harmless distress calls!" the explorer complained. "I never imagined Arkangel would pick them up! Who ever heard of a radio signal traveling that far? Some freak of these boreal climes, no doubt. . . . Anyway, it's done me no good, as you can see. I've been holed up here for *hours*, hoping to sneak aboard that Huntsman airship and make a break for it, but there's a dirty great sentry guarding it, and a couple more inside. . . ."

"We saw," said Tom.

"Still," the explorer went on, brightening, "now that you're back with your *Jenny Haniver*, it doesn't matter, does it? When do we leave?"

"We don't," said Hester. Tom turned to look at her, unsettled by her response, and she went on quickly, "How can we? We owe it to the Aakiuqs, and Freya and everybody. We've got to rescue them."

She left them staring at her and went to the kitchen window, peering out through the prisms of the frost. Aimless snowflakes eddied in the cones of light beneath the harbor lamps. She imagined the guards aboard their ship, their comrade out on the docking pan stamping the cold from his toes, the rest of Masgard's crew up in the Winter Palace warming themselves with the contents of the Rasmussens' wine cellar. They would be dozy and confident and not expecting trouble. They would have been no match for Valentine. Perhaps, if she had inherited enough of his strength and cruelty and cunning, they would be no match for her.

"Hester?" Tom stood close behind her, frightened by her icy mood. It was usually he who came up with rash plans to help the helpless. Hearing Hester suggest such a thing made him feel as if the world had come off its bearings. He laid his hand gently on her shoulder, and felt her stiffen and start to flinch away. "Hester, there are loads of them, and only three of us. . . ."

"Make that two," Pennyroyal chipped in. "I don't want any part of your suicidal scheme. . . ."

Hester had the knife at his throat in one swift movement. Her hand trembled slightly, setting the reflections shivering on the blade's bright edge.

"You'll do what I tell you," said Valentine's daughter, "or I'll kill you myself."

Valentine's Daughter

"EAT UP, LITTLE MARGRAVINE!" called Piotr Masgard from the far end of the table, waving at Freya with a half-eaten chicken leg.

Freya stared down at her plate, where the food was beginning to congeal. She wished she were still penned in the ballroom with the others, eating whatever slops and scraps the Huntsmen had given them, but Masgard had insisted that she dine with him. He said that he was only showing her the courtesy she deserved, and that it would hardly do for a margravine to eat with her people, would it? As leader of Arkangel's Huntsmen it was his duty, and his pleasure, to entertain her at his own table.

Except that the table was Freya's, in her own dining room, and the food had come from her own larders and been cooked in her own kitchens by poor Smew. And every time she glanced up, she met Masgard's blue eyes, amused and appraising, full of pride at his catch.

In the first horrible confusion of the attack on the Wheelhouse, she had consoled herself by thinking, *Scabious will never stand for this; he and his men will fight and save us.* But when she and her fellow captives were herded into the ballroom and she saw how many of her people were already waiting there, she understood that it had all happened too quickly. Scabious's men had been surprised, or busy fighting the fires the rocket attack had started. Evil had triumphed over good.

"Great Arkangel will be with us in a few more hours," Masgard had announced, circling the huddle of prisoners while his men stood watchful guard, with guns and cross-bows at the ready. His words boomed from the loudspeaker horns on his lieutenant's helmet. "Behave yourselves and you may look forward to healthy, productive lives in the gut. Attempt to resist and you will die. This city is a pretty enough prize; I can afford to sacrifice a few slaves if you insist on making me prove how serious I am."

Nobody insisted. The people of Anchorage weren't used to violence, and the Huntsmen's brutal faces and steam-powered guns were enough to convince them. They huddled together in the center of the ballroom, wives clinging to hus-bands, mothers trying to stop their children from crying or talking or doing anything that might draw them to the atten-tion of the guards. When Masgard called for the margravine to dine with him, Freya thought it wisest to accept: anything to keep him in a good mood.

Still, she thought, prodding at her rapidly cooling meal, *if dinner with Masgard is the worst I have to endure, I shall have got off lightly.* It didn't feel that light, though, not when she glanced up at him and felt the air between them crawling with threat. Her stomach lurched, and she thought for a moment that she was going to be sick. As an excuse not to eat, she tried making conversation. "So how *did* you find us, Mr. Masgard?"

Masgard grinned, blue eyes almost hidden under their heavy lids. He had been a little disappointed when he got here—the townspeople had given up far too easily, and Freya's bodyguard had turned out to be a little joke of a man, not worthy of Masgard's sword—but he was determined to be gallant to his captive margravine. He felt big and handsome and victorious, sitting there in Freya's throne at the head of the table, and he had a feeling that he was impressing her. "How do you know it's not my natural skill at hunting that led me to you?" he asked.

Freya managed a stiff little smile. "That's not the way you work, is it? I've heard about you. Arkangel's so desperate for prey that you pay people to squeak on other cities."

"Squeal."

"What?"

"You mean 'squeal on other cities.' If you want to use underdeck slang, Your Radiance, you should at least get it right."

Freya blushed. "It was Professor Pennyroyal, wasn't it? Those stupid radio messages he sent. He told me he was just trying to reach a passing explorer or a merchantman, but I suppose he's been signaling to you all along."

"Professor *who*?" Masgard laughed again. "No, my dear, it

was a *flying* rat who did the squealing."

Freya felt her eyes dragged toward his again. "Hester!"

"And you know the best part? She didn't even want gold in exchange for your city. Just some boy, some worthless scrap of air trash. Name of Natsworthy . . ."

"Oh, *Hester*!" whispered Freya. She had always thought that girl was trouble, but she'd never imagined her capable of such a terrible thing. To betray a whole city just to keep hold of a boy you didn't deserve, who'd have been much better off with someone else! She tried not to let Masgard see her rage, because he'd only laugh. She said, "Tom's gone. Dead, I think . . ."

"He's had a lucky escape, then." Masgard chuckled through a mouthful of food. "Not that it matters. His quail's vanished; she flew off before the ink was dry on her contract. . . ."

The door of the dining room banged open, and Freya forgot about Hester and turned to see what was happening. One of Masgard's men—the fellow with the loudspeaker horns—stood in the doorway. "Fire, my lord!" he gasped. "Up at the harbor!"

"What?" Masgard went to the window, tearing the thick drapes aside. Snow whirled across the gardens outside, and behind it a red glare flickered and spread, throwing the gables and ducts on the roofs of Rasmussen Prospekt into sharp silhouette. Masgard rounded on his lieutenant. "Any word from Garstang and his boys at the harbor?"

The Huntsman shook his head.

"Fangs of the Wolf!" bellowed Masgard. "Someone set that blaze! They're attacking our ship!" He drew his sword, pausing next to Freya's chair on his way to the door. "If any of your verminous townspeople have harmed the *Clear Air Turbulence*, I'll skin them alive and sell their hides as hearth-rugs."

Freya tried to make herself small, pressing down into her chair. "It can't be one of my people; you are holding them all. . . ." But even as she said it, she thought of Professor Pennyroyal. She hadn't seen him in the ballroom. Perhaps he was free? Perhaps he was doing something to help? It seemed unlikely, but it was the only scrap of hope she had, and she clung to it while Masgard heaved her out of her chair and flung her at his lieutenant.

"Take her back to the ballroom!" he shouted. "Where are Ravn and Tor and Skaet?"

"Still guarding the main entrance, my lord."

Masgard ran, and left the other man to drag Freya out of the dining room and shove her along the graceful curve of the corridor toward the ballroom. She supposed she should try to escape, but her guard was so big and strong, and so well armed, that she didn't dare. Her relatives' portraits stared down at her as she passed, looking as if they were disappointed in her for not fighting back. She said, "I hope somebody *has* set fire to your precious airship!"

"Won't make any difference to us," her guard growled. "It's you who'll suffer for it. Arkangel'll be here soon. We won't need an airship to get off your stinking town once it's in the Scourge's belly!"

As they neared the ballroom door, Freya could hear a rising babble of voices coming from inside. The captives must have seen the fire too, and were talking excitedly while their guards hollered for quiet. Then something flashed past her head, and Masgard's lieutenant went backward without a cry. Freya thought he'd slipped, but when she turned there was a crossbow bolt jutting from the front of his helmet and a thick dribble of blood starting to drip from one of the horns.

"Eww!" she said.

In an alcove beside the ballroom door a long shape unfolded itself from the shadows.

"Professor Pennyroyal?" Freya whispered. But it was Hester Shaw, already fitting a fresh bolt into the big crossbow she was carrying.

"You're back!" gasped Freya.

"Oh, what a clever piece of deduction, Your Radiance."

Freya flushed with anger. How dare the girl mock her? It was her fault this was happening! "You sold our course! How could you? How *could* you?"

"Well, I've changed my mind," said Hester. "I'm here to help."

"*Help?*" Freya was speaking in a hoarse, furious whisper, fearful that the guards in the ballroom would overhear. "How can you *help*? The best help you could have given us was to have never come anywhere near my city! We don't need you! Tom didn't need you! You're selfish and wicked and cold and you don't care about anybody but your horrible self. . . ."

She stopped talking. They had each remembered, at the same instant, that Hester was holding a loaded crossbow, and that with a slight twitch of her finger she could pin Freya to the wall. She considered it for a moment, touching the tip of the bolt to Freya's breast. "You're right," she whispered. "I'm evil. I take after my dad that way. But I do care about Tom, and that means I have to care about you and your stupid city as well. And I think you need me now."

She lowered the crossbow and glanced down at the man she had just killed. There was a gas pistol stuffed into his belt. "Do you know how to use that thing?" she asked.

Freya nodded. Her tutors had gone in more for etiquette and deportment than small-arms training, but she thought she grasped the general idea.

"Then come with me," said Hester, and said it with such an air of command that it never occurred to Freya to disobey.

The hardest part so far had been getting rid of Tom. She did not want to lead him into danger, and she could not be Valentine's daughter if he was with her. In the dark of the Aakiuqs' parlor she had pulled him close to her and said, "Do you know any back ways into that Winter Palace? If the place is crawling with Huntsmen, we can't just walk up to the main entrance and announce we're here to see Masgard."

Tom thought for a moment, then fumbled in the pockets of his coat and drew out a small, shining object that she'd never seen before. "It's a lockpick from Grimsby. Caul's people gave it to me. I bet I can get in through the little heat-lock behind the Wunderkammer!"

He looked so excited and pleased with himself that Hester couldn't stop herself from kissing him. When she'd finished, she said, "Go, then. Wait for me in the Wunder-kammer."

"What? Aren't you coming?" He didn't look excited now, only scared.

She touched her fingers to his mouth to hush him. "I'm going to scout around by the airship."

"But the guards—"

She tried to look as if she weren't frightened. "I was Grike's apprentice, remember? He taught me a lot of stuff I've never got around to using. I'll be all right. Now go."

He started to say something and then gave up, hugged her, and hurried away. For a second or two she felt relieved to be alone; then she suddenly needed very badly to have Tom back, to be in his arms and tell him all sorts of things she should have said before. She ran to the back door, but he was already out of sight, following some secret route toward the palace.

She whispered his name to the snow. She did not expect to see him again. She felt as if she were sliding too fast toward an abyss.

Pennyroyal was still crouching at the bottom of the stairs. Hester pushed her way back past him into the kitchen and took an oil lamp from a cupboard above the sink. "What are you doing?" he hissed as she lit it. The yellow glow gathered slowly behind the smoky glass, then spread, lapping across the walls and windows and Pennyroyal's soap-pale face. "Masgard's men will see!"

"That's the idea," said Hester.

"I won't help you!" the explorer quavered. "You can't make me! This is madness!"

She didn't bother with the knife this time, just pushed her gargoyle face close to his and said, "It was me, Pennyroyal." She wanted him to understand just how ruthless she could be. "Not you. I'm the one who sent the Huntsmen here."

"You? But Great Poskitt Almighty, *why?*"

"For Tom," said Hester simply. "Because I wanted Tom for myself again. He was to be my predator's gold. Only it didn't go how I planned, and now I've got to try and put things right."

Footsteps crunched through the snow outside the kitchen window, and there was a sigh as the outer heat-lock was tugged open. Hester slid backward into the shadows beside the door as the sentry from the docking pans pushed his way into the room, so close that she could feel the breath of cold coming off his snow-caked furs.

"On your feet!" he barked at Pennyroyal, and turned to check for other fugitives. In the instant before he saw her, Hester stuck out her arm and pushed her knife into the gap between the top of his armor and the bottom of his cold-mask. He made a gargling noise, and the twisting of his big body dragged the knife handle out of Hester's grasp. She flinched sideways as his crossbow went off, and heard the bolt slam through a cupboard door behind her. The Huntsman was groping at his belt for his own knife. She grabbed his arm and tried to stop him. There was no sound but their harsh breathing and the crunch of crockery under their feet as they stumbled to and fro, with Pennyroyal scrambling to keep out of their way. The Huntsman's wide green eyes stared out at Hester through the windows in his mask, furious and indignant, until at last he seemed to focus on something very far away beyond her, and his gargling stopped and he fell sideways, almost pulling her down with him. His feet kicked for a while; then he was still.

Hester had never killed anyone before. She had expected to feel guilty, but she didn't. She didn't feel anything. *This is what it was like for my father*, she thought, helping herself to the dead man's cloak and fur hat and pulling on his cold-mask. *Just a job that had to be done to keep his city and his loved one safe. This is how he felt after he killed Mum and Dad. Clear and hard and clean, like glass.* She took the Huntsman's crossbow and its quiver of bolts and said to Pennyroyal, "Bring the lamp."

"But, but, but—!"

Outside, snow swarmed like white moths under the harbor lamps. Crossing the docking pans, shoving the terrified Pennyroyal ahead of her, she glanced through a slot between two hangars and saw a big, far-off smudge of light on the eastern sky.

The hatchway of the *Clear Air Turbulence* stood open. Another Huntsman was waiting there. "What is it, Garstang?" he shouted. "Who've you found?"

"Just an old geezer," Hester yelled back, hoping that the cold-mask would muffle her voice, the fur cloak disguise her skinny outline.

"Just some old man," the Huntsman said, turning to speak to someone inside the gondola. Then, louder, "Take him to the palace, Garstang! Shove him in with the others! We don't want him."

"Please, Mr. Huntsman!" Pennyroyal shouted suddenly. "It's a trap! She's—"

Hester swung the crossbow up and squeezed the trigger, and the Huntsman went screaming backward. As his comrades tried to push their way out past his thrashing body, Hester grabbed the oil lamp from Pennyroyal and lobbed it in through the hatch. A Huntsman's cloak caught light, and fire blazed up inside the gondola. Pennyroyal shrieked in terror and fled. Hester turned to follow, but after two steps she found that she was flying, lifted up by a hot wind from behind and dumped into snow that was white no longer but a Halloween dazzle of saffron and red. There was no bang, just a great, soft *woof* as the gas cells caught. She rolled over in the snow and looked back. Men were scrambling from the burning gondola, slapping at the sparks that burrowed through the fur of their coats and cloaks. There were only two of them. One ran toward Hester, making her fumble for her fallen crossbow, but he didn't look at her, just clumped past shouting something about saboteurs, and she had plenty of time to slip another bolt into the bow and shoot him in the back. There was no sign of Pennyroyal. She circled the burning airship and met the last of the Huntsmen in a place where the smoke was thick and dark. Took the sword from his hand while he was dying. Thrust it through her belt. Ran toward Rasmussen Prospekt and the lights of the Winter Palace.

Uncle's device made tiny clicking sounds in the keyhole, and the heat-lock opened. Tom slipped inside, breathing in the familiar smells of the palace. The corridor was deserted; not even a footprint in the thick dust. He hurried through shadows to the Wunderkammer, where the Stalker skeletons scared him all over again, but the lockpick worked on that door too, and he padded into the cobwebby silence between the display cases feeling shaky but proud of himself.

The square of foil shone with a soft light, reminding him very clearly of Freya, and of the crab-cam that had watched from one of those grilles in the heating ducts overhead as he kissed her. "Caul?" he said hopefully, peering up into the dark. But there were no burglars aboard Anchorage now, just Huntsmen. He felt suddenly, suffocatingly afraid about what Hester was doing. He hated to think of her out there, in danger, while he waited here. There was a flickery glow in the sky, somewhere near the harbor. What was happening? Should he go and look?

No. Hester had said she would meet him here. She had never let him down before. He tried to distract himself by choosing a weapon from the display on the wall: a heavy, blunt sword with an ornate hilt and scabbard. Once it was in his hand, he felt braver. He paced to and fro between the cases of moth-eaten animals and old machines, swinging the sword, waiting for her to come so that they could save Anchorage together.

It was only when the gun battle began in the ballroom and the shouts and shots and screams came booming along the palace corridors that he realized she had come in through the main entrance anyway, and had started without him.

The gas pistol was heavier than Freya had expected. She tried to imagine shooting it at someone, but she couldn't. She wondered if she should explain to Hester how scared she was, but there didn't seem to be time. Hester was already at the door of the ballroom, beckoning Freya forward with quick jerks of her head. Her hair and her clothes stank of smoke.

Together, they heaved the big door open. Nobody turned to see them enter. Huntsmen and prisoners alike were watching the windows and the great sinuous wings of fire that swayed above the harbor. Freya clutched the gun with sweaty hands, waiting for Hester to shout "Hands up!" or "Nobody move!" or whatever it was one was supposed to say in situations like this. Instead, Hester just lifted her crossbow and shot the nearest Huntsman in the back.

"Hey, that's not—" Freya started to say, and then flung herself to the floor, because as the dead man pitched forward, the man beside him turned and sprayed a long burst of gunfire at her. She kept forgetting this was all real. She squirmed on the floor and heard the bullets kick chunks out of the door and skip off the marble beside her. Hester snatched the pistol out of her hand, and the Huntsman's face turned into a splash of red. Smew pulled his gun away from him as he fell and turned it on a third guard, caught in the swirling panic of the captives. "Rasmussen!" somebody shouted, and suddenly the whole room took up the shout, the ancient war cry of Anchorage, left over from times when Freya's ancestors had led battles against air pirates and the Stalkers of the Nomad Empires. "Rasmussen!" There were shots, a scream, a long, rattling xylophone trill as a dying Huntsman crashed against one of the mothballed chandeliers. It was all over very quickly. Windolene Pye began organizing people to tend to the wounded while men helped themselves to the dead Huntsmen's swords and sidearms.

"Where's Scabious?" shouted Hester, and somebody pushed him toward her. The enginemaster looked eager and clutched a captured gun. She said, "Arkangel's coming. I could see its lights from the air harbor. You'll need to get this old place moving pretty quickly."

Scabious nodded. "But there're Huntsmen in the engine district, and the stern wheel's shot. We can't do more than quarter speed on the cats alone, and we can't even do that until the wreckage of the stern wheel's cut away."

"Get cutting, then," said Hester, discarding her crossbow and drawing her sword.

Scabious thought of a thousand other questions, then shrugged them away and nodded. He started for the stairways with half of Anchorage behind him, those without weapons grabbing chairs and bottles as they passed. Freya, frightened as she was, felt she should go with them and lead the attack like one of those long-ago margravines. She joined the growing rush toward the door, but Hester grabbed her, stopped her. "You stay here. Your people are going to need you alive. Where's Masgard?"

"I don't know," said Freya. "I think he was heading for the main entrance."

Hester nodded, a quick, small tic of a nod that could have meant anything. "Tom's in the museum," she said.

"Tom's here?" Freya was having trouble keeping up.

"Please, Your Radiance, keep him safe when all this is over."

"But . . ." Freya started to say, but Hester was gone, the bullet-riddled door swinging shut behind her. Freya wondered if she should follow, but what could she do against Masgard? She turned back into the ballroom and saw a knot of people still cowering there: the very old and young, the injured, and those who were just too scared to join the fight. Freya knew how they felt. She screwed up her hands into tight fists to stop them from shaking and put on her best margravine's smile. "Don't be afraid. The Ice Gods are with us."

❀ ❀ ❀

Tom, heading for the ballroom, met Scabious and his people pouring toward him, a dark tumble of running limbs, light glinting on metal, a pale surf of set faces stark in the lamp-light. They filled the corridor like the sea pouring into a foundering ship. Tom was afraid that they would mistake him for a Huntsman, but Scabious saw him and shouted his name, and the tide picked him up and swept him along, the surf breaking into grinning remembered faces: Aakiuq, Probsthain, Smew. People reached out to pat his shoulders, punch his chest. "Tom!" shouted Smew, tugging at his waist. "It's good to see you back!"

"Hester!" Tom yelled, struggling in the tide as it carried him out of the palace. "Where's Hester?"

"She saved us, Tom!" Smew shouted, running ahead. "What a nerve! Came into that ballroom and cut down the Huntsmen, merciless as a Stalker! What a girl!"

"But where— Mr. Scabious, is she with you?"

His words were lost in the clatter of feet and the shouts of "Rasmussen, Rasmussen!" as the crowd swept past him and away, funneling down a stairway toward the engine district. He heard shouts and gunshots echoing under the low roof, and wondered if he should go and try to help, but the thought of Hester held him back. Calling her name, he ran through the Boreal Arcade and out into the swirling snow on Rasmussen Prospekt. Two lines of footprints dotted the snow, leading toward the air harbor. As he hesitated, wondering whether one of the tracks was Hester's, he saw a face watching him from the doorway of a shop on the far side of the street.

"Professor Pennyroyal?"

Pennyroyal darted sideways, stumbling in the snow, and vanished into a narrow alleyway between two boutiques. Coins sprayed from his fists as he went. He had been filling his pockets with loose change from the shop's cash register.

"Professor!" shouted Tom, sheathing his sword and running after him. "It's only me! Where's Hester?"

The explorer's clumsy footprints led to the tier's edge, where a stairway descended to the lower city. Tom hurried down it, setting his feet in the big, bearlike prints of Pennyroyal's luxury snow boots. Near the bottom he stopped suddenly, his heart beating fast, startled by a glimpse of black wings, but it was not a Stalker-bird, only the sign outside a tavern called the Spread Eagle. He jogged on, wondering if he would have a fear of birds forevermore.

"Professor Pennyroyal?"

Masgard had not been waiting at the palace entrance, among the bodies of the men Hester had killed on her way in. *Maybe Scabious's lot got him,* she thought. Or maybe he had heard the sounds of fighting and figured out which way the wind was blowing. Maybe he was hurrying back to the harbor in the hope of finding a ship there that could take him home to Arkangel.

She pushed her way out through the heat-lock. The cold-mask cut off her peripheral vision, so she threw it away and went down the slope onto Rasmussen Prospekt, with the snowflakes stroking her face like cold fingers. A long line of fresh footprints reached away from her, already filling with snow. She followed them, measuring the long strides. Ahead, a man was silhouetted against the dying glare from the air harbor. It was Masgard. She quickened her pace, and as she drew closer, she could hear him calling the names of his dead companions. "Garstang? Gustavsson? Sprüe?" She could hear the panic rising in his voice. He was just a rich city boy who enjoyed playing pirates and had never expected anyone to stand up to him. He'd come looking for a fight, and now that a fight had found him, he didn't know what to do with it.

"Masgard!" she called.

He spun around, breathing hard. Beyond him the *Clear Air Turbulence* had burned down to a charred metal basket. The docking pans seemed to jostle one another in the last mad light of the guttering fire.

Hester lifted her sword.

"What are you playing at, aviatrix?" Masgard shouted. "You sell me this city, then you try and help them take it back. I don't understand! What's your plan?"

"There isn't one," said Hester. "I'm just making it up as I go along."

Masgard drew his sword and swished it to and fro, practicing flashy fencing moves as he advanced on her. When he was a few feet away, Hester lunged forward and jabbed her blade at his shoulder. She didn't think she'd done much damage, but Masgard dropped his sword and put his hands to the wound and slithered in the snow and fell over. "Please!" he shouted. "Have mercy!" He fumbled under his furs, pulling out a fat purse and sprinkling the snow between them with big, glittering coins. "The boy's not here, but take this and let me live!"

Hester walked to where he lay and swung the sword at him with both hands, bringing it down again and again until his screams stopped. Then she flung the sword aside and stood watching while Masgard's blood soaked pinkly into the snow and the big white flakes began to bury the gold he had thrown at her. Her elbows ached, and she had an odd feeling of disappointment. She had expected more of this night. She wanted something other than this dazed, hollowed-out feeling that she was left with. She had been expecting to die. It seemed wrong that she was still alive, not even hurt. She thought of all those dead Huntsmen. Other people had been killed in the battle too, no doubt, all because of what she'd done. Was she not to be punished at all?

Somewhere among the warehouses on the lower tier, a single pistol shot rang out.

The trail of footprints had led Tom into familiar streets, lit by the glare of the fires in the harbor above. Beginning to feel uneasy, he rounded a last corner and saw the *Jenny Haniver*, sitting where he had left her in the shadow of the warehouses. Pennyroyal was fumbling with the hatch.

"Professor!" shouted Tom, walking toward him. "What are you doing?"

Pennyroyal looked up. "Damn!" he muttered when he realized he'd been found, and then, with something of his old bluster, "What does it look as if I'm doing, Tom? I'm getting off this burg while there's still time! If you've got any sense, you'll come with me. Great Poskitt, you'd hidden this thing well! Took me ages to spot her. . . ."

"But there's no need to leave now!" said Tom. "We can get the city's engines started and outrun Arkangel. Anyway, I'm not leaving Hester!"

"You would if you knew what she'd done," said Penny-royal darkly. "That girl's no good, Tom. Completely insane. Unhinged as well as ugly . . ."

"Don't you dare talk about her like that!" cried Tom indignantly, reaching out to drag the explorer away from the hatch.

Pennyroyal pulled a pistol from inside his robes and shot him in the chest.

The kick of the bullet threw him backward, into a snow-drift. He tried to struggle up, but he couldn't. There was a hot, wet hole in his coat. "That's not fair!" he whispered, and felt blood flood up his throat and fill his mouth, hot and salty. The pain came in like the long, gray breakers at Rogues' Roost, steady and slow, each wave fading into the next.

There was a crunch of footsteps in the snow. Pennyroyal crouched over him, still holding the gun. He looked almost as surprised as Tom. "Oops!" he said. "Sorry. Only meant to scare you; it just went off. Never handled one of these things before. Took it from one of those chaps your loony girlfriend spiked."

"Help," Tom managed to whisper.

Pennyroyal twitched Tom's coat open and looked at the damage. "Eugh!" he said, and shook his head. He groped in the inner pockets and drew out the *Jenny*'s keys.

Tom felt the deck plates under him begin to shudder as the city's engines came back to life. Saws were howling up at the stern as Scabious's men cut away the wreckage of the wheel. "Listen!" he whispered, and found that his voice sounded like someone else's, faint and far away. "Don't take the *Jenny*! You needn't! Mr. Scabious will get us moving again. We'll outrun Arkangel. . . ."

Pennyroyal stood up. "Really, what an incurable romantic you are, Tom. Where do you think you're going to run *to*? There are no green bits in America, remember? This city is headed for a cold, slow death on the ice or a quick, hot one in the gut of Arkangel, and either way I don't intend to be around when it happens!" He tossed the keys up in the air and caught them again, turning away. "Must dash. Sorry again. Cheerio!"

Tom started trying to drag himself through the snow, determined to find Hester, but after a few feet he had forgotten what it was he meant to tell her. He lay in the snow, and after a while the burr of aero-engines reached him, rising and then fading as Pennyroyal lifted the *Jenny Haniver* out of the maze of warehouses and steered her away into the dark. It didn't seem to matter much by then. Even dying didn't seem to matter, although it seemed odd to think that he had outflown Fox Spirits and escaped Stalkers and survived strange adventures under the sea only to end like this.

The snow kept on falling, and it wasn't cold anymore, just soft and snug, heaping its silence over the city, wrapping the whole world in a dream of peace.

Thin Ice

JUST AFTER SUNRISE A CHEER ran through the engine district as the wreckage of the stern wheel was finally cut away and the city began to move again, swinging south by southwest. Yet with the wheel gone and just the cats to drag it forward, Anchorage could manage only a crippled crawl, making barely ten miles per hour. Already, in the breaks between the snow showers, Arkangel could be seen looming in the east like a polluted mountain.

Freya stood with Mr. Scabious on the stern gallery. The enginemaster had a pink bandage on his forehead where a Huntsman's bullet had grazed him, but he was the only casualty of the battle to retake the engine district: The Huntsmen had quickly seen that they were outnumbered, and fled onto the ice to await rescue by Arkangel's survey-suburbs.

"Only one hope for us," muttered Scabious as he and Freya watched the low sunlight kindle reflections in the windows of the predator city. "If we run far enough south, the ice'll grow thinner and they may break off the chase."

"But if the ice is thinner, won't we go through it too?"

Scabious nodded. "There's always that danger. And if we're to keep ahead, we can't afford to bother with survey teams and scout parties; we'll have to keep going as fast as we can and hope for the best. America or bust, eh?"

"Yes," said Freya. And then, feeling that there was no point in lying anymore: "No. Mr. Scabious, it was all a lie. Pennyroyal had never been to America. He invented the whole thing. That's why he shot Tom and took the *Jenny Haniver*."

"Oh, aye?" said Scabious, turning to look down at her.

Freya waited for something more, but it didn't come. "Well, is that it?" she asked. "Just 'Oh, aye'? Aren't you going to tell me what a little fool I've been, for believing in Pennyroyal?"

Scabious smiled. "To tell you the truth, Freya, I had my doubts about that fellow from the first. Didn't ring true somehow."

"Then why didn't you say something?"

"Because it's better to travel hopefully than to arrive," said the enginemaster. "I liked your idea of crossing the High Ice. What was this city before we started west? A moving ruin; the only people who hadn't left were the ones too full up with sorrow to think of anywhere to go. We were more like ghosts than human beings. And now look at us. Look at yourself. The journey's shaken us up and turned us about, and we're alive again."

"Probably not for very long."

Scabious shrugged. "Even so. And you never know; perhaps we'll find a way. If we can only stay out of the jaws of that great monster."

They stood in silence, side by side, and studied the pursuing city. It seemed to grow darker and closer as they watched.

"I must confess," said Scabious, "I'd never imagined Pennyroyal would go as far as shooting people. How is poor young Tom?"

He lay on the bed like a marble statue, the fading scars and bruises of his fight with the Stalker-birds standing out starkly on his white face. His hand when Hester held it was cold, and only the faint fluttering pulse told her he was still alive.

"I'm sorry, Hester." Windolene Pye spoke in a whisper, as if anything louder might attract the attention of the Goddess of Death to this makeshift sickroom in the Winter Palace. All night and all day the lady navigator had been tending to the wounded, and especially to Tom, who was most badly hurt. She looked old and weary and defeated. "I've done all I can, but the bullet is lodged against his heart. I daren't try to extract it, not with the city lurching about like this."

Hester nodded, staring at Tom's shoulder. She could not bring herself to look at his face, and Miss Pye had pulled a coverlet over the rest of him for modesty's sake, but the arm and the shoulder nearest to Hester were bare. It was a pale, angular shoulder, slightly freckled, and it seemed to her to be the most beautiful thing she'd ever seen. She touched it, and stroked his arm, watching the soft down of hair spring back as her fingers passed, feeling the muscles and tendons strong under the skin, the faint tick of a pulse at his blue wrist.

Tom stirred at her touch, half opening his eyes. "Hester?" he murmured. "He took the *Jenny*. Sorry."

"It's all right, Tom, it's all right, I don't care about the ship, only you," said Hester, pulling his hand against her face.

When they had come to find her after the battle and told her that Tom was shot and dying, she had thought there must be some mistake. Now she understood that it was not so. This was her punishment for delivering Freya's city into the jaws of Arkangel. She must sit in this room and watch Tom die. It was far, far worse than her own death could have been.

"Tom," she whispered.

"He's unconscious again, poor dear," said one of the women who had been helping Miss Pye. She reached across to brush Tom's brow with cool water, and someone brought a chair for Hester. "Maybe he's better off out of it," she heard another of the nurses whisper.

Outside the long windows it was already growing dark. The lights of Arkangel sprawled on the horizon.

The predator city was closer still by the time the sun rose again. When it wasn't snowing, you could make out individual buildings: factories and dismantling mills, mainly, the endless prisons of the city's slaves, and a great spike-turreted temple to the wolf-god squatting on the topmost tier. As the predator's shadow groped across the ice toward Anchorage, a spotter ship came buzzing down to see what had befallen Masgard and his Huntsmen, but after hovering for a moment above the burned wreck of the *Clear Air Turbulence*, it turned tail and sped back to its aerie. No more came near Anchorage that day. The Direktor of Arkangel was in mourning for his son, and his Council saw no sense in wasting yet more ships to secure a prize that would be theirs by sundown anyway. The city flexed its jaws, giving the watchers on Anchorage's stern an unforgettable glimpse of the vast furnaces and dismantling engines that awaited them.

"We should get on the radio and remind them what became of their Huntsmen!" vowed Smew, sitting in on an impromptu meeting of the Steering Committee that afternoon. "We'll tell them that the same thing will happen to them if they don't back off."

Freya didn't answer. She was trying to pay attention to the discussion, but her mind kept drifting away to the sickroom. She wondered if Tom was still alive. She would have liked to go and sit with him, but Miss Pye had told her that Hester was always there, and Freya was still afraid of the scarred girl—even more so after what she had done to the Huntsmen. Why could it not have been Hester who was shot? Why had it happened to Tom?

"I think that might just make things worse, Smew," Scabious said, after waiting a decent time for the margravine to give her opinion. "We don't want to make them any angrier."

A deep boom, like cannon fire, rattled the glass in the windows. Everyone looked up. "They're shooting at us!" cried Miss Pye, reaching for Scabious's hand.

"They wouldn't do that!" cried Freya. "Not even Arkangel . . ."

The windows were blurred with frost. Freya pulled on her furs and hurried out onto the balcony, the others close behind. From there they could see how near the predator was. The hiss of its runners as it raced across the ice seemed to fill the sky, making Freya wonder if this was the first time cities had come to break the silence of this unmapped plain. Then came that great boom again, and she knew that it was not gunfire but the sound everyone who lived aboard an ice city dreaded: the crack of sea ice breaking.

"Oh, gods!" muttered Smew.

"I should be in the Wheelhouse," said Miss Pye.

"I should be with my engines," murmured Scabious.

But there was no time, and neither of them moved; there was nothing now that anyone could do but stand and watch.

"Oh, no!" Freya heard herself saying. "Oh, no, no, no!"

Another boom, sharper this time, like thunder. She stared up at the cliff face of Arkangel, trying to see if the predator city had heard the noises too and applied its ice brakes. If anything, it was still gaining, gambling everything on a last mad dash. She held tight to the balcony railings and prayed to the Ice Gods. She wasn't sure that she really believed in them anymore, but who else could help her now? "Make us swift, Lord and Lady," she begged, "but don't let us go through the ice!"

The next boom was louder, and this time Freya saw the crack open, a dark grin widening a quarter mile to starboard. Anchorage lurched and veered away. Freya imagined the helmsman trying desperately to steer a course across a jigsaw of breaking ice. Another lurch, and glassware fell and smashed somewhere inside the palace. The booms and cracks came very close together now, and from all sides.

Arkangel, sensing that it could not stay on this course much longer, put on one final burst of speed. Its jaws swung wide, wide, and the sun glittered on banks of revolving steel teeth. Freya saw workers scurrying down stairways toward the predator's gut, and fur-clad onlookers gathering on high balconies much like her own to watch the catch. And then, before the jaws could close on Anchorage's tail, the whole edifice seemed to shiver and slow. A sheet of white spray lifted into the air, like a curtain of glass beads being drawn between the two cities.

The spray crashed across Anchorage as freezing rain. Arkangel was trying frantically to reverse, but the ice beneath it was fragmenting and its drive wheels could not gain a purchase. Slowly, like a mountain falling, it tipped forward, and its jaws and the forward parts of its lowest tier bowed down into a widening zigzag of black water. Geysers of steam burst up as the cold sea sluiced through its furnaces, and it let out a great bellow, like some huge, wounded creature cheated of its prey.

But Anchorage was in trouble too, and no one aboard had time to celebrate the predator's defeat. The city was tilting steeply to larboard, tracks screaming as they struggled to keep a hold on the ice, gouts of spray thrown up on all sides.

Freya had never felt movements like this and did not know what they meant, but she could guess. She grabbed Miss Pye's hand, and Smew's, and Miss Pye was already clinging to Mr. Scabious, and they crouched there together, waiting for the gurgling black waters to come swirling up the stairways and drown them.

And waiting. And waiting. Slowly the light faded, but it was just night drawing on. Snow touched their faces.

"I'd better see if I can make it down to the engine district," said Scabious slightly bashfully, disentangling himself and hurrying away. After a while Freya felt the engines shut down. The city's movements seemed to have eased a little, but the floor was still tilted out of true, and there was still a faint, strange motion in the fabric of the palace.

Smew and Miss Pye went back inside, out of the cold, but Freya stayed on the balcony. Night and snow veiled the wreck of Arkangel, but she could still see its lights and hear the howl of its engines as it tried to drag itself back onto firmer ice. What had befallen Anchorage she could not tell; there was still this weird wallowing motion, and even without engines the city seemed to be moving steadily away from the trapped predator.

A burly shape hurried across the palace gardens, and Freya leaned out over the balcony's brim and shouted, "Mr. Aakiuq?"

He looked up at her, the fur on the hood of his parka making a white O around his dark face. "Freya? Are you all right?"

She nodded. "What's happening?"

Aakiuq cupped his hands around his mouth and shouted,

"We're adrift! We must have reached the edge of the ice, and the bit we were on broke free."

Freya stared out into the dark beyond the city's edge. She could see nothing, but at least the strange rise and fall of the deck plates made sense now. Anchorage was water-borne, balanced precariously on its raft of ice like an over-weight sunbather drifting out to sea on an inflatable raft. So much for that thick plain of sea ice stretching all the way into the heart of the Dead Continent! "Pennyroyal!" she shouted at the empty sky. "The gods will punish you for bringing us to this!"

But the gods did not punish Professor Pennyroyal. He had used some of his stolen gold to buy fuel from a tanker pulling clear of Arkangel, and he was already far away, steering east by the broad scar the predator city had cut across the ice fields. He was not a very good aviator, but he was lucky, and the weather was not too rough with him. He met with a small ice city east of Greenland, had the *Jenny Haniver* repainted and renamed, and hired a pretty aviatrix named Kewpie Quinterval to fly her south. Within a few weeks he was back in Brighton, regaling his friends with tales of his adventure in the frozen north.

By then even the Direktor of Arkangel had been forced to admit that his city could not be saved. Already many of the rich had fled, pouring away to eastward in a stream of air yachts and charter ships (the five widows Blinkoe made enough money selling berths aboard the *Temporary Blip* to buy themselves a charming villa on the upper tiers of Jaegerstadt Ulm). The slaves who had seized control of the underdecks in all the chaos were leaving too, flying out on stolen freighters or taking to the ice in hijacked survey sleds and drone-suburbs. At last a general order to evacuate was given, and by midwinter the city stood empty, a great dark carcass that slowly whitened and lost its shape beneath a thickening mantle of snow.

In the deep of that winter a few hardy Snowmad salvage towns visited the wreck, draining its fuel tanks and landing boarding parties to harvest the valuables its fleeing citizens had left behind. Spring brought still more, and flights of scavenger airships like carrion birds, but by then the ice beneath the wreck was growing weaker. In high summer, lit by the weird twilight of the midnight sun, the predator city stirred again, shivering amid a great cannonade of splintering ice, and set out on its final journey, down through the shifting levels of the sea to the cold, strange world below.

That summer there was news from Shan Guo of a coup inside the Anti-Traction League: The High Council had been overthrown and replaced by a party called the Green Storm, whose forces were led by a bronze-masked Stalker. No one in the Hunting Ground paid much attention. What did it matter to them if a few Anti-Tractionists were squabbling among themselves? Aboard Paris and Manchester and Prague, Traktiongrad and Gorky and Peripatetiapolis, life went on as normal. Everybody was talking about the fall of Arkangel, and simply *everybody* was reading Nimrod B. Pennyroyal's astonishing new book:

NEW FROM FEWMET AND SPRAINT!

The latest interpolitan best-seller from the author of

AMERICA THE BEAUTIFUL & ZIGGURAT CITIES OF THE SERPENT-GOD

PREDATOR'S GOLD

by Professor Nimrod B. Pennyroyal

THE SEARING AND PASSIONATE *TRUE STORY* OF ONE MAN'S ADVENTURES ABOARD ANCHORAGE, HELD CAPTIVE BY A BEAUTIFUL BUT DERANGED YOUNG MARGRAVINE, OBSESSED WITH DRIVING HER DOOMED CITY ACROSS THE HIGH ICE TO AMERICA!

MARVEL at Professor Pennyroyal's battles with parasite-pirates from beneath the ice!

———

BOGGLE at his impressions of the wild snowscapes west of Greenland, and the savage cities that hunt there!

———

WEEP at the tragic tale of a disfigured young aviatrix, and how her hopeless love for Professor Pennyroyal led her to betray Anchorage to the fearsome predator city of Arkangel!

———

CHEER Professor Pennyroyal's spectacular one-man victory over the Huntsmen!

———

THRILL to his descriptions of the last days of Anchorage, most beautiful of the ice cities, and his daring escape as it drowned in the icy waters of an unknown sea.

The Land of Mists

BUT ANCHORAGE HAD NOT drowned. Borne away from Arkangel by strong currents, it floated into thick fog, the ragged raft of ice it perched on grinding sometimes against other drifting floes.

When daylight came again, most of the city gathered at the railings on the bow of the upper tier. With the engines turned off, there was little work for anyone to do, and little to talk about, for the future looked so bleak and brief that no one cared to mention it. They stood in silence, listening to the slap of waves against the ice and peering through gaps in the shifting fog for glimpses of this strange new sight, the sea.

"Do you think this might be just a big polynya, or a narrow stretch of open water?" asked Freya hopefully, walking out onto the forward observation deck with her Steering Committee. She hadn't been sure what a margravine should wear for Going to a Watery Grave, so she had put on the old embroidered anorak and sealskin boots she used to wear for trips aboard her mother's ice-barge, and a matching hat with pom-poms. She regretted it now, because the pom-poms kept bouncing in an inappropriately cheery way, making her feel she had to be optimistic. "Maybe we will drift across it and find good safe ice to run upon again?"

Windolene Pye, pale and tired from tending the wounded, shook her head. "I would guess these waters don't freeze until the deep of winter. I think we will drift on until we ground on some desolate shore, or the ice floe breaks up and we sink. Poor Tom! Poor Hester! Coming all this way back to save us, and all for nothing!"

Mr. Scabious put his arm around her, and she leaned gratefully against him. Freya looked away, embarrassed. She wondered if she should tell them that it was Hester who had brought Arkangel down on them in the first place, but it didn't seem fair somehow, not with the poor girl still sitting vigil at Tom's deathbed. Anyway, Anchorage needed a good heroine at the moment. Better by far to let the blame for the Huntsmen rest with that fraud Pennyroyal. He was to blame for everything else, after all.

She was still trying to think of something to say when a sleek black back broke the surface, just off the forward edge of the ice floe.

It came up like a whale through a wash of white waters, venting air in a hissing plume, and everyone thought a whale was what it was until they began to make out patterns of rivets on the metal hull: hatchways and windows and sten-ciled lettering.

"It's those parasite devils!" shouted Smew, running past with his wolf rifle. "Come back for more loot!"

The wallowing machine extended its spider legs to grip the edges of the ice floe, hauling itself up out of the water. Sleds were already speeding to meet it, packed with armed men from the engine district. Smew raised his rifle, taking careful aim as the hatch popped open.

Freya reached out and pushed the gun aside. "No, Smew. There's only one."

Surely it could not be a threat, this lone vessel surfacing so openly? She peered down at the stiff, skinny figure who came creeping up through the parasite's hatchway, only to be grabbed and pinioned by some of Scabious's men. She could hear raised voices, but not what they were saying. With Smew, Scabious, and Miss Pye at her side, she hurried to the head of the stairs that led down onto the city's skirts, waiting nervously as the captive was led up to meet her. The closer he came, the more grotesque he looked, his misshapen face colored purple and yellow and green. She knew the parasite-riders were thieves, but she hadn't thought they were monsters!

And then he was standing in front of her, and he wasn't a monster, just a boy of her own age to whom horrible things had been done. Some of his teeth were missing, and a terrible red weal scarred his throat, but his eyes, blinking out at her from a mask of scabs and fading bruises, were black and bright and rather lovely.

She pulled herself together and tried to sound like a margravine. "Welcome to Anchorage, stranger. What brings you here?"

Caul opened and closed his mouth but couldn't think of

what to say. He was out of his depth. All the way from Grimsby he'd been planning for this moment, but he had spent so much of his life trying not to be seen by Drys that it felt unnatural to be standing here in the open with so many of them. Freya shocked him a little too. It wasn't just the boyish haircut; she seemed bigger and taller than he remembered, and her face was rosy; she was not at all the pale, dreamy girl he had grown used to from the screens. Behind her stood Scabious, and Smew, and Windolene Pye, and half the city, all glaring at him. He began to wonder if it might not have been easier to die in Grimsby after all.

"Speak, boy!" ordered the dwarf who stood at Freya's side, jabbing Caul's belly with his rifle. "Her Radiance asked you a question!"

"He was carrying this, Freya," said one of Caul's captors, holding up a battered tin tube. The people crowding behind Freya drew back with nervous little gasps, but Freya recognized the thing as an old-fashioned document container. She took it from the man, unscrewed the lid, and pulled out a roll of papers. Looked at Caul again, smiling.

"What are these?"

The breeze, which had been rising unnoticed since the *Screw Worm* surfaced, tugged at the papers, fluttering their crisp, age-browned edges and threatening to pull them from Freya's hands. Caul reached out and grabbed them. "Careful! You need those!"

"Why?" asked Freya, staring down. There were red marks on the boy's wrists where cords had cut into the flesh, and red marks on the papers too: words written in old-fashioned script in rust-colored ink; latitudes and longitudes; the thin, wriggling line of a coast. A rubber-stamped notice warned "Not to Be Removed from the Reykjavik Library."

"It's Snøri Ulvaeusson's map," said Caul. "Uncle must have stolen it from Reykjavik years ago, and it's been sitting in his Map Room ever since. There are notes too. It tells you how to get to America."

Freya smiled at his kindness and shook her head. "But there's no point. America's dead."

In his urgency to make her understand, Caul gripped her hand. "No! I read it all on the way here. Snøri wasn't a fraud. He really found green places. Not great forests like Professor Pennyroyal imagined. No bears. No people. But places where there are grass and trees and . . ." He'd never seen grass, let alone a tree; his imagination kept letting him down. "I don't know. There'll be animals and birds, fish in the water. You might have to go static, but you could live there."

"But we'll never be able to reach it," Freya said. "Even if it's real, we'll never get there. We're adrift."

"No . . ." said Mr. Scabious, who had been peering over her shoulder at the map. "No, Freya, we can do it! If we can just stabilize this floe we're sitting on and rig up some propellers . . ."

"It isn't far," said Miss Pye, reaching over Freya's other shoulder and resting her finger on the map, where the head of one long winding inlet was labeled VINELAND. A spattering of islands showed there, so small that they might have been just inkblots, except that old Snøri Ulvaeusson had marked each one with a childish drawing of a tree. "Perhaps seven hundred miles. Nothing at all, compared with the distance we've traveled!"

"But what are we thinking of?" Scabious turned to Caul, and Caul took a few shuffling steps backward, remembering how he'd driven this poor old man half mad with his ghostly appearances in the engine district. Scabious seemed to be remembering it too, for his gaze turned cold and faraway, and for a long moment the only sounds were the faint, nervous stirrings of the crowd and the rustle of the breeze-blown papers in Freya's hands. "Do you have a name, boy?" he asked.

"Caul, sir," said Caul.

Scabious stretched out his hand and smiled. "Well, you look cold, Caul, and hungry. We shouldn't keep you standing here. We can discuss all this at the palace."

Freya remembered her manners. "Of course!" she said as the crowd around her started to break up, everyone talking excitedly about the map. "You must come to the Winter Palace, Mr. Caul. I'll ask Smew to make hot chocolate. Where *is* Smew? Oh, never mind, I can do it myself. . . ."

And so the margravine led the way along Rasmussen Prospekt with Scabious and Miss Pye close behind, Caul walking nervously between them, and others hurrying to swell the strange procession as word spread that the boy from the sea had brought new hope: the Aakiuqs and the Umiaks and Mr. Quaanik, and Smew pushing his way to the front, and Freya waving Snøri Ulvaeusson's map in its old tin holder and laughing and joking with them all. It wasn't very dignified behavior, and she knew that her mama and papa and her mistress of etiquette and her ladies-in-waiting would not have approved, but she didn't care: Their time was gone; Freya was margravine now.

35

An Ark
of Ice

WHAT A HAMMERING AND banging filled Anchorage in the days that followed! What a glow of work lamps in the long nights, and what showers of sparks as Scabious supervised the cutting of makeshift propeller blades out of spare deck plates, the building of outriggers from the old cat cowlings! What a stutter and grumble of engines being tested, camshafts and drive belts repositioned! Caul used the *Screw Worm* to bore through the ice floe, and the new propellers were lowered carefully down into the water beneath the city while Scabious experimented with a jerry-rigged rudder. None of it worked very well, but it all worked well enough. A week after Caul's arrival the engines started up in earnest, and Freya felt her city stir purposefully beneath her and begin to push itself slowly, slowly through the sea, water chuckling along the edges of its ark of ice.

And slowly the days grew longer, and the icebergs fewer, and there was warmth in the shafts of sunlight that pierced the fog, for Anchorage was steaming into latitudes where it was still only late autumn.

Hester took no part in the parties and planning meetings and singalongs that occupied the rest of the city in those last weeks of the journey. She didn't even attend the wedding of Søren Scabious and Windolene Pye. She spent most of her time in the Winter Palace with Tom; and later, when she looked back on those days, it was not the landmarks she remembered—the dead islands and thick jams of drift ice that Anchorage had to nudge its way past, the lifeless mountains of America hunched on the horizon—but the smaller milestones of Tom's recovery.

There had been the day when Miss Pye summoned all her courage and all the knowledge she had been able to find in her medical books and cut Tom open, reaching in with long tweezers among the wet, dark pulsings of his body until—well, Hester had fainted at that point, but when she came to, Miss Pye handed her the pistol ball, a little dented snub of blue-gray metal that looked as if it could never have harmed anyone.

Then there had been the day when he first opened his eyes and spoke: feverish, meaningless stuff about London and Pennyroyal and Freya, but better than nothing, and she held his hand and kissed his forehead and eased him back into twitchy, murmurous sleep.

Now that Tom was no longer expected to die, Freya often came to visit him, and Hester even let her take a turn at sitting with him sometimes, for she was feeling unwell herself by then, as though the motion of the floating city disagreed with her. Things were awkward between the two girls at first, but after a few visits Hester steeled herself and asked, "Are you going to tell them?"

"Tell who what?"

"Tell everyone that it was me who sold you to Arkangel?"

Freya had been wondering about that herself, and she thought for a while before she answered. "What if I did?"

Hester looked down at the floor, smoothing the pile of the thick carpet with her scuffly old boots. "If you did, I couldn't stay. I'd go off somewhere, and you'd have Tom."

Freya smiled. She would always be fond of Tom, but her crush on him had faded somewhere on the Greenland ice. "I am the Margravine of Anchorage," she said. "When I marry, it will be for good political reasons, to someone from the lower city, perhaps, or . . ." She hesitated, blushing a little at the thought of Caul, so sweet and awkward. "Anyway," she went on quickly, "I want you to stay. Anchorage needs someone like you aboard."

Hester nodded. She could imagine her father, in some chamber of High London long ago, having just such a conversation as this with Magnus Crome. "So when there's trouble, like if Uncle and his Lost Boys find your little settlement, or air pirates attack, or a traitor like Pennyroyal needs quietly killing, you'll turn to me to do your dirty work?"

"Well, you do seem rather good at it," said Freya.

"And what if I don't choose to?"

"Then I'll tell everyone about Arkangel," Freya said. "But otherwise, it'll be our secret."

"That's blackmail," said Hester.

"Ooh, is it? Gosh!" Freya looked rather pleased, as if she felt she was finally getting the hang of running a city.

Hester watched her carefully for a moment, then smiled her crooked smile.

And at last, very close to journey's end, there came a night when she was woken from her half-dreams in the chair beside Tom's bed by a small, familiar voice that said just "Het?"

She shook herself and leaned over him, touching his brow, smiling into his pale, worried face. "Tom, you're better!"

"I thought I was going to die," he said.

"You almost did."

"And the Huntsmen?"

"All gone. And Arkangel stuck in trap-ice somewhere behind us. We're heading south, right into the heart of old America. Well, it might be old Canada, technically; nobody's sure where the border used to run."

Tom frowned. "Then Professor Pennyroyal wasn't lying? The Dead Continent is really green again?"

Hester scratched her head. "I don't know about that. This old map's turned up—it's complicated. At first I didn't see why we should believe Snøri Ulvaeusson any more than Pennyroyal, but there are definitely patches of green here. Sometimes, when the fog lifts, you can see twisty little trees and things clinging on for dear life to the sides of the mountains. I suppose that's what gave rise to all those airmen's tales. But it's nothing like Pennyroyal promised. It's no

Hunting Ground. Just an island or two. Anchorage will have to become a static settlement."

Tom looked frightened, and Hester squeezed his hand and cursed herself for scaring him; she'd forgotten how much townies like him feared life on the bare earth. "I was born on an island, remember? It was nice. We'll have a good life here."

Tom nodded and smiled, gazing at her. She looked good: rather pale, and still nobody's idea of beautiful, but very striking, in new black clothes she told him she'd taken from a shop in the Boreal Arcade to replace her prison slops. She had washed her hair and tied it back with a silvery thing, and for the first time that he remembered, she did not try to hide her face while he watched her. He reached up and stroked her cheek. "And are you all right? You look a bit white."

Hester laughed. "You're the only person who ever notices how I look. I mean, apart from the obvious. I've just been feeling a bit queasy." Better not tell him yet about what Windolene had found when Hester went to her complaining of seasickness. The shock might make him ill again.

Tom touched her mouth. "I know it feels awful, those men you had to kill. I still feel guilty about killing Grike, and Pewsey and Gench. But it wasn't your fault. You had to do it."

"Yes," she whispered, and smiled at how unalike they were, because when she thought of the deaths of Masgard and his Huntsmen, she felt no guilt at all, just a sort of satisfaction, and a glad amazement that she had got away with it. She lay down on the bed beside him and she held him, thinking of all the things that had happened since they first came to Anchorage. "I'm Valentine's daughter," she said softly, when she was sure he was asleep, and it seemed a good thing to be as she lay there with Tom in her arms, and Tom's child inside her.

Freya awoke to find a sliver of gray daylight showing between the curtains. Voices were calling out, down in the street outside her palace. "Land ho! Land ho!" It was hardly news, since Anchorage had been close to land for days now, nosing cautiously down a long, narrow inlet toward the place that Snøri Ulvaeusson had called Vineland. But the shouting went on. Freya climbed out of bed and pulled on her dressing gown, opened the curtain, opened the long window, stepped out into the cold on the balcony. Dawn was breaking, clear as ice. On either side of the city black mountains squatted over their reflections, striped with snow, and among the crags and scree slopes, small starveling pines showed like the first growth of hair on a shaven head. And there . . .

She gripped the balcony rail with both hands, glad of the bite of the frosty metal that proved she was not dreaming. Ahead, the outline of an island was hardening out of the mist that hung above the still water. She saw pine trees on the heights, and birches still holding up handfuls of last summer's leaves like pale gold coins. She saw steeps green with heather and rusty with dead bracken. She saw a lacework of snow on dark stands of rowan, aspen, oak; and beyond, across a shining strait, another island and another. And she laughed aloud and felt her city tremble beneath her for the last time as it yawed and slowed, bearing her safely into the secret anchorages of the west.

PHILIP REEVE was born in Brighton, England, and worked in a bookshop for many years before breaking out and becoming the illustrator of several highly successful children's book series in the United Kingdom. He has been writing since he was five, but MORTAL ENGINES was his first published book.

Mr. Reeve now lives on Dartmoor with his wife, Sarah, and their son, Samuel.